THE
OTHER SIDE
OF INFINITY

Joan F. Smith

FEIWEL AND FRIENDS

NEW YORK

A Feiwel and Friends Book
An imprint of Macmillan Publishing Group, LLC
120 Broadway, New York, NY 10271 • fiercereads.com
Copyright © 2023 by Joan F. Smith.

Our books may be purchased in bulk for promotional, educational, or
business use. Please contact your local bookseller or the Macmillan Corporate
and Premium Sales Department at (800) 221-7945 ext. 5442 or by email at
MacmillanSpecialMarkets@macmillan.com.

Library of Congress Control Number: 2022034600

First edition, 2023
Book design by Samira Iravani
All emojis designed by OpenMoji, license: CC BY-SA 4.0
Feiwel and Friends logo designed by Filomena Tuosto
Printed in the United States of America

ISBN 978-1-250-84338-8
10 9 8 7 6 5 4 3 2 1

*For Lucy and Teddy, who are still young enough to
believe this book is about a lifeguard and a know-it-all.
How lucky am I to love you on this side of infinity?
And for those who wish they knew the unknowable: I see you.*

It made you wonder: How much of our lives was just luck or good timing, and how much was actually choice? How could it be that tiny serendipitous events could change everything? And if lucky events could change everything, could minor mishaps have the same power?

—**Aditi Khorana,** *Mirror in the Sky*

What people have the capacity to choose, they have the ability to change. **—Madeleine Albright**

CHAPTER ONE

Nick

DROWNING WAS QUIET. That was drilled into my head from day one of certification class, and even though it was hard to believe, I was prepared for that. Every time I sat on the sunbaked cement across from the lifeguard chair, breathing in the smell of chlorine, coconutty sunscreen, the occasional drift of cut grass from the new landscaper, I reminded myself: Head up, Nick. Some of the kids in my cert class said they listened to podcasts while on duty, one earbud snaked into their ear, but not me. I rotated my position on schedule, keeping my shoulders squared to the pool.

The red rescue tube with its crisp white letters—I always traced the *D* in *GUARD*—balanced on my bathing suit shorts like a foam safety bar on an amusement park ride. I'd scanned the pool as I'd been trained: Up the trio of long lanes, the barriers bobbing obediently. Mr. Francis, the biology teacher at my high school, working his way up and down, as he did every morning at ten o'clock. A traditional individual medley. Butterfly, backstroke, breaststroke, and freestyle. Each of the sixteen laps ended with an easy flip turn before he returned to his coffee and sudoku puzzle.

In the water, Mr. Francis didn't cry out. He didn't shout, *Nick, help me*. He didn't crash during a flip turn or get caught in the lane line. Instead, what caught my eye was the most minute motion—or, really, the absence of motion—of the only other person at the pool that morning, a girl sunbathing beside the lifeguard chair.

I'd only spotted her around our complex once or twice before. Here, she shielded herself with a sun hat—one of those mom-looking ones, worn by girls in the 1950s—propped over her face, instead of on her head. Black and white, with geometric hexagons, the hat looked like someone had taken a soccer ball, sliced it clean in half, and dropped it on an oversized Frisbee. From my vantage point on the dock, all I could see was the hat and her long, tanned legs, which I determinedly did not stare at even though they were what my grandma would've called *a great pair of gams*, because I was not in the business of objectifying people. Her bare feet bobbed in rhythm to music I couldn't hear.

People say these things happen in the *blink of an eye* or a *split second*, and I guess clichés are what they are because they're true. In no time at all, Mr. Francis wound down lap eight—backstroke; Mrs. O'Malley's Chevy Lumina pulled up to the unloading spot, full of pool gear; and the girl's foot, tapping to what seemed to be an up-tempo tune, abruptly stopped.

Something in the air felt wrong. Off. A gnawing sense of dread poured into me, like the way Mom dribbles icing on cinnamon rolls. Immediate and encompassing, creaking into places it didn't belong. In this roughly three-second span, it dawned on me that all I heard was the wind. Not the churning swirl of water generated by Mr. Francis's smooth, zippy breaststroke.

My focus snapped to the pool. Mr. Francis lay floating, when only seconds before he'd been swimming. Something that looked like strawberry juice—blood, of course it was blood—marred the water on the left side of his head.

I scrabbled to my feet, the red rescue tube clutched in my numb fingers. My heart pounded everywhere but in my chest: my ears, the sweaty backs of my knees, my stomach. I prepared to dive in, my brain screaming *do it Nicholas go get Mr. Francis will he need CPR is this a heart attack no, no, there's blood, I need to do CPR it's thirty compressions per minute followed by a breath what's the song what's the song to keep in beat they sang it on* The Office *it's the Bee Gees' "Stayin' Aliiiiive"* . . .

But my feet wouldn't move. I glanced at them, sunscreen glowing white on my white toes. They were glued to the hot, pebbly cement, fiery coals beneath my skin. My knees jerked forward in preparation for my dive, but . . . nothing. It was as if the soles of my feet had grown roots, shooting through the cement and burrowing deep in the ground below.

Again. I willed myself to move.

Once more.

Move Nick move move move

All of this, only fractions of seconds, another blink or wink of time. But long enough for the girl with the no-longer-tapping foot to tear the hat from her face and launch herself from the lounge chair into the pool in three athletic and graceful strides. Midrun, she locked eyes with me.

"Why are you just standing there? Come on!" she shouted. "Do something!"

As if her words released me from a harness, I lunged into the water with an ugly, painful slap. Punishment for not moving. Underwater, my brain cleared even further. I gritted my teeth together. Why hadn't I moved?

When I surfaced, the girl was within feet of Mr. Francis, who still floated very much the wrong way. "Support his neck and flip him over!" I called, mentally scrambling through my first aid training.

The girl dove forward but stayed at the surface of the water, skimming along like a Bright Acres Condo Complex mermaid.

I propelled toward them with the fastest freestyle of my life, furious with myself—*why hadn't my body behaved?*—and as scared as I've ever been.

If Mr. Francis died . . . I gagged. Couldn't complete the sentence.

If he did, though, could I forgive myself for pausing? How much does a second count?

Lifeguard Certification 101: Every second counts.

The girl reached Mr. Francis, snared his neck in her palm, and turned him over. "He's not breathing."

My stomach boiled with panic. *Mr. Francis.* I was supposed to have him for my elective next year. I grunted. The rescue tube slowed my stroke.

Finally, finally, finally, I reached Mr. Francis and the girl, who'd gently steered him toward the edge of the pool. "Can you switch to his legs?" I asked.

"Yes."

"Mr. Francis," I said. His jaw was slack, his cheeks drained of their ruddiness. "Mr. Francis, it's me, Nick. Can you hear me?" Nothing. I exhaled. "Okay, let's transfer. Give me his neck on three."

Absurdly, when I counted to three, I heard Mom's voice. She used to head up the lottery for the French immersion program at her school, which my parents wanted me to take until they realized my dyslexia meant academics were already a stressor in my native language.

Un, deux, trois.

On three, I slipped my hand beneath the girl's palm, replacing her grip on the nape of my teacher's neck. His hair was wet and bristly

4

against my fingertips, and all I could think was how raw and wrong this felt to invade his space.

"It's not his spine," she said, moving to secure Mr. Francis's legs.

"I don't know that yet." I coughed, water catching in my throat. "Okay. On three again, let's get him up to the deck."

Together, we heaved Mr. Francis out of the pool. I cradled his neck as I'd been taught in cert class, ensuring it stayed in alignment with his vertebrae. Mr. Francis's skin was gray-toned and cool to the touch. Beneath his nose was a watercolor of pink.

"I'm calling 911." The hat girl stood.

"Use the phone attached to the pool house wall." I clamped my pointer and middle fingers together and pressed them to the artery that ran beneath Mr. Francis's jawline. "It's a landline, so it's linked to this address."

Fear sat on my vocal cords. I forgot how to breathe. My vision pixelated, righted itself. I stared at the droplets of water in his iron-colored hair, a tiny whimper escaping my mouth.

The girl returned. Sidled beside Mr. Francis. I moved opposite her, kneeling at his chest. "He doesn't have a pulse."

Her dark brown eyes scrutinized me. "He needs CPR."

A kind of nervous energy, lush and feathered, filled me. I recognized it in the space of one blink.

Doubt.

I'd paid attention—real attention, *this is serious* attention—to this step in training. Another kid in the class had pretended to dance with the CPR mannequin, flaming a surge of irritation in me.

At the condo pool, lives were in my hands. Human lives. I'd bargained that if I paid attention to training, I'd never need to put it to use.

But now I did. And this crackling hum of dread was as recognizable to me as my own face, only magnified. It was as if I was asked to read aloud while naked and juggling. I cleared my throat. "I know."

"Have you done CPR before?" the girl asked.

I shook my head. "Do you know it?"

Her mouth worked back and forth. "Yes."

I tilted Mr. Francis's head and fitted my mouth over his lips, blowing two quick, nonexpert breaths in, thankfully remembering not to blow too hard and burst his lungs. "Okay," I muttered, my brain cycling through the steps. *Stayin' alive.* "Chest compressions."

"Wait." The girl's voice was louder than it had been before. Tighter. She held up a palm. "I'll do those. You do the breaths."

My relief was a wriggling chocolate lab puppy, so strong I could pick it up and cradle it. "You sure?"

She rose on her knees and placed her hands on his chest. In a steady rhythm, the girl hiked her body weight down. With each pump, Mr. Francis's body jerked beneath her. "C'mon," she muttered. Thirty compressions later, she sat back.

I leaned over and blew two rescue breaths in his mouth. "Why isn't it *working*?"

"It—" she began, her hands already back on his chest, when Mr. Francis's face tightened.

Instinctively, I turned his head. And there it was, beneath my thumbs: a pulse. The bass drum of blood, slow, but gaining momentum. A hummingbird in his neck. Water geysered from his mouth, splashing across my thighs and soaking the cement. His eyes opened, and he coughed. Once, twice. Another cough, another heave of water-vomit. Followed by breath. Steady breath.

Breathing.

"Mr. Francis! It's Nick. Can you hear me?"

Cough. "That was . . . ," he said, wheezing. "Unpleasant." He closed his eyes.

My limbs rattled with adrenaline after-shakes, my face burning with the weight of the last several minutes, the heaviness of what could have been. A dead teacher. The hesitation, the exertion, the pool's almost moment—almost going from outdated but well-maintained condo pool to scene of a death I was trained to prevent.

I lifted my gaze to the girl. "We did it. *You* did it."

Her eyes—such a rich brown, the color of topsoil, especially situated against the aqua of the pool—locked onto mine.

The girl tilted her head. "What happened?"

"What do you mean?" I asked, even though we both knew what she meant: my pause. The moment I should have moved but didn't. My shoulders slumped. A breeze gusted over all three of us, but only the girl and I shivered. "I don't know. I also don't know how to thank you."

She glanced down at the puddle of water formerly inside Mr. Francis. Her face contorted. "I—I have to go."

I cocked my head, hearing the *wee-oo, wee-oo* whoop of sirens. "Go? Where?"

"Home."

"Wait." I shook Mr. Francis, whose eyelids fluttered open and closed. His breath was still even. "Why?"

The girl was already back at her lounge chair. She shoved her feet into a pair of flip-flops and hitched her bag over her shoulder, jogged to the gate, and stumbled. "I just do," she said, righting herself.

"But . . ." I looked at Mr. Francis, then at her. "What's your name?"

Across the lot, an ambulance banged over the speed bumps. The girl put her hand on the metal post and turned to look our way. "December."

"Wait. I'm Nick. Please—*wait*, okay?"

"I'm sorry," she said, gripping the edge of her bag. She took off, her hair streaming behind her.

I stayed put, puzzled. When someone sneezes, you bless them. When your ear itches, you scratch it. When your kid sister trips, you help her up.

When someone performs a life-saving measure, they stick around. Don't they?

CHAPTER TWO
December

I RAN FROM the pool with the single goal of getting home as fast as humanly possible. Sweat slicked my temples. Dotted the part of my back right above my bathing suit bottom. My feet slapped the pavement faster and faster, my wet hair thwacking against the bare skin of my shoulders. I sucked air into my lungs, trying to quell my terror because I'd really, truly messed things up by saving the life of a stranger.

Maybe not the most ordinary reaction to a pivotal moment, but I wasn't exactly a conventional thinker. And to be fair, I'd only had this particular feeling one time before.

I didn't enjoy it then, either.

Now my knees pumped and legs ached, because something was happening, and as much as I tried to race by it, avoid it, deny it—

I could not outrun myself.

You were supposed to witness that, not change it.

Goosebumps lifted the hair from my arms, despite the warmth of the sun, the burn of exertion. I braced myself for my impending skid ten steps from now. Everyone knows you're not supposed to run in flip-flops, but I knew with dead-on accuracy that four

three

two

steps from now, I'd roll my ankle on the brick that jutted out from the walkway, where a decade ago, a mason had been texting his girlfriend while laying mortar.

And . . . one. Done.

As I plummeted to the ground, I tried to cushion my landing by rolling up and over my ankle. I was greeted with the uncomfortable, gritty sensation of torn skin against cement. After a few seconds, I caught my breath and sat up to inspect the cut. My pool-soaked body darkened the pavement beneath me.

I wished more than anything that all of this wasn't happening right now. I didn't want any of what came next—not the headache, not the fatigue, not the adjustment to the way the world would carry on—and all of it my fault.

I'd changed something pivotal in the Way Things Were Supposed to Be. Broken the rules. Not that my game of life came with directions, but still. I brushed gravel from one of my palms. "Ow," I grumbled.

I closed my eyes, taking the smallest of moments to picture my simplest pleasures—the thick, fuzzy blanket Uncle Evan got me for Christmas, the feeling of the sun beaming on my forehead in the outdoor shower at the old summer cottage we'd stayed at way back when—before Mom left, before Cam's health declined.

I'd give anything to only think about the world through my own lens. It was straight-up exhausting to enjoy anything when you knew everything. I tucked my knees and rested my head on them, trying not to cry.

Before I'd gotten to the pool, my understanding of that particular moment was that, unlike other major things also happening simultaneously in the world:

(a mall shoplifter in Yokohama, a baby born in wing 204 at the fancy hospital in downtown New York City, preschoolers melting crayons in Barcelona)

I was present. A physical witness to this drowning.

—

Imagine memory as a collection. A glass jar of multicolored gumballs, with more streaming in every moment. Some visible and easy to grasp, others buried. Yours to keep until death do you part. And like cereal box tops or McDonald's Monopoly playing pieces, you generally move along and collect 'em all, until you end the game.

My own memory is unlike anyone's. I kicked off life with not only all (okay, most) of my own future gumballs/memories, but also everyone else's who has ever and will ever exist.

I get a general impression of peoples' feelings and motivations, but I don't know what they're thinking. It's omniscience with sunglasses on. And the world's memories don't exactly come time-stamped, but I can guess when they happen with some clues—the age of the people I know, the clothing, whether it's something that happened in the past (firm and unyielding in picture quality) or the future (milky, somehow, mostly accurate but somewhat malleable).

Science would define me as precognitive. Science would also define me as not real because I have not been proven. Still, there I sat, on the pink bricks at a just-on-the-right-side-of-well-kept condo complex. But what I know, what I've always known? That's both the simplest and most complicated part of all. I know everything that will happen, with one very personal exception.

Maybe you've heard time described as a line, or a string, or different dimensions. Maybe you've heard Alzheimer's patients, like my grandmother, Cam, thinking of time as this string crumpled up in a ball. It's not like that at all.

I know the string; I know its weaver, the person or being who plucked the threads and dyed them in the richest of colors.

—

This particular moment at the pool was my own gumball. *I* saw Mr. Francis drown.

There are two types of drowning: fatal and nonfatal. Mr. Francis was supposed to experience the second kind, technically surviving the drowning, because Nick was supposed to save him.

(Yet.)

I'd seen Nick frozen in some kind of private crisis, rendering Mr. Francis without oxygen for too long, followed by improper chest compression technique, which would effectively incapacitate Mr. Francis's brain.

This, in turn, would lead to a lifetime of doubt that would bring this boy to his emotional knees and punt him into a future of anxiety and inertia. The lifeguard would carry that loss with him, doubting himself every second for the rest of his life.

I was not supposed to alter this event because I can't change what happens. Believe me. I have tried. No matter what I've done, things somehow happen as they're meant to. I knew what I was supposed to do:

Lounge on chair.

Witness sad yet heroic incident where both Nick and Mr. Francis would be irreparably altered.

Move on.

(But.)

But.

I couldn't stand it. I couldn't stand watching him hesitate, waiting for the events to play out. Observing Nick through my half-closed lids, my ears plugged with music, I'd felt a tug. A pull. A desire to shield him. There was something about him I was drawn to in a way I hadn't expected to feel, something warm and melty and weirdly protective.

Most of the time, while my brain whirred and clicked through the ocean of all events past, present, and future, I didn't lay my own two eyeballs on them. My sockets were reserved for my own mundane—my uncle's grass-and-gasoline-stained jeans, a mover dropping a packed box, the occasional movie or show or book to kill time, even though I was a walking spoiler alert.

But in that moment, I was very much in attendance. The plastic of the lounge chair had stuck to my back in wet, uncomfortable stripes, and I had the bone-marrow-sucking realization that I was supposed to just . . . *observe* that event in real time. Kick back, relax, and take in the catastrophic ending of life as those two knew it.

I couldn't do it. And even though I'd tried to change other things a million times, when I tried this time, without believing I could do it, I *did*.

My whole life, I've had to shove my feelings into an imaginary dam. The weight of the world couldn't exactly be measured on a Target-brand scale, and skating near those highs and lows left about as much room for error as a surgeon operating with a chain saw. But now the thing that held my insides solid broke. I sighed, a deep, shuddering one, and gave up trying not to cry.

CHAPTER THREE

Nick

IN THE STRETCH of minutes after Mr. Francis almost died, time both picked up and slowed down, forever circling back on the moment my feet had made the most gigantic pause of their lives. While we waited for the ambulance to arrive, Mr. Francis mostly closed his eyes and rested. I monitored his pulse, thinking that if I'd let him die, my best friend, Maverick, would have destroyed me. He had an actual countdown on his phone for when he'd finally get to have Mr. Francis as a teacher.

"Nick Irving," Mr. Francis said, his voice hoarse. "You rescued me."

"Not only me, Mr. Francis."

He frowned. "Take the credit, son."

I looked off in the direction the hat girl had fled. "I had help. A girl named December."

Sirens screaming, the ambulance pulled to a halt. Two paramedics burst out. In seconds, I moved aside and they hovered over Mr. Francis, affixing an oxygen mask to his mouth and checking his pupils.

Mr. Francis pushed the mask away. "I knocked my beak on the flip turn. Can't stand the sight of blood. Get all"—inhale, exhale—"woozy. I must've fainted."

"BP is ninety-one over sixty."

The paramedic tried to replace Mr. Francis's mask, but he batted it out of the way and gestured to me. "This kid's a hero."

The paramedic gave me a brief smile. "Good work, kid."

"I wasn't alone," I insisted. "A girl was here, too. She did the chest compressions."

"Where'd she go?" the shorter paramedic asked.

"She took off." And then I spotted it, abandoned on the pool deck: the black-and-white hat. "See?" I pointed. "The girl left her hat. December. She's the one who called 911."

Outside the fence, Mrs. O'Malley and her three kids watched the paramedics work on Mr. Francis. The twins shook the chain links, and I was shocked into the reality that it had only been a few minutes since the squealing brakes announced their arrival.

There's a sometimes-dangerous thing people do after flying in an airplane, where they plug their nose and gently blow into it to unblock their ears, and I imagined myself mentally doing that. Clearing out headspace. Because somewhere between the grinding of the O'Malleys' brakes and right now, I knew I was in the middle of something that would follow me for the rest of my life. One of those life-changing moments you think back on as *oh, the time I figured out something pivotal*, or the *instant I can pinpoint with clarity from childhood*. The ones that key into whatever makes up a person. For me, it's: putting my dog to sleep. Winning free Yasso frozen yogurt bars for a year. Grandma dying.

Now, this.

"Mrs. O'Malley, did you see where that girl went?" I called. "Black bathing suit? Long dark hair?"

Mrs. O'Malley nodded. "Took off down Copeland."

15

Mom called Mrs. O'Malley *Mrs. Bright Acres*. Of course she'd seen December. "See?" I said to Mr. Francis. "The girl was here."

My future science teacher sat up fully now, a cloud of cotton gauze shoved into his nose. A scrape across its bridge had reddened, and a purple bruise steeped beneath his eye. "I only remember you. Say, how do I look?" He pointed at his face.

I gave him a weak smile. The nose gauze reminded me of an episode of *Mystery Buff*, my favorite true-crime podcast. Each week, the anonymous host of *Mystery Buff* starts the episode by "solving" the crime from the week before, then leaves listeners—aka "Buffys"—clues to a new crime he'd reveal the following week. My fellow Buffys take to the forums to try to solve the crimes, and the host, who donates all the ad revenue to victim organizations, sometimes gives out sponsored prizes if a Buffy nails it. The white-and-red wad of cotton brought me right back to the episode where a convenience store clerk hit himself in the nose with the cash register tray and falsified a robbery, pocketing a few thousand dollars but unaware of the surveillance video recording him.

I didn't usually haunt the podcast forums—they weren't screenreader-friendly, and I remember information better when I hear it. The sans serif font gave me the washout effect, where letters faded and ran together, making word decoding that much harder. But there was something satisfying about thinking through the crimes myself, especially when I was able to solve one. It was a ball of yarn I could unravel while I swam, cooked with Dad, or rode to school. For a kid who'd spent a lifetime untangling words, working to guess through a mystery with a guarantee the pieces would come into place the following Monday had an undeniable appeal.

"You've never looked better," I lied.

"I called your mom, Nicky," Mrs. O'Malley hollered.

Fantastic.

Before long, a crowd of my neighbors appeared, standing at what they probably imagined was a respectful distance, beneath the shade of the pine trees. Two police cars blocked the handicapped spots. The officers joined the paramedics.

A man I recognized immediately, even though he was taller than I'd thought and bigger-seeming than his headshot, broke free of the crowd and walked in the gate. Brazen move. His T-shirt looked like it had been washed too many times, but not in the good, broken-in way—in the way that made it both too wide and too short. He clutched something in his hands. "Joe DiPietro, with the *Woodland Gazette*," he said. "Mind if I chat with you, kid?"

"Me?"

"Permission to record our conversation?"

I stepped back, thinking of what my dad might've said to a client pre–mild-midlife-crisis career change, if he still wore the defense attorney hat. *Not without a parent present, kid.* "No, thanks."

"Old-fashioned way, then," the reporter said. The thing in his hands was a notebook.

Boom. The panic anvil. My heart picked up speed, staggering in my chest. "I don't really—"

"I hear you're a hero," he interrupted. He snaked a pen from behind his ear like a bad magic trick, using it to gesture toward the crowd. "Lady outside says you're Nicky Irving? You're a junior at Woodland High?"

I flushed. *Nicky.* "It's Nick. And yeah, I'll be a senior."

"You look pretty strong, kid. You keep in shape?"

"I'm on the swim team."

"For Woodland?"

I nodded.

"This your first save?"

"Uh, yeah. I've only been a lifeguard for three weeks. But it wasn't just me."

"Three *weeks*!" DiPietro crowed, scribbling. "Uh-huh, uh-huh. That's great. Fresh on the job, survival instinct takes over. What did it feel like to do CPR?"

Feel like? "I don't know. I mean, it was scary. I didn't really think about it, though. We just did it."

He tapped the pen against his lip. "Brave. Very brave."

I stared at him, trying to shake away the strangest feeling of disappointment. For years, I'd grown up with this guy in my living room via the nightly news. He'd made a whole splash about moving back to Boston after a stint in LA to "get back to his roots," and my parents had been thrilled for weeks.

"I was just doing my job."

"And humble, too." His eyes brightened.

"No, it's not that." I rubbed my temple, trying to massage away the icy headache that had dropped its way into my skull. "I didn't want anything bad to happen to Mr. Francis."

The reporter's hand flew. "You *know* the drowning victim?"

"Well, yeah, he swims here every day. And he's a teacher at the high school."

"First name's Ronaldo," Mr. Francis said from the cot the paramedics had set up. "That's an *o* on the end. Portuguese. You got questions for me, you can ask 'em. I've been at Woodland High for thirty years. Nicholas here is my hero."

"Beloved teacher," Joe DiPietro whispered, his pen looping across the page. "This is great. I'll be right over to you, sir."

One of the officers looked in our direction. "Move it along, DiPietro. He's a kid."

"Yep, yep. Not a bother." He scurried backward, writing furiously. "What are you, sixteen?"

"Seventeen."

"Yeah, okay, great. You do your training down at the Y?"

"Yeah, I finished in the spring. But . . ." I swallowed. "What about December?"

The reporter waved his hand. "I think we're good."

"No," I said. A trickle of the chlorinated water made its way down the back of my neck. "December. The girl who helped me. Called 911. Did the chest—"

"Got it, got it." DiPietro flashed a smile, his teeth unnaturally white against his sallow, faux-tan skin. "Be on the lookout for this in the morning, kid. This is a feel-good. Could even go viral. Our readers could use a break from the political crap, the cantaloupe salmonella outbreak, you know?"

"Last chance, DiPietro," the officer said.

He waved. "You're tomorrow's paper, kid."

I waved back, but my stomach clenched. The farther he got from me, the larger my unease grew. It seemed like everything was going to be okay, but I couldn't escape the feeling that something was still wrong. I had the strangest urge to call him back and trash his notebook, along with every other event from the morning.

CHAPTER FOUR

December

ONCE MY TEARS ran out, I gathered myself to my feet and walked home. I tried my grandmother's old trick, distracting myself with my surroundings: the thong of my flip-flops jabbing the skin between my big toe and my second toe on every other step. The stinging burn of the scrapes on my palms and knee. The condominium walkways, "paved" with these fake bricks—uncooked-tuna pink in color, which clashed with the chalk-blue vinyl siding of the condos.

Anything I could do to unfeel this feeling.

It didn't work.

My hands shook. Somehow, this was scarier than the time I changed things and accidentally lost my own mother.

I've learned the amount of true free will that exists was essentially the equivalent of a teaspoon of stardust in all the universe for the entirety of humankind. People exercise it *just* enough to make everything I know about the world ebb and flow. A true act of free will has a basic test: whether its impact saved a life or caused a death (*or* if it majorly affected the quality of human life). This time, I used my free will in a way I had never been able to before. I changed something major. I saved Mr. Francis. Not his life, but his quality of it.

I picked up my pace, my injured ankle twinging with each step, but the pain was nothing in comparison to the dance party going on in my head. My brain was not pleased to acclimate to this large free-will change.

The world is generally as predictable as the ocean's tide. People, too. They're born, develop some measure of moral compass, and are exposed to media and entertainment that either challenges or reaffirms their biological instincts. Basically, we're all some unsolvable equation of who we are plus what we experience.

But at the pool today, I had made a very large choice. Used a crumb from the measuring spoon of stardust, ending with a cosmic shift of epic proportions that now slammed into my brain, event after event after event. I was like the world's most meddlesome aunt, and now I was suffering the consequences of altering the future of human history.

I rounded the corner to my walkway, a world of future memories crawling in the base of my skull. Fear raced in my veins, panic humming in my chest as I waited for everything to settle. I inhaled, but I was only able to inflate my lungs to day-old-birthday-balloon status.

The screen door of our unit—number 23—slammed behind me, nipping at my heel with a bruising *thwack*. I paced the floor, dripping water on the fake hardwood, cupping my scraped, bloodied hands over my ears, unable to silence the roar of the reorganizing gumballs, unable to rake it from my scalp as the ocean of knowledge

(except for the one thing)

(the blank page, the Blank Spot)

settled into its new rhythm.

All because I'd intervened by saving Mr. Francis. And now with this shift came a consequence.

I'd committed an act of free will. I'd altered the world's truth.

Panic cottoned my mouth. Buzzed beneath my fingernails.

I thought I'd been doing something right, but I'd changed everything.

How?

The ocean inside my skull brightened. Settled. Brought with it . . . *lightness*?

At the arrival of a new change in the world—*my* world—I halted in place, stunned. The kitchen made its quiet working sounds: the steady hum of the refrigerator, the metronome tick of the clock. All regular home sounds doing their regular home thing as joy bloomed in my chest at this brand-new reality.

(Nick and I were going to fall in love.)

Love?

Me?

No one would call me a romantic. In another life, I might have been, but in this one? I knew too much about too much. I'd ruin every promposal. Judge the cost of every Valentine's Day trinket. Anticipate every kiss. The idea of *me* plus *romance* was raw, unnatural, but it carried a pleasant shiver. My nerve endings crackled with possibility, absorbing the gumballs rearranging, swirling, righting.

And there it was. I grabbed on to the end of this new future, held on tight.

I saw Nick ducking his head while telling his parents about me. Me, the observer, the ceiling flower, running headlong into a world where *I* was part of an *us*.

I pressed my fingers against the grin threatening to overtake my face. I was dizzy. Floored. Oxygenated with possibility.

Me. December Jones. In love.

It was almost impossible to imagine. I was the silent audience to millions of people buying flowers and writing letters and logging on to online dating sites with the sheer hope of promise. I knew the hours my uncle had put into this thing, using the old computer that now sat powered off and boxed away in the crawl space below our condo.

Not me. Never me.

Now me. *Me?*

Love was emotional frivolity. It seemed to promise the things I craved. Comfort. Stability. Balance, eventually. But my body still couldn't relax. An hour ago, Nick was a lifeguard-sized blip on my wonky radar. Now he had suddenly taken the lead role of my life's play.

I needed air. I pushed open the slider and dropped onto the deck couch, my face buzzing but my brain nagging. This was not me. This was *so* not me.

I was the person who could tell you about love. That wolves and albatrosses were monogamous. I could explain that when you're flooded with it, the "love hormone" oxytocin decreases headaches. That we put wedding rings on our fourth fingers because ancient Greeks believed the vena amoris vein runs from there straight to the heart.

I sucked in a breath. In sixth grade, my teacher Mrs. Rizzo told my uncle that I was "cool as a cucumber" under pressure. (Evan tried to spar with this cliché, making a vague joke about how cucumbers are 95 percent water.) Right now, I felt like the complete opposite: peeled back. Exposed. Vulnerable to what someone else might think of me, feel about me. And now, somehow, I was playing Cupid's cousin, my brain rushing to reassure me that this future was big and magic and possible.

I climbed further through the still-sorting future memories, savoring each rung on my imagined ladder. Our story would be made of coconut and peony blossoms, summer kisses and autumn hand-holding, the deepest of conversations, and, eventually, the truth about my brain and how it worked.

A big, doofy grin slipped over my face. I reclined against the scratchy clearance-fabric couch, my limbs sagging as the last gumballs began their descent, unable to shake the idea that something was off.

Maybe it was that Nick and I were strangers? I unquestionably had the home-field advantage, to the point where it was more than borderline unfair.

So many other people my age were thinking about this kind of thing all the time. Figuring out their preferences, maybe catching feelings. But not me. I rarely fantasize. I'm not impulsive because I always know what's next. I wasn't ever evaluating people on whether or not they gave me crush vibes. I'd always assumed this was not in my deck of cards, so this was a big deal for me. Ordinary teenager kind of stuff. I lifted my feet to the coffee table, but my ankle sang with a fresh wave of pain. I sighed. Antiseptic ointment and bandages were also in my near future.

I stood, stepping over my uncle's compost bin and wholesale soil bags, and went back inside. As I yanked the junk drawer for the medical kit, I tried to dismiss that one worry. The remaining pieces were settling in, and—

I dropped the Neosporin.

The last image was so out of place with the rest of the new future memories that I couldn't believe it at first. Didn't want to.

But I watched, horror-stricken, as the final gumball dropped into my jar with a soft, menacing *ping*.

In it, I saw Nick, lying on the ground, wearing a sherbet-orange T-shirt and a look of blank surprise and something heavy on him, his cheek pressed into the earth, and blood, too much blood, and his parents and young sister folded in half at his funeral, and me

(my heart)

bashfully open and bruised and wide, shredded.

Here in number 23, I fell to the floor, slamming my hip. I inhaled breath after ragged breath, my body somehow getting it entirely wrong. I felt all flipped around, as if I breathed in carbon dioxide and out oxygen, a green plant doing her earthly duty.

What had I done?

I was going to love Nick.

Nick was going to love me. And then he was going to die.

And I had no ability to stop it.

I closed my eyes and pressed my cheek into the cool flooring.

That didn't mean I wouldn't try to anyway.

CHAPTER FIVE

Nick

THE MORNING AFTER Mr. Francis lived, I joined my parents at the kitchen table, where Mom had made a whole fuss. Eggs, bacon, toast with strawberry jelly and butter, and the good orange juice from the farmers market were arranged in mismatched dishes on top of my grandmother's old tablecloth, the lacy one Mom tended to pull out for special occasions. Thanksgiving. Christmas. The full week each summer my dad's parents came to visit.

"You must be *exhausted*," Mom said, tipping a carafe of coffee over her favorite chipped purple mug. She brushed a kiss on my temple. "What a day yesterday."

I dunked a spoon in the bowl of eggs and slathered butter on toast. "I'm okay."

Dad slid a gray sheath of paper in my direction. "Hey, if you're tired, you earned it. Look who's on the front page."

Staring up at me was . . . me. Cropped from last year's swim team group picture and grainy as hell, but anyone I went to school with wouldn't have to look twice. I froze. "What the heck is this?"

"You want the screenreader?" Mom asked.

I did. It was a lot easier for that thing to read out loud, but I ignored her. I'm a slower reader in general, but the real problem is sometimes I have trouble holding on to all the words. Most readers with dyslexia—myself included—outgrow reversals, where they confuse letters like *d* and *b* because they look like sticks with a bubble on the end. Right now, *d* and *b* were two of the five letters making up the word that sucked through my veins like mud for as long as I'd been me.

Doubt.

Anxiety sweat bloomed beneath my armpits.

IN THE NICK OF TIME
Local boy, 16, saves beloved teacher
BY JOE DIPIETRO

Nicholas Irving has barely gotten his feet wet on the job, but he's already clocked his first save.

The lifeguard, a rising junior and superstar swim team captain at Woodland High School, heroically revived a swimmer who suffered a medical emergency at the Bright Acres Condominium Complex pool Tuesday morning.

Irving single-handedly rescued the victim, identified at the scene as 64-year-old Ronaldo Francis, a teacher at Woodland High School, after he suffered an accident that included a nosebleed and a loss of consciousness during his morning swim.

Irving immediately entered the pool and pulled the man out, then resuscitated him using CPR. "Nick Irving is my hero," says the popular science teacher.

But the teenage lifeguard brushes off the accolades. "It was scary, but I was just doing my job," Irving says.

Irving completed his water safety certification and guard training at our local YMCA in December. Francis was treated and released at Beth Israel hospital in Boston.

I read the article through twice, trailing my palm along the smooth, grayish page to cover the words below so I could focus on what was in front of me because *what the hell was in front of me*? Sixteen? Junior? Swim captain? Incorrect month of certification, instead of the name of the person who'd actually saved him?

This was the garbage he published? Joe DiPietro, the journalist I'd followed for years, was a snake.

I pushed the plate of food away. "This is all wrong." The words were caught in my throat, thick and contagious with the threat of tears.

Mom blinked. "Tom, he needs the screenreader."

"I don't need the screenreader."

"You sure, buddy?" Dad asked. He paused his forkful of food half-way to his mouth. "I can get it. I think it's in Sophie's room, but it's time for that kid to get up, anyway. You two are screwed when school starts."

"So are you," Mom murmured. Dad, a law and ethics teacher at the high school in the next town over, fell out of the early morning routine as soon as summer started. Mom was on the admin side of things, so she still got up.

"You sure you don't want it?" Dad asked again.

"I'm sure."

He pulled the article toward him, two vertical divots appearing between his brows as he read. It was his big tell, the one that said he was deep in thought or massively confused. "You know, Nick. It's an okay thing to accept a compliment."

I swallowed twice, trying to arm-wrestle the balloon of tears. "This. Is. All. Wrong," I repeated, poking the page with my finger to emphasize each word.

Mom skimmed a spoon through the orange juice, removing the

pulp. "What do you mean, honey?" She leaned over and glanced at the article. "Oh, they got your age wrong. They do that all the time."

"Not only that. I mean the entire thing. 'Superstar swim team captain'? I'm not the captain. I'm going to be a senior, not a junior. And I didn't finish my training in *December*. The girl was *named* December."

Mom and Dad exchanged their trademark Irving Parent Glance. Mom sighed. "Sometimes, news articles aren't exactly accurate. But, hey, you *are* a superstar."

I shook my head. "You're missing the point. Yesterday didn't happen 'single-handedly.' The girl—December . . ."

Mom slipped an arm across my shoulders. "My Nicholas," she said, her voice all throaty. "C'mon, honey. You don't need to be so modest. I've never been prouder in my life."

A grin broke across Dad's face. "Plus, you saved a man's life. You're a hero."

The word *FRAUD* banged into my head, inflating until it took up all the space in my skull. The letters bubbled, twisted and ugly, like an early morning alarm before a funeral.

I almost opened my mouth and told them *everything*. About my knees jerking in place, and December's rhythmic compressions, the 911 call, her swift departure. Despite the

F

R

A

U

D

I hesitated for the second time in two days.

It's not as if Mom and Dad were ever outright disappointed in me, though if they knew what I'd done in May, they would be. Instead, they were my dual defending champions, celebrating my academic wins instead of celebrating me for, well . . . being me. Constant examples of patience and cheer, determined to help me navigate my dyslexia, no matter what. They decried school curriculum for being narrow, but they also rejoiced when I did okay with it.

It's why they wouldn't get it. If our condo burned down, they'd be all, *Oh, well, at least we have one another. These are all just things!* Instead of acknowledging the very real truth that life would suck with a burned-down home.

"By the way," Mom said, using the voice she used when she tried to sound casual. "You did put in your application for the elite team, right?"

I nodded. An Olympic champ had moved to Boston and started this ultra-competitive training team that some of the best swimmers in the school league joined, either during or after high school. A couple kids even took a gap year for it. The farm team is a feeder system of sorts, helping people make it onto college swim teams— accompanied by a nice scholarship. For people with the end goal of competing in the Olympics, the farm coach helps them train toward qualifying for the Olympic trials. Even sniffing a seat ticket at one of those qualifying events can be tough. I didn't have high hopes of being the next Michael Phelps, but with two educators' salaries, a scholarship was a nice alternative to a lifetime of college loans.

Mom smiled, satisfied. "Good."

"I'm not going to make it. They only take fifteen people a year."

"Certainly not with that attitude," Dad said.

I braced myself for one of his *you get what you get* speeches, but my sister saved me by wandering in the kitchen. She wore an old BU Law T-shirt of Dad's, and two sweatbands encircled her wrists, left over from a Halloween eighties workout costume. "You left your phone in the bathroom," Sophie said, tossing it to me. "Maverick texted you."

I snatched it out of the air, only then noticing the newspaper ink stain along the side of my hand. "Don't go through my phone."

"Don't throw technology," Dad said at the same time Mom said "Sophie, *please* be gentle!"

Sophie slugged a sip of Mom's orange juice. "Mav wants to hang later."

"You read my texts, too?"

"I'm only in fourth grade. I'm still learning boundaries. Plus, your passcode is *1111*. You make it too easy." Sophie knelt on the empty chair. The table was round, and for some reason, we'd never done what most families did—each claim a chair. She picked up a slice of toast. "Time to carbo-load."

"Where on earth did you hear that term?" Mom asked, smoothing her palm over Sophie's sleep-tousled hair.

My sister dodged Mom's hand. She ripped off a hunk of bread, dragged it across the pat of butter, and shoved it in her mouth. "You-Tube says runners carbo-load before races." Sophie and her little band of cronies had run in these town-sponsored races all summer long, undefeated.

I groaned. "On that note, I'm out."

Sophie swallowed. "You don't want to know where that girl December lives?"

"You were eavesdropping, too?" I paused. "You know her?"

"Her uncle is the new lawn guy. He showed Mom and me how to prune the tomato plants in the community garden. Remember, Mom?"

Mom nodded. "The complex's new groundskeeper," she said to

Dad. "Do you know that if tomatoes don't ripen on the vine, you're supposed to pick off the flowers?"

"Mrs. O'Malley calls him a *stud muffin*," Sophie said. "Which means he's hot."

"Where do they live?" I picked up my plate.

Sophie leaned over, swiped my uneaten toast, and gave Mom a look meant to say, *oh, Nick.* "They moved into the condo that used to have all the wind chimes outside."

I got up from the table and moved to the trash, scraping my congealed breakfast inside.

"Aren't you hungry?" Mom asked. "Is everything okay, sweetie? This has been a lot of excitement for you."

"Fine," I grumbled, keying in *1111* to unlock my phone. Five messages, all in Mav's ALL CAPS trademark:

Maverick: YO, IRVING
Maverick: YOU WORKING TOMORROW?
Maverick: I'LL COME BY
Maverick: BE THERE IN THE NICK OF TIME
Maverick: GET IT?

I got it all right. The whole town was under the impression I'd completed a heroic solo mission I hadn't done, recorded for the rest of time in our only local newspaper and undoubtedly shared on every social media adults had access to. All morning, my parents had looked at me knowingly, as if all their parenting had paid off because of this one act. They mistakenly believed I'd followed through with my training and rescued a fellow educator.

I could turn around right now and tell them everything. Explain that among the falsely printed words in the article, the reporter had missed the fact that December had been the one to save Mr. Francis. That I'd lost my nerve, choking on my own lack of confidence before I could muster my training and do what I was supposed to do.

I'd already been lying to everyone I knew since May. I couldn't stomach doing it again.

Or I could let the details remain . . . muddy. At least for a little while. I bit my upper lip. I could let my parents keep looking at me this way, full of pride in how they'd raised me, advocating for anything and everything on my behalf.

I rolled my shoulders back and inhaled. My parents had finally half timed their constant academic surveillance once they'd felt I had learned to stand up for myself.

Maybe it was time I proved them right.

CHAPTER SIX
December

I GRIPPED THE serrated edge of the packing tape clinging to yet another box and lifted. The rip of adhesive echoed in the eggshell-white walls of our living room. "Here," I said, sliding my uncle the box. "This one's yours. Those antiaging gardening gloves are in there."

"What a scam." Evan laughed, stashing his phone. Even though he spent approximately ninety seconds a day creating videos, my uncle was mildly TikTok famous for, of all things, gardening tips. He went from taking seven seconds to tell people to dip rose cuttings in honey for its natural rooting-hormone properties to grow a whole new rosebush to having BuzzFeed slide into his DMs to feature him in articles like "28 Tips to Up Your Apartment Garden Game" or "12 Ways to Hack Your Grass from GardenTok."

"Trade you." Evan slid me a medium-sized box marked *DEC*. "You're acting awfully chipper today."

I stopped humming. "Am not." I was caught in the crosshairs of falling in love and trying as hard as I could to save the person I was about to love from dying. Standard afternoon.

"What's with this mood?"

"I don't have a mood."

"You *are* a mood. Usually. But this?" He waved his palm between us, scattering dust motes from the air in whatever apartment these were packed in previously. "This is not my beloved niece. You're a sun-shower right now—all smiley one second, cloudy the next."

I groaned and pulled a folder from the box, then promptly stuffed it into the one marked *TRASH*. "Chance of precipitation is zero percent."

"There she is," Evan said, rescuing the folder from its demise. Shaking his head, my uncle pulled a pair of rusty gardening shears from another box. He made a face and tossed them into the discard pile. "Why do I keep this stuff?"

"Because Cam?"

"Because Cam," he said, his eyes softening as they always did at any mention of his mother. Cam was someone who had kept everything. "So." Evan wiped his hands. "We're unpacking our stuff. This is new."

I avoided his gaze. "We are." We were home—*home* home, long-term—for the first time. That, at least, hadn't changed in the swamp soup that was the result of me saving Mr. Francis.

"We never unpack after a move."

"Correction. We also did after the fifteenth-ish one or so. The apartment above the laundromat."

Ever since I moved in with Evan, we held the same pattern. Move, settle, disrupt, repeat. As soon as we'd find our stride in a new place, I'd mess it up by shocking a teacher with the news of her husband filing for divorce, or advising a playmate to choose the pink cast before they fell off the monkey bars and broke their elbow. We'd move again. With zero complaints from Evan. We'd pack up, he'd apologize to Paul or Saul or Raul for breaking up with them, and we'd hop in his Jeep for the next stop.

All that, before I learned better. Before I learned to not score 100s on all my tests, before I learned my own gumballs were not for others to chew.

Evan has been my all. My only parent hightailed it out of my life without a backward glance, and my uncle didn't just step up to the plate—he cartwheeled right over it. He made sure my socks were clean and my clothes were folded. He was better than a place. He was home.

"I guess this means you're feeling good about the condo," Evan said.

"Mmm." Noncommittal.

"Good, like we'll be staying here for a long time?" he pressed.

"Don't," I warned. Our agreement had one rule: Don't talk about the elephant in my head. "Your work is solid here. That's all." His landscape and design business usually paid the bills in more of a paycheck-to-paycheck than thriving-business way. Evan had long quit being concerned, since I never worried about it. I guess it's hard to have work stress if your all-knowing niece doesn't seem bothered.

He thumbed open an aging manila folder, stuffed with page after page of watercolor-crinkled landscapes. "Oh, Dec. Your art!"

Early on, a preschool teacher had told my mom she was concerned about me because my pictures rarely had people in them—and when they did, they were doing boring adult things like drinking coffee at a conference and spring cleaning. I remember drawing some potentially warning-label-worthy ones, too, but I instinctively knew not to show my teachers those. Before I could explain to my mom how I was different, art was how I made sense of the world. I hadn't picked up a non-school-issued art utensil since she left. "Let me see." I held my palm out.

His smile was something. Wistful? "You used to love this stuff," he said, handing it over.

Page after page of age-stained sheets furiously painted by my eight-or-so-year-old self stared back at me. The stone cover of a natural pool beneath the hot Aruban sun, an abstract field of fawn lilies beside Mount Hwaya in Gapyeong, a waterfall in Gabon. Places I'd never seen in person.

"Do you want more art supplies?" Evan asked. "Remember how you used to do those charcoal drawings of New York? The building silhouettes?"

I pressed my lips together and shook my head. "Drawing reminds me of Mom."

Pop quiz. My mother was:

A) In San Diego, working as a college admissions counselor.
B) A housekeeper in a prewar co-op across the street from
   Central Park on the Upper West Side of Manhattan.
C) In Omaha, working as a waitress at a diner.

Other options: Kansas. Ohio. Oklahoma. Vegas. All wrong. Or maybe all right. As far as I knew, my mother was:

D) All of the above, and
E) None of the above.

I knew she was *somewhere*—occasionally, I got a flash of something that felt real, such as her eating ramen, blending blush on her cheek, jutting her elbow out the driver's side window. But she was also nowhere, because her presence

(or absence . . . ?)

in the world is empty.

Some part of my gift had broken in my head when she left. My mother was my mind's sole exception, the one thing I could not grasp, no matter how hard I tried. She was the dotted areas in my vision, as if I'd stared at the sun too long and burned my gift's retina. Instead, when I would lie in bed at night, or ride beside my uncle in the car, I made up stories about what she was doing. To fill it. Blank Spot.

I can only remember her the same way most people would be able to recall a mother who had left them when they were seven. She was in my episodic memories—the coins in my own personal piggy bank. Those memories of my mother were weird. Backlit and pockmarked, almost.

Now my uncle and I worked for the better part of an hour, keeping a spatula, a French press, this strange fancy barometer he used in grad school. We tossed almost everything else—old tax forms, mildewed pillow covers, a guidebook on disc golf, which Evan mimed throwing like a Frisbee to make me laugh.

I picked up the last of the boxes, hearing the rattle of a leftover item inside. My breath caught in my throat. What was going to come out would remind me of the one woman my mind was able to forget.

Evan glanced at me, waiting.

"It's the wishing well." My words tumbled out, sharp and clipped. I ran my finger along the scuffed edges of the itty-bitty figurine. Mom had always tucked it in her purse for good luck. Until the day she left it behind for me.

"Ahh, right," Evan said, pressing the trash items into the box harder than necessary. "How unbelievably kind of her to gift the memento to you."

"Your sarcasm is showing."

"Wasn't trying to hide it." Evan might be the best parental figure in human history, but he still has moments where he lets his resentment fly. After all, my mother didn't only saddle him with me—she ditched her own mother, too, leaving her brother to figure out Cam's care.

The thing was, I got it. Sometimes I missed her so much my stomach hurt. Other times—especially whenever I met someone new and explained that I lived with my uncle—I felt like the word *ABAN-DONED* had been stamped on my forehead.

Now, though, I popped his shoulder with my knuckles. "Too bad this wishing well isn't even *useful*," I said, struggling to keep a smirk from my face. "Not like those antiaging gardening gloves."

His glare turned into a snort, and we both cracked up. I breathed a sigh of relief. Mood restored.

CHAPTER SEVEN

Nick

THERE WAS SOMETHING deeply unsettling about waking up to the sound of a falling object.

My bedroom shared a wall with the living room of the unit next to us, which our neighbor—a fitness instructor—had transformed into a home gym. The sound that had woken me was suspiciously hard yet muffled, like a twelve-pound weight hitting carpet installed during Bright Acres's construction twenty years ago.

Bright Acres was the sort of place that seemed like it should be a stopover for people transitioning from one part of life to the next. College grads, town newcomers, the recently divorced. Instead, folks moved in, maybe with the best of intentions to move on, and stayed. We were on the first of six streets of condo units, each of which included two green spaces. Our direct neighbors were mostly single people who'd been here as long as I could remember, and one family with twin toddlers.

From next door came the dull, pulsating beat of electronic dance music, remixed to a hundred-fifty-plus beats per minute. Hooking my feet on the back bedrail, I draped myself over the edge of my loft bed, stretching my arms until my shoulder sockets popped. I scrabbled on the desk below, snagged my phone, and brought it back up to my nest of blankets.

Yawning, I keyed in my code to the lock screen. My eyes widened at the three-digit red bubble of notifications.

I bolted upright, smacking my hairline against the ceiling for the thousandth time in my life.

"I need a new bed," I muttered, clicking on the notifications. I'd been tagged in that news article by twenty different people overnight, mostly by parents or friends of my mom's. I groaned.

*You have **284** follow requests*

Thirty texts.

Inbox (14)

I shoved my phone under my pillow.

I had the horrible, sinking suspicion that this wasn't going to go away unless I did something about it. I swung my legs over the side and heaved myself off the elevated mattress, frustrated with my inertia.

I knew what I had to do.

—

Knowing what I had to do didn't stop me from promptly losing my nerve outside of Joe DiPietro's office.

I stood on the sidewalk, the wheels on my overturned bike still spinning. It wasn't much to look at—a house, really, only identifiable by a doleful wooden sign and a thin strip of parking lot. Unit 1E. Shady on one side, sunny on the other; cars whizzing by on a four-lane road.

I tried to summon the resolve to jog up the sidewalk, but again, I couldn't move. This time, though, my feet weren't stuck—my brain unkindly told them not to go up there.

What was I supposed to say? *Hey, remember that feel-good story you published yesterday? It's a crock of lies. Fix it for me, will you?*

41

My bike's wheels slowed, then stopped. I heaved a sigh and bent over, reaching for the handlebars, when the sound of a slamming door broke through the intervals of speeding cars.

I straightened, my chest vibrating at the sight of Joe DiPietro high-stepping down the brick stairs. His hair was wet, as if he'd recently showered, his jeans low-slung and his face all stubbly behind his definitely expensive sunglasses.

How do I know? When you have enough money for the basics but nothing left over for the luxuries in a high-luxury town, you know how much expensive sunglasses cost, because you can't afford them.

My resolve sagged further, until I realized he hadn't noticed me, I could blend in right here, he'd go by, and—

"Hey," I blurted out.

His face turned, at first with a casual glance, then a flicker of recognition. "Oh, it's you. Woodland's teenage dream." His pace slowed. "Did you fall off your bike or something? Good on you for wearing a helmet. Ninety-seven percent of bike fatalities don't. Wouldn't want to publish your obituary right after your big save."

I swallowed, flustered. "Hey. No, I didn't fall. I, uh. Can I talk to you for a sec?"

He shrugged. "Sure. My car's over there. I'm going to the café to bang out a story." He patted a messenger bag slung crosswise over his chest.

My mouth was dry. I picked up my bike, pushing it as I walked, trying to both keep pace with the reporter and avoid a pedal to the shin. "You got some of the details wrong."

"The news often does, kid."

"But the story's wrong."

He sighed. "Fine. I'll bite. What is it?"

"Uh." My tongue tripped over my words. "Lots. I'm gonna be a senior. I'm almost eighteen. I didn't finish my training in December; a girl named December helped me."

"Our fact-checker verifies every detail for the community newspapers in the state, kid. Sorry she got your birthday wrong."

I clenched my teeth. "Everyone's sharing the one you wrote."

He paused outside of a nondescript sedan. Toyota. I'd pictured him in something sharper. "Let me guess. Girlfriend wants the credit?" He opened the back door, unlooped the messenger bag from around his neck, and tossed it on the seat. Dude was careless with a laptop.

"That's not it. I don't even know her."

"No biggie. People barely read retractions, so it's really not worth the time. Enjoy the spotlight." He opened his car door. "Good luck."

The air left my lungs, my neck stiffening. My parents listened to this guy. *I* listened to this guy. We took him for his word. He'd had some major role in finally helping convict this local lawyer of murdering his wife a few years ago after he blew apart the guy's alibi a decade later. He'd been on three episodes of *Mystery Buff*. And all he did was take the easy road? All my pacing, chickening out, trotting along the heels of this Z-lister's coffee run—for this? I blinked away my rage. "Wait."

He paused. "What is it?"

My heart thumped. "Please," I said finally. "It means a lot to me. I don't want to take the credit for this. Saving someone's life is a big deal. And it's not ethical to not tell the truth."

He lowered himself into his car, rolling down the windows to let the hundred-plus-degree air out. "Tell you what. If your girl comes in and corroborates your story, then fine. I'll print a retraction." One side of his mouth dimpled, his nostrils flaring slightly.

I resisted the urge to clench my handlebars.

"Deal," I agreed, without any clue in the world as to how to make that happen.

CHAPTER EIGHT
December

EVEN THOUGH HE wouldn't be here until after nine, I'd been up for hours, heavy with anticipation and nerves. The former, because duh—here was the first boy I'd ever fall in love with. My candy-apple-red gumball.

And the latter because I was rarely uncertain about how things were going to play out, and yet here I was, a chapter torn from the center of my daily novel. That meant only one thing. Whatever was going to happen with Nick must have something to do with my mother.

At this moment in time, he was on his way here to try and convince me to do something for him, and right in the middle of our conversation, boom.

Blank.

I'd lain there, casting ideas out to the universe like fishing line, trying to strategize any possible scenario I could create to clear my Blank Spot's visibility. But it was like an active volcano protruding from the ocean. Untouchable.

I could go with him to the newspaper, but if I did that, then we would not fall in love, and he would die.

I could *not* go with him to the newspaper and wait until school started, when we'd be forced into the same setting every day, and feel the weight of his burning shame whenever he looked at me: a living reminder of his failure.

And again: no love. Ultimately, his death.

Every single scenario I committed to resulted in the same thing: no love. Just death.

I stood in my bedroom waiting for his knocks. I grazed my knuckles along my mother's wishing well. Heaving a sigh, I dipped my finger in a tin of lip balm, slicked it along my lips, and tried to psych myself up for what inevitably must have to happen: me giving up the part of myself that was most vulnerable.

From outside came a series of what would become familiar sounds: a bicycle kickstand, three quick steps, the scraping of rubber soles against the outdoor mat my uncle replaced seasonally, a carry-over habit he'd learned from Cam.

On Nick's phone was that beloved podcast of his. The one with the host everyone desperately wanted to know the identity of—everyone but me, that is, since I knew he was a part-time construction worker in Pennsylvania, living in his aunt's basement and going to grad school at night for poetry. On my way to the door, I squashed a sigh.

"It's you," Nick said by way of greeting. His features were blurry behind the screen door. Shadowed. He glanced above him. "There used to be, like, thirty wind chimes lining your roof."

"I know. We took them down. They were loud at night."

He wound the cord of his headphones around his wrist, swinging it ever so slightly. "Can I talk to you?"

Yes. "I guess so."

At the sight of the faint worry lines around his eyes, my heart, my soul—whatever made up my insides—fired on, like a burner flame going from low to high. Twin flames, actually: desire, or really the anticipation of it, a hot-coal orangey red. The other, a cool lemon.

Mellow yellow. It was the color of impatience, or maybe fake patience, because I had none of it but had to pretend I did. I tried to take a deep breath without being obvious, gearing myself up for something I was incredibly unaccustomed to experiencing. Pending uncertainty.

The next few minutes were locked in my mind's concrete, but after that? I had to endure whatever tangential way my mother touched this conversation to ensure he'd stick around long enough to fall in love.

Nick flipped his hat backward. "I need you to talk to the newspaper guy."

I lifted the door latch and pushed the screen open, forcing him to move aside so I could join him on the stoop. His face flushed, trace freckles visible on the slope of his nose. "What newspaper guy?"

"Joe DiPietro. The one who wrote the article. About the—about two days ago."

I fought to keep my expression blank. "What article?" *The one on my desk.*

"Oh, good. At least one person in town hasn't read it."

"I'm not a hundred years old. I don't read the local newspaper."

"The *Gazette* put it out. It's—Let's say it's inaccurate. It's all about me saving Mr. Francis. Nothing about you."

He was long and lean. He gave off the impression that he was born in a locker room, wearing Adidas slides and logging PR swim times in a notebook. This was the part of this gift that was weird (okay, maybe one of many): I did not know how this would *feel*. I didn't know nerves would dance like champagne bubbles in my belly, or that oxygen in my lungs almost had a taste. I arranged my face into a polite smile. "And what would you want me to say to this reporter, exactly?"

"I want you to tell him the truth."

47

I crossed my arms. "Why?"

A line beside his mouth deepened. Exasperation? Impatience? "Because it's not right."

I tilted my head, pretending to think. "No, I'm good." I turned around and put my hand on the door. "Need anything else?"

I'd never (personally) seen someone actually blanch before, but now was my time. The color drained from Nick's face, going from peach to paper. "Wait. What? Why don't you want the credit?"

I suppressed a smile. "Why do you need me to take it?"

"Because . . ." A furious adjustment of his hat. "Because it wasn't only me."

"Pretend it was, then," I said. "I don't need the attention. I'm already the new kid. I don't want to start senior year with my name in the news."

"But I didn't do it!" Nick's voice rose. "The reason why Mr. Francis is alive is because you were there. You helped me get him out. You did the CPR, you called 911—"

"So?"

He furrowed his brow. "So, me getting this credit is bullshit."

I leaned against the thin strip of vinyl siding between the screen door and the railing. "What is it? You don't like the attention?"

"It feels . . ." He paused, searching for the word. "Fraudulent."

I curled my tongue in my mouth, examining the pebbles of all my memories—an endless number of them, when you factor in this whole world's past and future events. Usually I didn't do this. Climb. The infinite search was exhausting; my skull cracking painfully with every memory I rattled. In my head, I held countless keys, but a thousand of them might fit into this lock—the reason why he was insistent about this. I tried to find the one that would tell me why this boy carried such a hefty weight around with him.

I found a missed goal at the final buzzer of soccer championships, a sobbing mess of a child after an experience putting his dog under anesthesia. Those weren't it.

I climbed further, pushing. Pressing. A dead grandmother. Head in his hands at a wooden desk, a green banker's light beside him, his father hovering behind him like a balloon. Surrounded by devices. Assistive technology. Screenreader, a pen that looked like a thermometer. Misery and struggle etched his face. His dad, folded arms, his smile both patient and sad.

The podcast.

Aha.

"What do your parents think about all of this?" I asked.

"I didn't tell them the truth," he said. His voice dropped. "Yet."

"So you think if the newspaper corrects its report—"

"That the town will quit losing its mind over the story. Yes."

"People barely read retractions."

He frowned. "Wait. How do you know?"

I shrugged one shoulder. "Twitter."

"Joe DiPietro, the reporter? He said if you came forward, he'd print a retraction." His eyes were wide and honest. "Will you?"

I shook my head. "I'm sorry. I really am."

His face twisted in disappointment. "I don't know what to say." He looped the headphones across his neck, tugging on the dangling buds.

I paused to collect myself, my gaze drifting upward. Finally, I pointed to his headphones. "Um. Listening to anything good?"

He blinked. "What? It's . . . *Mystery Buff*. It's a—"

"Podcast," I interrupted. "I know."

"You like it?"

I bit the inside of my cheek, about to deliver my last piece of knowledge of this moment. One last turn on my internal GPS before

I plunged over a cliff. "It's okay. I don't really do mysteries." I'd never listened to it. Hard to hook me with a mystery, with one pretty exceptional exception.

"Really? My dad got me into them. He used to be a criminal defense lawyer. Why don't you like them?"

And here we were. Uncharted waters. A fuzzy gray sensation enveloped the corners of my vision, cueing my Blank Spot. The biggest clue to what I had to tell him. Still, there was something almost impossible about giving this lifeguard *this part* of myself. It was as fragile as one of Evan's spring bulbs, and I was digging it up mid-bloom and crushing it in my fist.

Whatever my Blank Spot was made from, it was born when she left. It was as if my gift had malfunctioned with her loss. "My mom has been missing for nine years."

Confusion crossed his forehead. "Your mom? Oh, wow. That's a lot. I'm sorry."

Thinking about her opened a hole in my chest, and everyone knows that what goes into a black hole in the solar system never comes out. But if I did this—if I served this mystery-loving boy the story of a missing woman—I figured I'd be seeing him, more and more.

He'd be seeing me.

After all, I knew about the upcoming kiss at the foot of the driveway of a girl I hadn't met yet; I knew about the hot mugs in passenger seats and climbing trees by the condo pond. I could taste the ice cream in a waffle cone and feel the simmering catch of our eyes in the hallway at school.

I needed to keep him around because I'm selfish, and I wanted all that. It's not because I was desperate for a boy to love me—it's because I was desperate to *feel* instead of witness.

Besides, one quick climb through history told me people have

50

done out-of-bounds things for love. One guy faked his own death, complete with blood and a movie production team chronicling the whole thing, then stood up and proposed. He wanted to make sure the woman *pondered how badly her life would be without him* before signing on for life.

I didn't need to know how that would feel. Hard pass.

I wanted something like my favorite love story, about a Chinese couple named Liu and Xu. Their village forbade elder women from being with younger men, so they escaped to an isolated mountain cave with Xu's children. Over the next fifty or so years, Liu carved more than six thousand steps into the side of the mountain to make the much-older Xu's treks upward easier.

I mean, come on.

Love was a big motivation, sure. But these stakes were even higher. If I couldn't figure out how to keep Nick around, then he'd be dead, and it would be my fault.

"You have no idea where she is?" he asked, interrupting my spiraling thoughts.

"Not a clue. She did a good job of making it clear she didn't want to be found."

His face clouded. "That sucks. I'm sorry. So you live with . . ."

"Just me and my uncle," I said. "My mom's brother."

He nodded, seemingly understanding what wasn't said—no other parent in the picture. As our conversation hit this awkward point, my gift winked back on, unchanged from before. I'd played it right.

"I have to get to work." He retreated down my steps, his broad shoulders stiff enough to hang on a coat hanger. "Let me know if you change your mind about the article."

"I will." I wouldn't. And neither would he. I closed the door after him, my thoughts a jumble of anticipation, relief, fear, and regret.

CHAPTER NINE

Nick

THE POOL MANAGER, Trish, had been covering the first hour every Thursday to check the water's pH levels, so I still had more than a half hour before my shift. I pumped my feet on my bike's pedals, putting as much distance between me and December as I could. My bike jolted over a slightly upturned brick on her street, but once I hit the pavement encircling the pool, all I heard was the whirring of the wheel spokes beneath the hammering of the pulse in my ears.

I couldn't see that chlorinated blue rectangle without thinking about how I'd unwillingly hesitated to save Mr. Francis. And the moment I thought about that, guilt dropped into my stomach faster than a plot twist on *Mystery Buff*. I jumped the speed bump and swung into the main condo roadway. Once I hit smoother pavement, I stood to pedal, gripping the handlebars and sailing past the tiger lily wildflowers and tall, perfect pines that lined the concrete.

I crossed the road into the Little League fields adjacent to our complex. At three or four this afternoon, the dusty parking lot would be full of minivans and SUVs, with hordes of uniform-clad kids dragging baseball bats and chomping wads of grape- or bubble-gum-flavored Big League Chew. But this early in the morning, the fields were mine.

I steered around a fallen log, pedaled through the short forest path in four quick bursts, and coasted into the entrance. Nothing had changed since I had been here last summer, catching a game with Maverick. Dirt-and-gravel-strewn pathways led to each field, six in all, and right in the center was a snack shack where I used to trade Mom's empty seltzer cans for pretzel rods.

Growing up, anytime Mom worked late in the summer, Dad would send Sophie and me here for dinner. Five bucks for two foil-wrapped hot dogs and a tray of hot salted fries. Sophie dipped hers in vinegar; I soaked mine in ketchup.

Outside field 5, I skidded to a stop. Dust and gravel sprayed over the diamond-link fence, the wires rusted with age. I lifted the lock and ducked inside the dugout. It was smaller than I remembered. Darker, too, but it smelled the same. Fried dough and dirt.

I sprawled on the bench, staring at the cracks of sky visible through the wooden ceiling. Finally, honestly, truly alone.

When I was a kid, I'd been a consistently average player with a handful of amazing plays. Content to be in Mav's shadow. Because unlike at school, crammed into remedial rooms and aides who TALKED. LIKE. THIS. the second any student entered their space, I wasn't trying to defend my intellect. I used to think that everyone else thought I was dumb, and it took me a long time to figure out that they didn't—it was me worrying about something that had never even happened. Back then, this place was a respite. Here, I didn't need to be smarter than the kid next to me, whose baseball pants also came from Amazon and smelled of All-brand Free Clear detergent until they were covered in mud and sod stains. Here, it didn't matter that I read slower than anyone else and that I used to need to perform mental calisthenics to tell time on an analog watch.

But now I was back there. Except this time, I knew I was smart.

I also knew I was a coward, and I could not sit with that feeling any longer. I closed my eyes, surprised to find heat beneath my eyelids, the kind that signaled the start of tears.

I'd be the first to admit that in comparison to a lot of people in the world, I knew I was doing okay—I was fed, clothed, loved. My parents had drilled that into me since childhood.

But sometimes, it seemed as though I couldn't do anything right. Couldn't school right, couldn't lifeguard right. Didn't make swim captain, didn't make the farm team the first two times I'd applied, thanks to my shitty backstroke start.

There was no rewriting my body's hesitation. What was done was done.

Unless . . . what if I could somehow not rewrite what happened, but maybe redeem myself? What if I could do December a major solid and find her mother?

I was a binge listener often enough to know that clues would help, but it didn't take an *Unsolved Mysteries* reboot to know that many mysteries stayed, well, mysteries. But what if even the mere act of trying to do this—even if I failed *again*—sort of made up for the fact that I couldn't save Mr. Francis solo?

I opened my eyes, allowing myself to picture it for one moment. Permission to think about how it would feel if the prideful way my mother had looked at me after reading the article was justified, if the words Mr. Francis said to Joe DiPietro really did define who I was and what I thought and how the world perceived me.

If I really deserved the accolades. If I wasn't a fraud.

I thought of all the times the Buffys had guessed right. One week, the *Mystery Buff* host described a series of small-time robberies—twenty bucks from a woman at a bus stop, a handful of pickpocket incidents, and, more seriously, a twenty-four-hour gas station holdup—all linked to two people. Using Google Maps, the coordinates from a dropped Target receipt, and a cardboard cup from a bank, the Buffys narrowed down their identities; one internet sleuth then unearthed an accidental post to Instagram, meant for a DM, tagged #crimecomplete, which the prosecution must have paraded in court.

For years and years, I read Joe DiPietro's stories, watched crime docs, and listened to the podcast. All these stories, all these clues and details that drove people to the forums: They'd entertained me.

And for the first time in my life, I was sitting in the passenger seat of a real person's mystery. The intro music of *Mystery Buff* played in my head. I imagined the host's deep, self-assured voice opening an episode with:

> *Welcome, Buffys. We've got a special episode for you today. After one Massachusetts lifeguard bungles the save of a drowning victim, he manages to redeem himself by embarking on the quest of a lifetime. Can you solve the cold case of a mother missing by choice and not by chance?*

I sat up, filled with a flicker of something both powerful and ugly. Powerful if it were possible, ugly because it wasn't. Was it?

I rubbed my forehead. Last spring, I was one scrawny point away from a senior year spent at a new school. One my parents presented to me, hopeful I'd leap at the opportunity.

Innovative technology, Nick. A grades-free atmosphere. No standardized testing. Accessible curriculum.

No clock to chase you.

A confidence boost before college.

Cool. Also: Zero swim team. An hour each way in traffic. No Maverick.

All that was in the past now. Maybe soon enough, the whole hero thing would cease anyway. The town would move on during another news cycle. After all, it's not like a lifeguard saving someone is so extraordinary that it snags a Nobel Prize.

Right?

Right?

But I had a lifetime habit of being wrong, so why stop now?

My first clue that I was mistaken about the timeline of the heroic die-down should've been the Edible Arrangements truck easing over the speed bump as I biked back to the pool. It creaked down our lane, the red glow of the brake lights blinking every few feet until they stopped outside our door.

My stomach plummeted. Delivery trucks weren't uncommon, but this one at our unit certainly was.

The next clue that this whole hero thing wasn't about to end was far more obvious, and far more nerve-racking.

The pool deck was packed. Dozens of towels were cast to the end of the white plastic lounge chairs or hung over the fence. The air rang with the sound of kids' wet feet slapping the cement. I spotted a trio of immediately recognizable girls flipping magazines, guests of Bright Acres's own resident Woodland High popularity queen (but, to shock the high school cliché, super-nice girl) Maisie Cabrera.

We didn't exactly swim in the same circles, so I hadn't seen Maisie all summer, even though she lived less than a football field's throw away from the pool.

I resisted the urge to turn back—hunker beneath the shaded seclusion of the dugout, full of little-kid, starry-eyed dreams and the sound of American promises, when I heard someone—Mrs. O'Malley?—shout,

"It's him, it's him!" It was as if she'd pressed a button to reset a game. The crowd quieted, faces pivoted toward me. And suddenly, someone clapped. They all joined in, their hands blurring with applause and the air choking with undeserved cheers of my name.

Bile inched up my esophagus. I gulped, fighting the urge to leave. The hunch that I was in this thing way, way over my head clutched my gut, wouldn't let go. It dialed higher, intensifying, but I stayed where I was, raising a cold, clammy hand in greeting.

CHAPTER TEN
December

MY GRANDMOTHER'S ROOM was the last one on the right in the Alzheimer's wing of the Wisteria Hills Nursing Home, conveniently located seven minutes from Bright Acres Condos and one of the prime reasons Evan had accepted the landscaping gig there. Whenever we lived a reasonable radius away, Evan and I—and, before, Mom—made a weekly trek here to visit Cam. But about four years ago, when Cam started getting worse—moving from severe forgetfulness to almost no communication in the span of eight months—our visits had fallen off.

Her name was short for Camilla. She'd never wanted to be called Grandma, Nana, or one of the cutie ones, like Gigi or Mimi.

On those early visits, Mom's tactic was to flutter around the room, her voice bright as tinfoil in the sun, her hands a flurry of activity. Straightening sheets, wiping trays, fussing over the number of paper towels in the bathroom, back when Cam used it unassisted. Back when Cam's forgetful face was a pleasant, polite blank, instead of the slack one she wore now.

Evan plopped on a pleather ottoman near Cam's wheelchair. Elbows on his knees, face and voice both upturned, he described our new rug and wall frames for the condo. Through a process by which I do not understand, the room smelled like a smoothie made from apple juice, chicken patties, baby powder, and bleach. Super unfitting for a woman who wore vanilla-scented deodorant and said things like *being considerate is free.*

I despised these visits. Missing Cam, knowing she was here but gone—it was one of those impossible feelings too big to name. Blaring and bottomless.

". . . you'd love it, Mom. Business is good." He shifted his focus to me. "Why don't you say something?"

"Like what?"

He exhaled, scraping his knuckles along his beard, creating this muffled rustling sound. "Tell her something about her life. Help her remember."

"Evan, she's not in there."

He gave me a hard look. "Do you *know that* know that, or are you guessing?"

I wrinkled my nose and didn't answer. Evan and I did not skate into this territory too often. He used to slam drawers and throw glares at Mom when she'd press me about when to leave to pick up her friend at the airport, the amount of snow we'd get from a forecasted blizzard, or the existence of God(s).

I didn't need precognition to know my uncle was always on my side.

And Cam. My memories of her featured a neighborhood food truck that served spicy fish tacos and street corn and toasted turkey sandwiches. Museum visits and feeding ducks and watching movies on the couch, my wet hair lathered with Cam's special leave-in conditioner and tied atop my head, oily droplets soaking my back.

Those moments were remarkable for their unremarkability. They represented our family's normalcy, unlike the ones that shrouded

Cam's decline. Car keys in the refrigerator, a loaf of bread shoved in the linen closet. *Would you require a bathtub for dinner?* Two decades after 9/11: *Can you believe those planes hit the Twin Towers last week?*

Then, later. *Where's my daughter, Mara? That goddamn woman.*

Now Cam's unfocused eyes stared out the window.

In the corner chair, I crossed and recrossed my legs, the backs of my thighs peeling from the matching-ottoman pleather material with the sort of pain that told me I'd left half my skin cells behind. My lower back was heavy and tight because of one very particular gumball that had passed through my blanket knowledge this morning: This would be my third-to-last time seeing Cam.

Like my midnight kitchen raids for Uncrustables and Evan's weakness for *Love Island*, we did not speak of Cam's not-too-far-in-the-distance death. I knew what was coming for him. A bowed head over a casket, sleepless nights over insurance codes and hospital paperwork. Thankfully, selling the duplex had covered her stay here.

I sighed. This version of her saturated me with sadness. This helpless-as-a-newborn shell of her once strong, muscular, maternal self. Sometimes, when I stared at my ceiling at night, I worked myself up, wondering if the real her was still trapped inside. I massaged the back of my neck with my hand, chasing the stiffness along my vertebrae.

I cleared my throat. "I like your braid, Cam." Her hair was still shockingly dark for an elderly woman, and some young nurse had woven it into a thick French plait that divided her curved back in half. "My mom used to do mine like that."

A blank smile was on the side of her mouth, but it wasn't for me. She made the sort of clicking noise she'd taken to doing.

Evan shook his head. "Your mom didn't know how to braid."

I frowned. "Yes, she did."

"Nope."

"But I remember her doing it." Memories of my mom were fuzzy, but I had this one. I was sure of it. I furrowed my eyebrows, dipping instead into the foreknowledge bank for today's gumball and wincing when I saw what would come next. And as the proverbial cherry on top, now that I had wasted all this time applying my own thought process into considering it, I'd probably missed a thousand other things coming my way. See why this whole thing is exhausting?

"It was Cam. She did your mom's hair, too. When you came along, Cam braided yours, my humble plant."

Humble plant. I fell silent at the use of my old nickname. At all this information. You know how food commercials essentially rely on your perception of hunger to entice you into a restaurant? The way I *know* about what happens versus how I *experience* what happens is similar to that. Seeing painted-on grill lines on TV burgers does not equate to standing at the grill, smelling the sizzling meat and the smoke from the fire, and sinking your teeth into the burger. It's watching a movie kiss versus pressing your lips up against someone else's, feeling the heat and desire and emotional gravitas.

Right now, though, it was recalling the tug and pull and tweak of expert fingers in my long, coarse hair. Quickly, I abandoned my own memories in favor of the world's collection, climbing back and back and back until I confirmed it for myself. A small version of me, nestled between Cam's knees, reading books while her fingers, deft and nimble, wove my strands. "I guess I always thought it was Mom."

"Your mom was flighty, December. In and out. Graduated in major debt, gone. Came back with you. Gone. Back for a few months, skating off for a few, whenever—" He bit off his own words and swallowed them. I bet they tasted like *whenever it was convenient for her*. "She changed. So much. Like my dad."

I stared at him, stunned. Like his *dad*? My grandfather was addicted to opiates, a victim of an injury prescription. He'd overdosed and died way before I was born. "She left for *months* at a time?"

Evan's gaze flicked to Cam. Back to me. "You, of all people, don't remember?"

Did I not remember, or had my brain blocked it from me? It was a million-dollar question with a five-cent answer.

CHAPTER ELEVEN

Nick

MY DAD REVERES Malcolm Gladwell, the guy who went from *New Yorker* journalist to podcast guru. He's the dude who claimed ten thousand hours of practice makes an expert. Apparently, when the theory came out in the nineties, Dad subscribed to it as though it were the sole Law of Nature. When he quit being a lawyer, he kept a ten-thousand-hour log of learning how to cook. And perhaps as the sign from above that they were meant for each other, Mom insists it takes thirty days to acquaint yourself with a new Healthy Behavior. Her flavors of the month have included 9:45 P.M. bedtimes, morning yoga devotionals, and eight-minute meditation rituals.

Turns out it takes neither ten thousand hours nor thirty days to become an expert. All I needed was one afternoon and the fluttering eyes of three girls in my grade to make me develop the new habit of Forgetting You're Living a Lie.

—

My shift was so busy that Trish, the pool manager, had to stay on to maintain the legal ratio of guard to swimmer. Even then, we had to monitor how many people could be in the pool on a one in, one out basis.

The rectangular lanes, the blurry activity of all these people inside the fence, the coconut sunscreen and musty trace of artificial chemicals—it tumbled into my brain, assaulting me with the clear fact that two days ago was more than a scary one-time thing, a giant scar on my psyche. My heart did a sly little jig against my lungs every time I heard a splash.

One hour and two liters of sweat into my shift, I took a break in the pool shed. I ran my hand along a shiny tin box of medical equipment and dug my fingernails into a lime-green pool noodle, trying to calm down. The fact that I'd failed to act was one thing, but the sensory experience of being back here was a whole other kind of retrauma.

I was tempted to tell Trish I couldn't do it. Couldn't work here anymore. But at this point in July, where would I work? The two other places in town where teens landed jobs were Pire's Dairy Bar and the Spa, a bar-style pizza place nearly dreamlike in quality. Both places had enough applications to hire people for the next decade. Mom and Dad weren't exactly making it rain, and not working meant no money. No car insurance, no gas fill-ups, no athletics activity fee.

But what if? my brain wheezed. What if another swimmer needed my help? What if one of Mrs. O'Malley's kids swam beyond where their small feet could touch?

Would I halt in place again?

Okay, Nick. Talk yourself out of the thought spiral. I sucked the musty pool house air through my teeth and pulled my shoulders back in the most deliberate way possible, pinching my scapulae together like I was doing the butterfly stroke. Mom always claimed that if you held yourself with purpose, you'd forget you weren't confident in the first place. Besides, Trish was here. What better way to rip off the limp Band-Aid than with a professional on standby?

With that thought, I carried out the rest of my shift. I half watched Maisie Cabrera and her two friends, Stella Rose Goldman and Carrie Lee, as they scrolled their phones and hopped in and out of the pool en masse. I ducked congratulations and shoulder claps and accepted a wrapped plate of melty sugar cookies from the O'Malleys, who waited patiently until I tried one, choking on a bite that was dry, crumbly, and held together by a too-sweet glucose glaze.

When Joie O'Malley cannonballed into the pool, I sensed movement out of the corner of my eye. Maverick stood at the entrance, balancing a white box in his hands. His mouth worked around a wad of what had to be nicotine gum, and he was sporting a fresh cut, with three faded stripes etched in. (His cousin was a Black barber who had found national fame on Instagram. He lived a futile life of trying to "keep Maverick cool.") I cleared my throat again, and my chest caved in partway when I thought about trying to keep up this savior facade with my best friend.

"Yo, Irving," he said. "Your new hero status is some real college-essay-level shit, huh?"

And my chest pulverized itself. "You don't know the half of it."

He handed me the box. "Stopped by your house. Your mom made me bring these."

I lifted the lid and groaned. Chocolate-covered strawberries from Edible Arrangements.

"They're from the science department at Woodland High," Maverick said. "Your shift over?"

I checked my watch: 3:01. "Hey, I guess it is." I stood and signaled to Trish, who waved.

"Hey, Maverick!" Maisie called.

Maverick's head swiveled on his neck. His face morphed from surprise to delight as he witnessed the popular trio. "Oh, hey!" he called back, his words rising in surprise. When the girls stood and gathered their pool gear, he shot me a look, his eyes bugging from their sockets. "Why have you never mentioned the Angels come here?"

"The Angels?"

"Don't you follow them on Instagram? They tag themselves as the Angels. Ever since they were Charlie's Angels for Halloween freshman year."

I shrugged. More often than not, I skipped the captions. "Never noticed. And they don't come here."

"We heard about your big save yesterday, Nick," Carrie said as they approached. Her glossy dark hair spilled over one shoulder.

"Ah-ha." I turned to Maisie. "Haven't seen you here at all this summer."

She hiked her sunglasses on top of her head. "We've been at Stella Rose's pool."

"My mom says Mr. Francis is a national treasure," Stella Rose said. "So we decided to come see the guy who saved him in person."

I scrubbed the back of my neck with my hand. "You did?"

She angled her phone so I could see the screen. "I mean, you're practically a celebrity. Look." A selfie of the three of them, a blurry me in the background, the red rescue tube tucked beneath my arm. On duty. My gaze went down to the caption and the numbers, which I *could read* if I could focus, if her hand would stop its slight imbalance, but if she noticed how long it would take and—

"'Pool day with hashtag theRealWoodlandKnight,'" Mav read over my shoulder. "Dude. 6,586 likes. Over three hundred comments."

My ears burned. A glow of something golden and fast spread through my veins as I pictured it: A senior year made for a movie. Riding in Stella Rose's Wrangler, traveling the hallways in a pack, these girls coming to my swim meets.

"That's way more than usual," Carrie said.

"Algorithms do all kinds of things," I said, my voice sounding strangled.

"Algorithms don't write these comments." Stella Rose dashed her index finger on the screen and read, "'Whoa, he's in my grade.' Well, duh. 'OMG I know him.' 'The fact that someone I know saved a life has me deceased rn.' Oh, look at this one—"

My face must have betrayed my panic, because Maisie held up her hand to interrupt. "We're heading to Stella Rose's now. Let's all hang out sometime?"

"Sure," I said. "See you around, maybe."

After they left, Maverick pantomimed his mouth closing. "Areyou-kiddingme. You should save people more often, Irving."

Pressure built in my throat, my head, my ears. And, like I was a human Instant Pot, the only valve to release this steam was the truth. "I didn't save anyone." I walked to my bike, toed up the kickstand, and began walking alongside it. "We gotta talk."

"Come again?"

"The whole saving thing? I didn't do it."

Maverick opened the Edible Arrangements box. "Strawberry?"

While Maverick devoured the strawberries, I pushed my bike around the condo complex and spilled the truth of the last few days. How, when faced with the single most alarming moment of my life, I was unable to move. How my feet had hot-glued themselves to the cement. The way December's foot stopped tapping, the way she pinned her palms on Mr. Francis's chest to do CPR. Joe DiPietro and his article of lies that had spawned a small crowd at the pool, the Edible Arrangements delivery in my best friend's hand. December's missing mother.

"Forget college essay," Mav said when I was done. "This won't fit

67

in six hundred fifty words or less." He punctuated his point by tossing the empty cardboard box in a recycling barrel near the condo's dumpster. "So what now?"

I took a breath. "You know how I have the world's guiltiest conscience?"

"Do I ever." Maverick clasped his hands together, imitating me as a child. *"Mom, I stepped on one of your flowers. Dad, I think I pulled on the doorknob too hard. It's wiggly."* He shook his head. "You have nothing to be guilty about. Make peace with the fact that you helped save my favorite teacher of all time and do what my mother says."

"Move on past, nothing lasts," I said, quoting Maverick's mom, but behind my smile, it simmered. The smallest of blips. He was wrong, but he didn't know it. I *was* guilty of something, and everything that had happened the last few days only added to it. "But I can't."

"Extrapolate."

I watched his face as I spoke. "I'm going to find December's mother."

"Come again?" Maverick groaned. "That effing podcast."

"You don't think I can?"

"It's not that." Maverick punched my arm, rattling my bike. "Why do you think I made you my chem lab partner?"

"Because I'm your best friend?"

His glance was withering. "I want to be a neurosurgeon. I'm hardly going to campaign to have you as a partner because we're pals." He made a scoffing sound. "You really . . . I know you've struggled with your dyslexia, but it's more than that. Something like one in five people have some form of dyslexia, so it's common enough. You see the world differently than anyone I've ever met."

"What do you mean?"

"I'm granular. I'm all up in brains. I like to think about neurons and pathways and chemicals. I get lost for hours opining about scopes and the weird smell anesthesia gas gives off. But you?" He tapped his forehead. "Your brain seeks an alternate route. Sometimes it's longer, sometimes it's shorter, but you always get to where you need to. You've got this . . . global view of things. Bird's-eye." He snapped his fingers. "Mr. Turcotte's rubrics."

English class, last September. Junior year. The new teacher had put our feedback in the wrong box on the online rubric, so the grades posted incorrectly. People got angry, parents called the school, and Mr. Turcotte took a billion screenshots to explain. In class, I'd opened the rubric and simply unchecked a native setting, pushing feedback to the place where the system recorded it. "So?"

"So? You solved three days of issues in a single click."

"That was just logical."

"Lots of people don't see logic, accidental hero. They get bogged down in the deets." He wiped his hands on his shorts. "But the thing about your mystery podcast is that they're not really mysteries. They're solved stories about real people."

"I obviously know they're real people, Maverick."

"Of course you do. But I think—I know, actually, because there are studies on it—people lose sight of humanity when it comes to true crime stuff. We conflate that shit because we're used to movies and stories as fiction."

I bit my lip. "That's probably accurate."

"The sheer concept of a seventeen-year-old kid looking for a woman whose disappearance has been a cold case for almost a decade . . . it's a lot. But you're a stubborn ass. And if anyone's gonna do it, I believe in you. Just—make sure *you* remember that some-times things have no explanation. Sometimes we have no idea how the brain works. Sometimes mysteries aren't solved."

"Got it." I flicked my fingers across his shoulder, and he soft-punched me again. But my mind was already working ahead of itself, thinking about what I'd do later that night.

Go to the pool shed, get December's forgotten hat. Return to her front stoop and leave it there, along with a note.

Meet me at Welsh Park tomorrow night at 5.

CHAPTER TWELVE
December

AT WELSH PARK, a hundred or so elementary school kids and their parents milled about the wide oval track, here for the weekly town races. Parents sat in clusters, drinking iced tea while their kids played tag. I stood beneath an oak tree's dappled shade at the entrance, fidgeting.

For the second time in as many days, my Blank Spot was alive and well, thrumming beneath whatever was about to happen with Nick and me. The sensation was not as strong as it had been yesterday—sort of paling this gumball in spots. I didn't like it, but I was here in the name of speeding along our love story. I couldn't wait to dive into the feelings my vision promised.

(But the faster your timeline, the quicker the death, I reminded myself. Remember *that*? Remember the stricken look on his face, and the blood everywhere, and the orange T-shirt?)

From across the field, Nick raised an arm in greeting. He sat on the top row of the concrete bleachers that horseshoed the track, which, coupled with the swarms of competitive mini-humans, created the effect of a suburban Colosseum.

I cut across the grass and trotted up the scuffed bleacher steps, hoping I gave off a *this is effortless* vibe, yet only succeeding at increasing my heart rate and challenging my quadriceps. At the top, I smiled in greeting. "Hey. Thanks for dropping off my hat."

He bent and scratched his ankle, giving me a peek at the back of his hair curling against his neck. "Hey. No problem."

"You running today?" I joked, gesturing at the track.

He hitched a brow. "I wish. I loved these as a kid."

"They seem fun. Do you like to run now?" I sat, the concrete rough and hot beneath my thighs.

"Not really. I mostly focus on swimming."

"Oh, nice. Competitively?"

"Yep. Since elementary school."

"What's your favorite stroke?"

"Backstroke, but I'm best at butterfly." He tilted his head. "What about you?"

"Me? I don't have a favorite stroke."

He smiled. "No. Hobbies. You know, the things people do when they aren't at school, working, or sleeping?"

"I like being summoned to parks via cryptic notes," I deadpanned.

His eyes were ordinary and brown. I wanted to stare at them for hours. "I don't have your phone number."

"This is a semi-convoluted way of trying to get someone's number," I said, my voice much steadier than my insides, which screamed with *oh my God, is this what flirting feels like? Am I flirting?*

He flushed, and I bit back a smile. "I'm not—" He paused when he saw my face. "Ha. Okay. Before I go on, any chance you've reconsidered, and you're willing to go to the newspaper office with me?"

I laid my fingertip on my own pulse, pushing away all the gumballs until I could only sense the smooth warmth of my skin, the gentle bump of my veins moving beneath the pressure. A distraction from the thing I was trying to keep sacred for Nick. His life. "I'm sorry, but no."

"Look. You saved my ass this week. What if I could trade you something?"

I dug my nails into my palms. My Blank Spot reared its head. I lifted my eyebrows, waiting.

"It would make me feel a lot better if I could make up for what happened."

I studied him. "Sometimes bad things happen," I said carefully. "You don't need to, like, I don't know, *atone* for those things."

He shook his head. "I do. Personally."

"People make mistakes."

"Everyone does. And I like to balance them out." He faced me. "I know this sounds wild, but . . . what if I found your mother?"

Here it was. I sighed, pretending to mull it over. "You won't be able to find my mother," I said gently.

"Why not?"

"She's been gone nine years. Ten, this Christmas."

His expression took on one of disbelief. "She left on Christmas?"

"Two days after." I pursed my lips. "It's her choice to stay away. My grandmother isn't doing well, and if Mom kept tabs on her own mother, she'd come back."

My climb into his past told me Nick had lost his own grandmother, and his paling face confirmed it. "That sucks. Why haven't you and your uncle hired a private investigator?"

"We didn't have the money."

He nodded, accepting that instantly. Everything about him had shifted almost imperceptibly in the last minute or so. His shoulders unspooled in my direction, his face losing its practiced mask, like stale gum being chewed. "I'm good with solving the episodes on *Mystery Buff*. Gimme a shot? I really think I can do it." He paused. "Or at least figure out where she went."

You're not going to. This isn't about finding her. It's about buying time to spend with you. It's about saving your life. "Even if you could find her . . . if enough time passes, then won't people think it's weird that the newspaper would be bringing it back up then?"

"I'll say I thought it wasn't going to be as big of a deal as it became."

It wasn't the most romantic way to start a relationship—find my missing mother and I'll come clean to the media! But it might be a way for me to buy enough time to come up with a plan to save him. Satisfaction settled into my belly. "Okay."

"Okay?"

"Sure. Find out where my mother went, and then you can consider the favor returned."

"You'll go to the newspaper office with me and tell the truth?"

"I will."

His face softened. He offered his hand, and I clasped it. His wrists were thick, forearms straining with lean muscle. "I think this is the part where I actually do get your number," he said.

I banished the ridiculous smile that threatened to break across my face. "You could've just asked for it. We've known each other two seconds, and we're already trading traumas."

He handed me his phone. "I obviously had to make sure we could get through a life-or-death situation first."

I tapped in the digits, willing my fingers not to shake. "Typical."

"Great, then." He stood, sidestepping me. "I'm gonna go join my parents. My sister's about to race."

I swallowed against the urge to ask him to stay. He barely knew me. I knew the freckle on his shoulder, the way one side of his mouth smiled a few degrees higher than the other, his proclivity for calzones. He knew I was a resistant stranger who had done him a major favor. I was still nothing to him; he would be everything to me. "Good luck to her," I said. "Meet me at Pire's Dairy on Saturday? I'll bring everything you need."

"Deal," he said, tossing me a wave in farewell.

I stayed in the bleachers, watching Nick's sister, a serious-looking brunette with a major case of swagger for such a little kid, and her friends. They cheered for the younger kids, hyping them up while they waited for their turn to race.

There were no playing instructions accompanying this gift, so I was responsible for self-regulating it. I did my best to give people privacy, though I'd spent a fair amount of time when I was twelve interested in the life of Cam's long-dead aunt. She was a flapper in the 1920s who'd never married. She lived a life I used to dip into when I was bored, as if I were watching clips from a biopic movie, until I figured out that doing so gave me a cracking migraine. The more I tried to hunt for one person's experiences, the more depleted I became.

It was one thing to have this secret capability, I thought, watching Nick trot down the concrete steps and join his parents. But it was definitely another to memory-stalk. I fisted my hands, pressing my knuckles into my temples. It took a certain amount of mental contortion to climb, like rubbing a scab somewhere in my brain. And everyone knows that when you catch a scab too many times, it can leave a scar. But with Nick, I couldn't help it. I craved learning more about him, impatient to entangle my memories with my future experiences. To *feel*.

Desperate to fall in love.

But more important, most important: desperate to keep him alive.

CHAPTER THIRTEEN
Inside the Blank Spot

ONCE UPON A time, there was an extraordinary little girl and a mom she adored more than anything else on the planet. On hot summer nights, they would lie in the mother's bed because the mother had a double bed and the only room with an AC unit in the window. And on cold winter evenings, the radiator would clang and give off a scalding heat only the other side of the house could control, which is what happened when you lived in a duplex converted from a single home. An unnatural division of the house, a slapped-in second kitchen, and an out-of-code heating system made for unbearable coolness in one house hemisphere and astonishing heat in the other. So the girl and her mother would lie in the same bed with the window open, desperate for the relief of the frigid, dry air.

The mother would rub the little girl's back to help her sleep, which wouldn't work. After a while, they would face each other, the little girl winding fistfuls of her mother's dark hair around her tiny wrists. Hung on the plaster wall was a set of nails where her mother kept her favorite accessories—beaded necklaces, stiff metal bangles, a scarf with ponies stampeding along it, a black-and-white sun hat.

It was only in the dark the mother would ask questions.

In the daytime, the little girl would say something like *Don't go that way. There's an accident* or *Mama, turn on the TV, that actor you love is dead.*

At first, her mother balked. She shook her head and grinned at the girl's imagination. Her creativity! She might ask, *How could you know that, honey?*, or say, *It's not nice to speak about people that way.*

In the ocean, barnacles can pile onto anything. Whales, rocks, coral, mussels. They can even attach themselves to ships. If enough do, then they affect how a ship steers. Barnacle-laden boats consume more fuel and travel with more heft than clean ones. They drag.

Like those barnacles, the little girl's statements became coincidences piled high enough to have an impact. So after a while, her mother would simply nod and believe her. She switched to buying a new lockbox once a month, covering her hand every time she made up a new key code.

Because the little girl—December, of course—was always right.

Since birth, December had slept fitfully and never more than a few hours at a time. She woke up, screaming, when the Ugly Thoughts raced through her mind.

In a year, there would be a dead blond girl her age in the tall grass in Missouri. In two months, a father, sober for fourteen years, his head bent low over an open bottle of alcohol, a salty tear dripping off the beak of his nose.

December would be four, five, six, seven. She would try to make all these things stop. She couldn't. She *tried*.

In the dark, her mother would trace December's cheekbones, her forehead. She would tell her daughter stories about the vee of birds that cut through the sky, or about the swirls of fabric on the city streets of New Orleans, about the cricket-bright color of the green chiles in Las Cruces. On the winter nights, they had the comforter pulled up to their shoulders, single-digit-degree night air skimming across their overheated cheeks.

—What made you this way, December?

I don't know, Mama. It's part of who I am.

—Okay. Let's play a game. What's going to happen tomorrow?

In the world?

—In the world. Or in our world.

Um. That politician lady you watch is getting her own news show. In our world? Evan met a new boyfriend. We'll meet him at Christmas.

—Even I could've guessed that one.

Ha.

—What about . . . tell me why you can't change our lives.

How?

—Well. For instance, why can't you tell me the winning lottery numbers?

I can.

—Then why don't you? Don't you want to get out of this neighborhood?

No. I love it here. I don't want to move.

—Fair enough. But why . . . ?

Because I just don't, Mama. I don't change what happens. I could tell you the winning numbers, but I won't, because I don't. Because that's not our life. It's not what happens.

—But you could make it happen.

Not really. I know I don't tell anyone what the numbers are. If I break the real story and tell someone, then those numbers could change. Or worse, everything could.

—But even if it's not what you see . . .

I don't see anything. I know it.

—Okay. But what if you told me them, and I didn't do anything about it?

I don't know. But then someone might do something to make them change, and you'd be out of the money for a ticket. Or something bad could happen. You could win, and someone could rob you, or things would change too much. And it's not what happens, so it doesn't matter.

The girl would snuggle closer. After a while, Mama's voice would drop off, drowsier but braver, her hand heavy on December's shoulder.

—Do you know what happens when we die?

Door.

— . . . Door?

That's locked up tight behind the door, Mama. It's a heavy one. I know there's something behind it, but I can't get in, I don't think.

—Have you tried?

The girl thought. She'd learned to slam a door of her own. She had to. Otherwise, everyone's feelings brought her soul to its knees, decimated her mood. Left her shaking in bed, unable to eat or drink or think. One mother's pain of losing a child, cooped up and wailing on the ninth floor of a children's hospital in Ireland. The unbridled joy of a kid in South Africa learning to ride a bike. Different situations, over and over again, joy and pain and joy and pain and—

She had to shut the door, separating what she *knew* from what she *felt*. Even if it meant purposefully ignoring things she knew, sometimes, or thinking around them. Climbing.

Door.

Silence for a while, except for the hum of the air conditioner. It blew December's hair across her cheek, tickling her.

— . . . Honey?

Yes, Mama?

—Tell me something you think I should know.

December told her mother . . . something.

Whatever she said, life changed. December's gift grew the Blank Spot, where her memory went static. Buzzed, grayed out, speckled and pixelated.

Two days after Christmas, December awoke with that unfamiliar shift in the world's truth. Mama was gone. Not gone like she was sometimes gone—with phone calls and letters. Gone gone.

The girl emerged from the bedroom to find her uncle sitting at the scarred wooden table, his hands curled around a steaming mug of coffee.

He observed her without a trace of wariness. "Do you want to talk about it?"

She reached in the cabinet and pulled out a box of Cinnamon Chex Evan had brought with him and already stored away. A swell of gratitude rose within her. Her uncle remembered she liked the cinnamon kind. On the left side of the fridge, there would even be a fresh gallon of milk. "Nope."

CHAPTER FOURTEEN

Nick

I PLUNGED A paintbrush into the open can and scraped it against the side to remove the excess. Carefully, I ran its bristles down the horizontal length of wooden deck Dad had built last weekend. There was something oddly soothing about watching the whorls and grain of the wood disappear beneath the deep navy-gray color that complemented the condos' siding. The painted stripes stacked on one another until they accumulated into rectangles, then squares, until each railing was covered. I stepped back and admired our work.

Our yard was situated on an end unit of the first set of buildings, so our front door cut into the side of our condo. When I stepped outside, I was immediately faced with seven porches, all bearing traces of our neighbors' lives. Some with charcoal grills or herb gardens, two with clothing racks drying in the sun, one with ashtrays and a recycling bin. This meant that on any given day, we could hear the couple with the baby two doors down fighting in the morning, Mrs. O'Malley's Top 40 music, and even the distant sound of splashing in the pool.

The air was still and heavy with fumes. Beside me, Sophie stopped humming an overdramatic rendition of "We Are the Champions." She swiped her forearm across her sweaty forehead, the sight of which somehow made me even hotter than I already was. It was in the nineties and a terrible day to paint, overall, but we'd promised Dad we'd get it done before the end of the week, and, well: Saturday. "What would you name this color?"

I adjusted my hat, then grabbed the stick of sunscreen where it lay on the grass. I swiped it, all greasy and half-melted, along my nose and cheeks. "Hmm. Gray Matter."

Sophie wrinkled her nose. "Why?"

"That's a nickname for the brain."

"That's a bad nickname."

"How come?"

"Because brains are mostly pink. With all these gross red blood vessels that look like a road map. Or as if someone took a broom to a spiderweb."

"Nice visual." I stirred the paint with the wooden stick. "Who told you that?"

"Maverick."

I dipped my brush in again. "Oh, yeah? Well if you're so good at it, what would you name it?"

"The Winning Gray." Sophie tapped the gold medal around her neck, which she hadn't taken off since the races on Friday night. "Get it? Instead of the winning *play*?"

"I got it," I said drily. "You better not get paint on that."

Sophie flicked her paintbrush at me.

Around the corner, our screen door slammed. Mom rounded the edge of the condo holding her phone. "I got an email." She squinted at her palm.

"Congratulations." I mimed clapping. "Is this your first?"

She made a face at me. "The email is from a news affiliate in

82

Boston. A podcast." She thumbed the screen. "They want you to come on the show and talk about saving Mr. Francis!"

The paint fumes wafted toward me, dizzying with their intensity. The sunbaked marker smell was suddenly overpowering.

This was not going away.

I wiped my hand on my gray-stained shirt. "Not interested."

"But you love podcasts." Mom blew out a breath of air. "You don't *have* to do it—"

"Good. Because I don't want to." I failed to ignore the quiet roll of my stomach.

"I'll do it," Sophie said, throwing her paintbrush to the burned-out grass. "This is boring."

"Honey, I don't think it's the same thing if you do it."

"No one's doing it." I turned around, fully aware of Mom's critical eye boring holes into my back. "I really want this whole thing to blow over."

"Is something the matter?"

Everything. "No."

The truth was left unsaid, filtering into the sound waves of the podcast I'd never do.

I didn't do what you think I did.

I'm terrifically ashamed.

Don't praise me.

My confession threatened to twist into the space between us, drilling me with the thousand-pound weight of disappointment my parents would send my way.

"Okay," Mom finally said. "But take a shower before you go out for ice cream with Maverick. You stink."

—

A few hours later, Maverick edged his car onto the brick pavement outside my unit. "We've got a problem, Nick."

"What's up, man?" Half greeting, half question. I slid into the passenger seat of his car.

His eyebrows were all scrunched together, which, if the melo-drama wasn't enough, was his typical tell that something was both-ering him. Mav had been my best friend since he moved here in third grade. His mom worked long hours, and she was sometimes late picking him up from the after-school program. Mom, then a vice principal, would tell all the aides to go home while she stayed with us.

"I'm so sorry," Mrs. Tate would say, flying into the cafeteria with her shoes making ticking sounds on the tile floor.

Mom would look up from whatever paperwork she scrawled on while Mav and I raced around the empty cafeteria, sliding under the rows of tables folded in half like place cards. "Don't mention it," Mom would say. "You do important work, Cindy." Mrs. Tate ran an award-winning statewide organization that paired young girls of color who needed or wanted mentorship of some kind with high-powered women in Boston.

Now, at the sight of his eyebrows, I sighed. "Spit it out, Mav."

"Holly and I broke up."

I paused. I'd been jangly all day in anticipation of meeting up with December at Pire's, my nerves lighting off firecrackers, but this news pulled the fire away like smoke in a downdraft. ". . . You were still together?"

He gave me his *uh, duh* look. "Yes. You have to be with someone to break up with them, don't you?"

"The last time you mentioned her, you were kind of not all about her."

"You know why." He made a scoffing noise and shifted the car into drive. "She would *not* stop talking about *DuckTales*."

"Hey, you love—"

"Being a fan of the *Walking Dead* is not the same thing as only discussing talking cartoon ducks for three hangouts in a row."

"How'd you break it off?"

"I didn't!" he shouted. "Holly dumped me. She said it's because we haven't seen each other enough this summer. But I got o-chem, you know?" He'd enrolled in the pre-college organic chemistry class through Harvard. For *fun*. He shook his head and swung out of my too-crowded complex onto Wheelock Road, giving way to large, sprawling, faux-farm–style houses. "After that, the writing was on the proverbial wall, my friend." Maverick picked up a tin tray of his nicotine gum and crinkled it in his hands, making the same sound as a drag-and-drop of a file to the Recycling Bin.

His tone was light, but . . . those knit eyebrows. I cleared my throat. "Sorry. That sucks."

He wrinkled his nose. "Yeah. It does." He tossed the foil at my feet.

I stepped on it. "When are you going to quit this nasty gum habit, anyway?"

A half smile.

He rolled down the windows then, letting the yellowed late-afternoon air rush into the car. The wide road soon gave way to tight S-curves, punctuated at predictable intervals by telephone poles and electric lines. This time of year was so leafy and overgrown, it was tough to see through the trees, so Mav coasted, steering with caution until he swooped into the parking lot of Pire's Dairy Bar.

Mav cut the engine. "You want to tell me more about what the hell we're doing here?"

I lifted my hand toward the figure sitting on one of the picnic benches, recognizable even at a distance because of her posture. Something radiated off December, distinguishing her from the classmates in our high school hallways. Where their shoulders curved in on themselves, December almost presented herself to the world, her chin lifted, collarbones wide open.

She must've gotten here early to get that seat. The parking lot was full of SUVs with their trunks jacked open, kids kicking their feet, their faces sticky with ice cream and summer heat. Not December. She sat, her head framed by that black-and-white hat and her feet crossed at the ankles, dipping an extra-long spoon into a waffle cone. "Mav. Any chance organic chemistry teaches you how to find a missing person?"

Mav laughed and nudged open the car door. "Not quite. O-chem has taught me that everyone is far less intelligent than they think they are."

CHAPTER FIFTEEN
December

I'D ARRIVED EARLY

(because I knew I would)

(because of what was about to happen)

so I'd spent the last twenty minutes enjoying my favorite order of Moose Tracks ice cream. Vanilla base, fudge swirl, and peanut butter cups stuffed inside a monster-sized waffle cone. I'd need sustenance for the night ahead of me.

When Nick and his friend got out of the car, I forgot to swallow. The ice cream gathered in the back of my throat and trickled down, glomming into an uncomfortable dairy belly pool. The cone crunched beneath my fingers. Half-soggy pieces crumbled into my palm. I'd gripped it so hard it'd shattered.

The sherbet orange shirt.

Shit.

Nick had on the shirt he wore in my vision of his death.

They joined a line of people waiting for ice cream while I analyzed my mistake. I'd spent so much time gathering all the items that collectively made up my mother's legacy that I'd neglected to climb hard enough. I'd surfed through my foreknowledge of this event, checking off the boxes—presentation of mother-related artifacts (which, because they were mine, I could see). Meeting Maverick. The incident that would prevent me from getting home before midnight.

I shivered. Melted ice cream dribbled onto my bare thigh. I wiped it with a napkin, trying to quell my racing pulse by going through my foreknowledge of all our upcoming moments in time. I drew in a breath, exhaling through my nose. It worked. He might be wearing the shirt, but he wouldn't die today.

From across the table came a throat clear. "December, meet Maverick Tate. Also known as Mav."

"Sorry we were a few minutes late," Mav said, settling onto the picnic bench across from me with his order. "I got dumped."

"Ah. Sorry about that."

He sipped from a Raspberry Lime Rickey, then jabbed a spoon into a cup of strawberry ice cream covered in M&M's. "Thanks. It's all good. Half our conversations were about *DuckTales*."

"Never make your fandom your main personality trait," I said solemnly. Mav cracked a smile.

Nick folded himself beside Mav, holding his own waffle cone. Mint chip. Both rainbow and chocolate sprinkles, which struck me with its adorableness. "What did you bring for me?"

I glanced at Maverick, who pointed with his spoon.

"Don't worry," he said. "I know all about your agreement. Irving here filled me in."

Nick flicked a stray sprinkle from the cone's paper. "Let's get on with it."

Even though he had on the T-shirt I couldn't stand to look at, I had to admit the guy wore his clothes well. Unlike all the other times I'd seen him, his hair wasn't covered by a hat. It was disheveled but not unkempt—a kind of purposeful disarray. I stuffed down the urge to put it back into place, instead pulling out a tote bag stenciled with

REDUCE, REUSE, RECYCLE from beneath my feet. "My mom left me with my uncle when I was seven. These are the only things she didn't take with her."

I pulled the items from the bag, steeling myself against the pain each object brought with it. While the boys ate, I explained what they were: A travel journal, which chronicled things like the weather and food on a mere handful of trips she'd taken. Her wishing well figurine she'd never left the house without. The black-and-white sun hat on my head.

A series of pictures. The ones that helped me remember her best. Her alone, the hood of a sweatshirt pulled up over her hair, beaming on a whale-watching excursion off the coast of Province-town. One with four-year-old me on her lap. My head is thrown back, mouth open with laughter, but her face locks eyes with the camera, squint-smiling. The last one was a few months before she left. Thinner, her hair a bit more wild—she'd straightened it for years, and had taken to letting it dry naturally toward the end—her eyes a bit darker as the quality of the photos improved, still a spark of a smile in them.

Every time I introduced a new thing, I watched Nick's face. I wanted so desperately to get on with it—with what would become *us*. But I had to be patient.

"Your mom was always there, and then she was"—Maverick flicked his hand—"gone?"

"She was gone a lot already." I drummed my knuckles on the rough wood of the picnic bench, thinking. Combing my memories for my own gumballs—for my life before. So much of it was redacted, like a government report on a sensitive subject, as if the disappearance of my mother would be labeled in a folder next to *The Assassination of John F. Kennedy* and *UFOs* files. "My uncle said she was 'flighty.'"

Here, I air-quoted. "But she wasn't gone so much that I'd forget her or anything. She would be with me for long stretches at a time."

A crease appeared on Mav's forehead. "That really sucks. Growing up without your mom."

Nick blinked, as if this fact were news to him. As if me telling him that my mom was missing was just another thing—a lost kickball, a lonely sneaker—and he hadn't stopped to consider that I might be missing her in a way that was real and raw and affective. A flash of annoyance burst in my gut. I straightened up.

Nick's gaze met mine. "That must be really hard."

"It is. But my uncle is the best."

"Maybe you should write down her old number and email, too," Maverick suggested. "Not that it's as easy as calling her, but maybe they'll be helpful?"

"They're on the inside cover of this notebook." I tapped the journal. "I've tried emailing and calling before, but everything comes back 'Delivery has failed' or out of order."

"Have you ever put something online? That kind of story goes viral all the time. You see people finding biological parents every couple months or so."

I shook my head. "We've never done that. She doesn't seem to be on social media, either. My uncle . . . he's angry with her. For leaving me. I don't know if he wants to find her. And I've always sort of let her go."

Nick clicked his tongue. "But this is what I'm stuck on."

"What?"

"Well, if you're going to try to track her down, then shouldn't you start by figuring out what would make her leave?" He ducked his head, as if he were embarrassed to ask.

I was startled by the flare of pain that stumbled through me. In my stomach, the ice cream coagulated to gelatin. "Don't you think that if I knew that, I wouldn't be sitting here with you two?"

Nick's eyes were soft. Unfocused. They were thinking eyes. Beneath them, he had two small patches of sunburn thumbing his cheeks like eye black worn by football players. He wiped his lips with a napkin and tossed his trash in a nearby metal can. "I don't know that we even need to start with all this stuff."

"What do you mean?" I asked, unable to peel my focus from that same metal can. The one with the sticky paper, the spoiled milk smell. The one with a cracked plastic shard sticking out that was the main character in my vision for today. The antagonist.

No, I decided.

I would not go near the can.

(It was not a Mr. Francis moment. Not a big world tilt. It was the flipping of a clamshell, the light pounding of a foot on the ocean floor, a resettling cloud of sand.)

". . . everyone's focused on data and clues," Nick was saying. "We can internet search the hell out of this"—here, he gestured to everything I'd set in front of him—"but we need the bigger picture. We need her motivation, or whatever set her on her path away from you and your family."

Maverick tapped his chin and nodded. "You're right."

I didn't like how my memories of my mother were suspect to the hands of time. I trained my eyes to the other side of the parking lot, where a rolling green pasture of cows were penned in with a wooden fence. "What do you mean?"

Maverick glanced at Nick, then back at me. "We need to know, basically, whatever set her off. Think about fear, for instance. Fear is something that's wired in our biology—it's built to protect all of us against perceived threats."

I nodded. People reacted out of fear all the time. When they observe something that scares them—a lion, an oncoming car, a relationship commitment—they act accordingly. Fight or flight or freeze.

"More specifically," Nick said, leaning forward, "what makes a parent leave a kid they've been raising for seven years?"

(Here was the heart of the matter, wasn't it?)

(Wasn't it my fault she was gone?)

This Story of My Mother's Departure was something my gift had subconsciously buried, like an unpopped kernel in a bag of popcorn. It belonged in the trash. It was a dud. As the memories I'd made with my mother faded, I'd grown more and more certain of one thing: I was the reason she left. I didn't have a precise answer to fill in the blank, but I knew it in my bones. Maybe it was all her questions, or the examining look she'd give me through squinted eyes.

Or maybe it was the suddenness of her leaving, right at the end of the month with which I shared a name.

Gone gone.

"I mean," Nick continued, breaking my thought spiral, "if I think outside of your mom, about why anyone would leave, I think: Fear. Desperation. Shame. Specifically, addiction, drugs or otherwise. Or maybe something else. A big family rift over politics. Disagreements about religion. Cults, or mental illness. She didn't leave a note or anything, right?"

I shook my head. "No. Nothing. She hid it well if she was dealing with any of those. Plus, she and my grandmother were as close as it gets." A few summers after my mother left, I caught Cam crying in the kitchen. I had gotten up early to find her paused midway through making coffee, clutching my mother's wishing well, Cam's face wrinkling with time but her hair still so strikingly dark. She'd flushed, knowing she was caught in a raw moment, but something I loved about her was she didn't try to hide it from me. Instead, she had dropped a kiss on the crown of my head and given me the plastic spoon so I could count seven scoops into the filter.

Trying to find my mother gave me dry mouth, sawed through the base of my skull, ruined any sense of agency I had. Her absence festered in my entire body. I was like an inside plant turning to flower toward a window, even in the dead of winter. I closed my eyes for the briefest of moments, for whatever reason picturing the exact sound a coconut makes when it drops on the sand and cracks open: a thump, a shift in the earth to make room for it, a break, the flow of milk. "I want some closure."

"Understandable. Do you want to help me search?"

"Nope. Thinking about her is kind of a lot."

Nick glanced at Mav. "All right, then." He'd dropped a line of ice cream on his ill-fated orange shirt, the sight of which opened the door for fear to clamor inside my heart and crush its walls. "Ughhh. Why."

Fight or flight or freeze.

Waves of pain in anticipation of my future experience of Nick's loss

(his death his death his death when he dies)

rolled over me. I set my face into a mask. My saliva vanished, leaving my tongue dry and heavy.

And then I had no more thoughts left because they were too painful to think. To buy time, I lowered the empty tote bag to my feet at the precise moment Maverick's elbow knocked into his Raspberry Lime Rickey, and *oh*.

Since I had avoided the trash can, this was where it would happen.

The anticipation of pain was a funny thing. All my life, I'd been able to guess with a decent success rate what my major "events of pain" would be. The broken wrist in the McDonald's playground, the time I flipped my bike while riding to the convenience store for a slush, a cartwheel gone awry, running from the pool after saving Mr. Francis and rolling my ankle (though that one was less painful than I'd thought). And now, right before it happened, I flinched and wondered if either of them had noticed my instinctive recoil.

The fizzy drink spilled, splashing over Nick's shirt.

(Please, please, let it stain.)

Impulsively, I lurched back from the spreading liquid. Every part of me moved freely away, but my arm stayed put, tethered. A stray nail jutting from the bottom of the table had made its way into the base of my innocent bicep. The velocity of my body forced the nail to sear its way down, hooking over the curve of my elbow and nestling in the middle of my forearm.

For the most minute slice of a moment, the sensation was similar to the one you feel when you know the water you've turned on is too hot and your thoughts cognitively understand this before your nerves transfer the actual feeling to your head. I knew what was about to come. But I was unprepared for the white-hot space my brain would enter, the gush of blood rushing over my skin waking me to the pain.

I sucked air through my teeth. Horror spread on Nick's and Maverick's faces at the sight of the massive, gaping gash, the blood on my skin, my clothes, the picnic table, the crumpled napkins. I swallowed my nausea and gripped the wound with my other hand, trying to stanch my blood by holding flaps of skin together. "Hospital," I managed to say.

Maverick was on his feet at once, jogging to his car. "I'll pull up," he called.

Nick pulled his fated shirt over his head and half ran around the picnic bench. He wound it around my arm, and blood soaked through it immediately.

Somehow, a small part of me found the space to be satisfied as my blood ruined his shirt. I wondered if I'd feel the lightest of changes as the ocean of my knowledge adjusted, ebbing and flowing into new memory paths without the shirt, but I didn't.

Nick tightened the cloth tourniquet. My arm throbbed. Tears streamed from my eyes, but I figured if I opened my mouth, I wouldn't be able to close it from my screams.

Nick put his other hand in the air between us, reaching for my leg, backing away, and finally wrapping me in an awkward hug. He smelled of sweat and Dove soap and sugared ice cream and, faintly, something chemical. The paint from earlier, I realized, and almost commented on, but then I remembered he hadn't told me he was painting earlier and this was all so hard to keep straight sometimes, so I closed my eyes and waited for this boy's best friend to drive up and help me to the car, where I'd bleed all over the interior.

CHAPTER SIXTEEN

Nick

THE TRIAGE AND treatment wing of our local ER was slammed. Across the bay, a gray-faced elderly man sat in stone-cold silence every time the guy he was with snuck out of the emergency exit to smoke cigarettes. A crying toddler with loosened pigtails and a burn from a vat of clam chowder on her forearm was off in the corner. Her mother kept giving her lollipops from the nurse's station, which was positioned like a nucleus among all the beds.

When we'd arrived, an intern had whisked us to an available bay, where he'd cleaned December's cut and sprayed it with numbing solution. But right when he was ready to stitch her, an emergency code sounded, so he temporarily fastened it with butterfly closures, elevated her arm, and left me with firm, terrifying instructions to make a racket if it started gushing.

I tried not to think about Mr. Francis recuperating here a few days ago. I slid my phone out of my pocket and checked it. No new messages since Maverick had dropped us off.

"If you want to head out, you can," December said. Again. She'd put the medical johnny on over her clothes. It swamped her. A thin sheet blanketed her legs.

I shook my head. "I'm happy to stay. I mean, if you *want* me to go,

I will." I flushed. "I don't want to make any assumptions, but . . . this kinda sucks. I wouldn't want to be here alone."

"Yeah. I guess it does." December stretched her foot in front of her and tapped her phone, which lay dark and unlit at the end of the thin bed. "My uncle doesn't always check his texts."

I shifted in the plastic chair. The thin strip of skin above my waistband kept crackling with static electricity. I'd had to throw on one of the white T-shirts crumpled in the back of Maverick's car, as mine was now laden with coagulated blood and stuffed in a hospital-issued bag. My friend wasn't a shrimp, but the sparks and snaps against my back were a healthy reminder of the extra four inches I had on the guy.

"Are you doing okay?" December asked.

"Me? I'm not the one with a Grand Canyon carved in my arm, am I?"

She shook her head, the hint of a smile playing on her lips. "I didn't mean this." She tapped above the ghost-white butterflies with her fingertip. "I meant in general, I guess. From everything that happened the other day."

Mr. Francis. The pause, the action, the aftermath. *Was* I doing okay? I moved again, wincing at yet another elastic-band *snap* shock. "I was going to say no one's asked me that, but I don't think that's really true." I met her eyes. "I mean, my parents have asked me if I'm doing okay. But they don't know the whole story."

"It was pretty scary."

I kept still to avoid more static electricity. "It didn't seem like you were scared."

I guess my voice sounded bitter, because December tilted her head and spoke with concern. "Everything happened fast. I didn't have time to be scared, honestly."

I twisted my mouth. "That's the difference between you and me. Fear ate me for breakfast."

And how do you plead, Nick Irving?

Guilty AF.

The guilt. Absolving myself of it meant living my life according to the false facts from the "In the Nick of Time" article, and I didn't deserve that. I couldn't stand replaying the memory. Knees jerk, hesitate. Mr. Francis, bobbing in the lane.

December pressed a button, lifting the head of the bed with a mechanical whir. She settled against the hospital pillows. "Please distract me," she said. "This really hurts. I feel like I shoved my arm into a food processor."

"That is a *brutal* image."

She pursed her lips. "Let's do an AMA."

"An AMA?"

"Yeah. Have you seen those on Reddit? 'Ask me anything.'"

"I know what an AMA is. I've never had one in person before."

"Great. We'll go back and forth."

"What are the rules?"

"There are no rules. We simply ask questions."

I squinted. "Anything?"

"Well, you can *ask* anything. It doesn't have to be any huge secret. When Obama did one, he answered questions about White House beer."

I laughed. "I don't know."

"Do you have a better idea? If you don't want to answer, then pass." She gestured around the curtained-off room with her uninjured arm. "There's no TV. I'm on low battery. And like you said, this sucks."

I straightened up. "Who's going first?"

"The honor is yours."

"Okay." I folded my arms, searching the pockmarked ceiling tiles for a question. "If you never had to sleep, what would you do with the time?"

Her grin spread across her face. "I'd do everything I could to change the world."

Impressive. "Vague. But good answer."

"My turn." She wrinkled her nose, thinking. "When was the last time you climbed a tree?"

"It's been a long time, actually. You know the pond out on the far end of our condos, next to the hill?"

"The hill?"

"The sledding hill. Anyway, Mav and I used to go ice-skating on the pond. There's this perfect pair of climbing trees there, too, and my mom would send us over in the fall or spring with stale bread for the ducks. So, wow. Maybe five years or so since I've climbed a tree?" Seventh grade? When did we abandon tree climbing? How often was I supposed to climb a tree, anyway?

She peered at her injured arm, grimaced, and turned back to me. "Your turn."

"Hmm. Is this the most pain you've ever been in?" I drew a line from above my elbow to the top third of my forearm, mirroring her injury.

She laughed. "Emotionally or physically?"

"Uh. I meant physically."

Her smile was wry. "I know. I'm teasing you. It's close, but I had a bad ankle break when I was in sixth grade after a botched cartwheel landing. Snapped the bone straight through."

I imagined the sound and mock-shivered. "Ouch."

"Yeah. But the scariest time was actually when I flipped over my bike's handlebars and knocked the air from my lungs." She frowned. "It was the worst."

"I did that once, on the pool deck." I remembered the sharp panic that took over when I'd realized that the air was all around me, but I couldn't draw in a single breath. "My coach said it's a blunt force spasm. It temporarily paralyzes your diaphragm, which makes you anxious that you're gonna die."

"Exactly that." Her nose twitched. "Okay, your turn. Name three things that frustrate you."

"That's not a question."

She mimed picking up a microphone. "I'll take 'What Are Three Frustrating Things for Nick?' for two hundred dollars."

"Ha," I said, not bothering to point out that her reply was also not a question. "Okay. One, people invading my privacy. Specifically, my parents in my schoolwork and my sister in my everyday existence. Two, teachers thinking I'm not on par with my classmates who don't need extra help to meet curriculum standards. Even though there were always a handful of us in class with dyslexia, some teachers really don't do a great job of normalizing needing extra help. And third and last is reading, the headaches that accompany reading, and sometimes writing, but not as much as when I was a little kid."

A dark lock of hair tumbled out of her loosened ponytail, catching the marigold light from the recessed ceiling discs. She swiped it behind her ear. "I sort of know something about your second frustration. A related one, at least. The 'me versus them' thing."

"How so?"

"Is that your question?" December flashed a smile. "Kidding. My uncle and I have moved around a lot. I've been the new kid more often than a celebrity gets canceled. It's brutal."

I stopped, considering. Growing up, every time the sound of fluttering pages filled a classroom, I'd feel anxious. I'd never been the new kid before, but I'd only narrowly avoided that one, and I could only imagine all that came along with it.

I'd built a wall against this girl. Against her inability to reveal herself as the person who'd really saved Mr. Francis. My frustration with her was only magnified by that goddamn article. Like that newspaper or a bad joke about a zebra falling down the stairs, I felt all black and white and gray about her.

But this—this common ground? This softened the gray into the bluish-purple hue of empathy. She knew how it felt to be anxious. To lose someone. "What would you do if you found your mother?"

"Oh. Wow." Her eyes flitted around the room. She seemed to struggle to pluck the words from wherever they swam, and string them into something that made sense. "I want to know she's okay, I guess. And I want my grandma to find a sense of peace before she goes." She was quiet for a moment. "It's so strange to think about how much I've changed since she left. I was so young. I used to paint and draw all the time. I don't do any of that anymore. She ditched me. I grew up."

This girl sat here with a guy she barely knew, her arm gaping open. Parentless. Alone. She had experienced the kind of losses I never had—being abandoned by her mother, her grandmother there but not really there, too.

Sure, I'd gone through the grieving process when we lost my grandmother. I'd never cried more in my life, barreling through boxes of Kleenex like I'd had a sinus infection, misery clouding every one of my breaths. Until, day by day, it didn't anymore. From storm cloud to cumulus to humidity-free. Now, every time I ate homemade macaroni and cheese or passed a thriller novel at Boston Book World, a Gigi-flavored ripple of nostalgia or sadness or loss chugged in my veins like a freight train, there and gone before I could hop on and take a nightmarish ride.

I leaned over, resting my elbows on my knees, thinking about how to express that sense of sorrow or empathy or comradeship at having

101

been in the same pool at the same time, when the hanging curtain pushed open with a *whoosh*. I rocketed upward, startled by the interruption.

December's eyes widened. "Evan. You're here."

"At least your observation skills are intact, humble plant."

Humble plant?

He crossed the tiny vestibule of a room. "Your friend Maverick came by and told me what happened. Please tell me you're okay. Are you okay?"

"Never better," she said, but her voice came out warbly.

"What did they give you for pain?" he demanded. "They didn't give you anything heavy, did they?"

"Just ibuprofen. Don't worry."

He brushed her hair away from her forehead before noticing me. "Oh. Hey. Do I know you from somewhere?"

I didn't know how to tell this giant guy with a strong sense of superhero energy that I'd ridden my bike by him, or that my mother and sister both revered him. I gave him a weak wave. "I'm Nick."

"He lives in our condo complex," December said.

Evan's face broke open, his mouth curving his beard upward. He leaned across the bed and gripped my hand. "I'm so grateful to you for keeping December company. Can I call you a rideshare?"

Before I could answer, the intern from before walked in the open curtain. "I can't apologize enough for this wait," he said. A waxen layer of sweat shone beneath his brow. "You ready to get stitched up, you shining unicorn of a patient?"

Evan crossed his arms. "How could you leave her here for so long?"

The intern frowned. "Who might you be?"

"The patient's family," Evan said, his voice morphing from superhero to supervillain.

The intern turned to December. "Is that tr—"

She held up her good hand and interrupted him. "True. This is my uncle. He's harmless. And much nicer than he seems."

The intern's eyes narrowed. "We're short-staffed tonight, and the unfortunate reality of this job is emergencies have rankings. Believe me. There was more than one code, and more than one minor here tonight. If I could've sewn her earlier, then I would've." He turned to December. "This'll take a few minutes to stitch. That's a jagged cut. And do you know when your last tetanus shot was?"

Evan's face paled. "She had one last year." He grunted and turned to me. "You want to step out?"

I checked my phone. When did it get to be nearly eleven? "Sure. I'll set up a ride."

"No way." December brandished her arm. "We're all going to the same place. I'll meet you guys in the hallway when Sim and I are done in here."

The intern—Sim?—smiled. "She remembers my name. This one's a good cookie."

Sim wheeled a tray beside the bed and removed a needle from a plastic sleeve, which I took as my cue to follow Evan toward the gaping hole in the curtain. "Oh, wait. My shirt." I swiped the plastic bag from its hook.

"Hey!"

I half turned around, a question on my face.

"That's covered in blood." December frowned.

"My dad is a laundry magician. He can get anything out."

"But." She shook her head. "It's ruined."

"No way." I smiled at her. "It's my favorite shirt."

And then I left the intern and the fake lifeguard to their task.

CHAPTER SEVENTEEN
December

THE FIRST YEAR of living with my uncle had been pockmarked with pain. Evan and I had skated around each other on the same sheet of ice, hovering on top of the slippery surface. I'd been able to see that I'd be with him for good, so I was secure in that—but I couldn't help but notice how much his life had changed. Gone were the late nights in Boston bars, gone were his trips with his buddies to away football games. Evan had become a de facto parent, and I never knew how he felt about it until the day I'd broken Cam's wedding vase. Practically the only thing of value we owned had shattered, the pattern cleaved into pieces at my feet.

I'd burst into tears. Beyond-my-regular tears. Crying was not in my wheelhouse that often, yet a full wave of it preceded a torrent of hysterical blabber, releasing worries and fears that went far beyond being such a burden for breaking a simple vase.

When I was reduced to hiccups, he had gripped my arms. "Look at me."

I lifted my head. "What?"

"What eight-year-old says they're a burden? You're not a burden."

"But it's how I *feel*," I said, subdued by what came next.

"If you don't feel like I'm here by choice, then I need to do better.

Because I'm choosing you, December. And I guess I need to do a better job of that." His eyes had lit up. "The *Mimosa pudica*."

I had frowned. "The what?"

"It's a plant. Comes in a few different forms, but my favorite is this beautiful pinky-purple color from countries in South and Central America. Now it lives in all kinds of places across both hemispheres. Sort of a spherical fern." He cupped his hands into an open circle. "It's sensitive to what it perceives to be dangerous. When you touch it, it folds up, only to reopen a few minutes later." He mimed this with his fingers.

I had scaled through the flip-book of my memories, coming to one about a plant scientist conducting an experiment by dropping the same species of plant over and over on the floor. "The plant *learns*?"

He'd tapped his head, grinning. "You're quick. It's nicknamed the smart plant, shy plant, sensitive plant, and humble plant, and, bingo: It doesn't forget. Even though, obviously, it doesn't have a brain."

I had climbed backward, watching

(an animal biologist, Monica Gagliano, realizing the *Mimosa pudica* can take in sensory data without a brain)

"It's sort of like how this other plant, the rock cress, can hear without ears. When you play that plant a recording of caterpillars munching on leaves, it secretes mustard oil, which is poisonous in large quantities." He had smoothed my hair down with his palm. "These kinds of things are what drew me to plants in the first place, December. Their resilience. Their ability to learn in ways we can't understand. Their capacity to know things." His voice dropped. "Kind of like you."

I'd spent that first year feeling like a burden. I wasn't one of these *Mimosa pudica*s or rock cresses, wowing researchers with my wisdom.

I was a leech. A barnacle on a boat. "I hear you," I'd said. It was a truth. I did hear him, but that time, it was louder, somehow. Everything was different when you lived it instead of simply seeing it.

His smile was sad. "Look, kiddo. You're the best thing in my life. We're family, sure, but we're also each other's chosen family. I'm choosing to be with you. Whenever you need the reminder, you can say it to me. Or I'll say it to you. It can be our thing."

I had answered his smile with one of my own. "Humble plant is our thing?"

"You tell me, humble plant."

—

The morning after my injury, the pain had somehow both dulled and sharpened. The cut hurt less, but now my muscles and flesh were sore.

But the pain did not matter. The pain did not quell the small turn I saw in Nick.

The one where his face changed from lifeguard to unguarded. Like swiping to a different filter on a photograph or washing a stiff piece of fabric so many times the fibers finally gave way to softness.

The one where he realized I wasn't some stubborn secret-keeper. I was a person.

Maybe an interesting one.

And right now, at this instant—trying not to bend my elbow too much, as I sat in our galley kitchen and ate left-handed spoonfuls of Cinnamon Chex (which Evan had set out for me alongside spare Tegaderm and Vaseline for my stitches), trying to climb to Nick to see how his day would go, a spot was grayed out.

Whatever he was doing involved my mother. Even after spending last night with me, an almost stranger, he was up and at 'em early.

Once I'd foreseen that ruined orange cloth shoved away, I'd left it. Who would want that bloody T-shirt back? Waiting in line for my waffle cone, I'd been distracted by the backroom antics of DC politicians, three prescription pill overdoses in Dubai, the locker room screams of a football coach in Johannesburg. It was enough to make anyone ragey. Enough to skip a climb.

My sole regret was stuffed inside that white hospital-issue bag, carried away by the boy I'd soon come to love.

—

A week after the ice cream incident, I stood in miserable August heat. The kind that was cloying, sticky, damp. Sweat sluiced from the Vaseline on my stitches, trailing down my arm, joining the swamp on my back. If I didn't move a muscle, it was possible I would melt straight into the community garden.

My uncle squinted at me. "You positive you're okay to do this?"

I'd sweat my butt off, but I'd be fine. And besides, I'd have some company. "Yeah. You can probably see my pit stains from space, but I'm good."

He gave me a look. "Hate to tell you this, dudette, but you can see them from beyond the universe."

I stuck out my tongue.

"Remember. The correct moisture content is key—"

I nodded, impatient. "You like it to read a five or six. I know."

"Will you note the fours, too?"

I was already walking in reverse. "I *know*."

"And drink water."

I pointed to the bottle at the foot of the tomato plants. The ice cubes inside had already melted. "Over and out."

I hightailed it to the center of the complex, ready to take on my chore: noting the moisture sensors of the individual compost bins. The air felt like a wall of fire. My cheeks pulsed with the heat, the sunscreen smeared on my nose thick and reeking of synthetic coconut. In the shade of the Bright Acres entryway sign, I stopped and pretended to be enthralled by my phone, planting myself like coincidences like these happened to me all the time.

"Hey, you," Nick said. He wore a low-slung bathing suit still dripping with pool water, a wet baseball hat, and a sweat-soaked cutoff T-shirt, like someone Taylor Swift would write a song about. My chest did that *I'm gonna explode* thing. "Kind of a weird place to hang out. How's the arm?"

I brandished it toward him. "Today it's an embarrassing display of my ability to perspire."

He slugged a sip of water. "Anyone not sweating today would be a freak of nature. It's *gnarly* out here. What're you doing?"

"Checking all the compost bin meters for my uncle. He'll collect them when they're ready."

"Huh. So he's the guy responsible for those things."

"He is." I spread my arm to the wall of flowers lining the sign. "And these."

"Bright Acres is really stepping up its flower game. Want help?"

"You really want to walk around in this?"

He made a shrugging motion. "Nothing else to do."

"Be my guest," I said, leading him toward the first street.

"Oh, hey. Meant to text you to let you know Maverick has all your mom's stuff safe in his car. I'll pick it up later in the week."

"Oh," I said, somehow flushing even more than I already was. "Thank you."

"No prob." He pointed to the first compost bin. "How do you know when it's good to use?" He paused. "Reuse?"

"Evan likes them at fifty to sixty percent moisture. Too low, they're biological trash. Too high, they can become air pollution."

"Gotcha."

"Yeah. The whole initiative was part of the reason why he was hired. He calls compost 'soil conditioner' to make it sound sexy."

"Irresistible," Nick deadpanned. He took off his hat, wiped his brow.

I sucked in a mouthful of air, which blasted my lungs with oven temps. "No work today?"

He shook his head. "I was just practicing," he said. "I'm waiting to hear from a farm team."

"What's that?"

"An extra team thing that helps train people at a higher level, but I sort of put it out of my mind as much as possible." He sighed. "My backstroke start is absolute garbage, so I was working on that to better my form. And time."

As I tried not to imagine Nick's firm, bare upper half slicing through cold water, we made our way up and down the first two streets. I showed him how to read the meters and logged each number in my phone.

"Three," Nick announced at his unit. "Not ready."

"You can add grass or leaves to speed it along." I dashed a hand across my upper-lip sweat. I was approximately as sexy as soil conditioner right now.

His sister appeared at the window screen. She had a wet washcloth draped over her forehead, presumably to cool off. "Niiiiick. Mom says *Nutella* isn't an acceptable play."

"It's not." He looked at me. "Slothful Scrabble. My parents made it up to get around the spelling pressure when I was a kid. We leave it out and play whenever. Family record's thirteen days."

Which I already knew but still found absolutely charming. Adorable. Nick was adorable.

Sophie banged the screen. "It's twenty-four points! Triple word. And it gets rid of all my one-pointers."

"It's a brand name. That goes against the rules."

"Slothful Scrabble already *is* against the rules," she protested. "It takes everyone, like, three days to come up with a single word."

"Hey, Sophie," I called. "You'll lose a letter, but try L-U-N-A-T-E. It means crescent-shaped, like the moon."

"Yes!" she shouted. "Score. I love your new friend." Sophie flounced from the window.

"Bring us freeze pops," Nick called back. He turned to me. "Hey, no fair. A word assist, after I escort you around to check on a neighborhood's supply of worm food?"

I bit back a smile. Something had softened between us. I knocked my palm against my forehead. "How silly. Heat must be getting to my head."

Even in this heat, I could take great satisfaction in the shape of the slightest dimple in his cheek. It was lunate.

CHAPTER EIGHTEEN
Nick

Maverick: YO, IRVING

Me: hey

Maverick: LET'S GET COFFEE

Me: I can't

Maverick: I HAVEN'T SEEN YOU SINCE I GOT DUMPED, DRAGGED YOUR ASS TO ICE CREAM, AND BROUGHT A BLEEDING STRANGER TO THE HOSPITAL. I COULD USE SOME COFFEE

Maverick: HELLO?

Maverick: WHAT ARE YOU DOING? I'M GONNA COME PICK YOU UP

Me: I'm at the lib

Maverick: YOU'RE AT THE LIBRARY. ON A SUNDAY MORNING. IN THE SUMMER.

Me: Confirmed

After years of tutoring, I'd seen the inside of our local libraries enough to know that the university library was ten times better than Woodland's. It had large, padded, *soundproofed* headphones and the same accessibility software I used at school.

The Sunday-morning college library was depopulated. I sank into a spinning chair and took my first sip of coffee while I waited for the desktop to load. The liquid ran a hot trail into my stomach. I winced.

Maverick: YOU'RE SERIOUSLY AT THE LIBRARY?
Me: Srsly
Maverick: WOODLAND OR THE U
Me: The u
Maverick: GOD, I LOVE THAT PLACE.

Early morning sunlight filtered through the massive stained-glass rotunda, leaving colorful, light-patterned shapes against wood the same color as the liquid in my cup. It would be the perfect setting to research if I had any idea where to begin.

On *Mystery Buff*, the search for a missing person always kicked off with friend, family, and witness interviews, tracing cell phone pings and credit card usage, and social media. Not the easiest way to find someone who's been absent for a decade. And even worse? December's mom left on purpose. She wasn't missing, she was deliberately gone, and so long as she set up care for her child, she had every legal right to be.

I typed her name in the first place I knew to look: Google. *Click. Click.* Stock photos of models populated the screen. No woman bearing resemblance to the mother of the girl named after the twelfth month of the year.

The name Mara Jones was too common. I leaned back in the chair, mulling what we'd discussed at Pire's Dairy. The reasons someone would leave their kid.

Could she have been afraid for December? Scared something she did would hurt her daughter or ruin her life? I dragged in another sip of coffee and let it mull in my mouth before swallowing.

I cleared the search and typed a new one. *Why do people voluntarily disappear?*

Hundreds of articles popped up.

Missing Persons, Inc.

Police reports with a bajillion case numbers.

News articles.

The FBI and mass.gov sites.

Top stories and Amber alerts.

The Images tab contained old scanned copies of flyers and milk-carton faces and . . . I shuddered. Hard pass.

I clicked on an NPR interview titled "Majority of Missing Persons Cases Are Resolved," plugged in my headphones, and clicked the PLAY button.

"That year, we recorded 661,000 cases of missing persons . . . quickly, approximately 659,000 of those were canceled, meaning those persons are located or deceased. At the end of the year, 2,079 cases remained unresolved."

Holy shit. More than two thousand people gone without explanation?

I chewed the inside of my cheek and X'd out. Clicked on the next article and hit PLAY.

"According to the FBI, in 2017 there were 464,324 NCIC entries for missing children," the audio recited.

Nearly half a million *kids*? The coffee roiled in my stomach. Here was the risk of internet research. One minute you're Alice-not-yet-in-Wonderland, reading a book by a river, and then next you chase a talking rabbit into bizarro world, where the National Crime

Information Center blows your heart into shreds. The stats kept coming: *91 percent endangered runaways, 1 percent family abductions.*

I clenched my fingers together and shifted in the seat. There was something deeply unnerving about the number, sure, but even trying to put myself in the place of one missing person made my stomach hurt.

As I considered the screen of depressing statistics, something else bobbed to the surface of my brain. I pushed the headphones down my neck, trying to harness this feeling of unsettlement, as if the puzzle pieces inside my skull included one Jenga piece. The unnamed thought *bop bop bopped* in my head, a buoy trapped beneath a dock.

I flipped my phone over.

Maverick: PLEASE GET ME OUT OF MY HOUSE
Maverick: I'M SORRY. I WILL NOT STAND IN THE WAY OF YOUR RESEARCH. I AM IMPRESSED YOU ARE DOING RESEARCH. RESEARCH IS ALMIGHTY

I snorted. I sat back, closing my eyes and thinking of my best friend itching to get out of his house. I loved his mom's grilled Cajun swordfish and his dad's daily requests to "play catch" out back. I loved that he was an only child, so going in his basement to play video games was completely uninterrupted by Sophie. I took one last, lingering look at the hellish facts on the screen, ripped the headphones off my head, and held the power button until the screen winked out.

As I mounted my bike, I paused, my foot hovering over the pedal. Was I quitting too early? Not trying hard enough?

Later, I resolved. I'd come back later. I pushed off.

CHAPTER NINETEEN
December

TWO WEEKS AFTER the incident at Pire's Dairy Bar, I stood at the foot of a dozen or so cement stairs leading to Woodland High School. Little speckles on each step glinted in the late-summer sunshine. In a town like this one, new students weren't exactly packing the halls, so the school treated freshman orientation as an open house for the stragglers. Including seniors. Like me. And one sophomore boy, who would soon breeze by me with a trio of kids from the track team.

Even through the hazy, gumballed events of this August day, including a catastrophic hack of the stock market, a kid fainting on a soccer field in Vermont from double-session soccer, and a nonfatal boating accident in the Ozarks, I was distracted by what I was about to experience.

I un-hunched my shoulders, lifted my chin, and mounted the first stair. At the top, I pulled open the freshly painted door of what would be (according to my wavy collection of predetermined events) my final high school, after a lifetime of new-kid sweaty palms and sticky loneliness.

Inside, I clenched my fist. The skin flexed against the bottom edge of my new, taut scar, which was freckled with black lumps of dissolvable stitches. My heart was a leaky faucet in my chest.

School and I did not mesh. We were not sandbox buddies. When

I was a kid, it was my gift that got in the way. And after that, it was faking my grades. My brain's recall gave me what one might call an unfair testing advantage. I was basically academically juicing before the big game. After we'd moved to Woodland, I'd finished out junior year with the gloriousness that was independent homeschooling. But because my uncle was perfect in nearly every way, he was insistent on me having a Senior Year Experience to last a lifetime. He was one of those rare birds who treasured his high school days. And he wanted the same for me.

I got it. But good intentions carry assumptions with them. They project and broadcast, and even when they're meant well, they simply don't always play out. One by one, I forced my fingers to relax.

At this event—this orientation/open house hybrid—I had a goal. After all, people didn't go to Stella Rose's end-of-summer party unless they knew Stella Rose. At this moment in time, I did not. Yet.

I followed the red-and-white arrows to the gym door. Inside, it had been organized into an information fair, with tables advertising the school's clubs lining the gym border. Student Council, Peer Leaders, Gender and Sexuality Alliance, and so on.

Toward the end of the first row sat Maisie Cabrera, the girl who lived at the same condo complex as Nick and me. Maisie, Stella Rose Goldman, and Carrie Lee commandeered the tables for the debate team, varsity soccer, and cheerleading, respectively, but Maisie and Stella Rose had pushed their chairs between booths, and Carrie was half perched on Stella Rose's soccer table.

"Hey," Carrie called. In response, Maisie shifted in my direction, and Stella Rose's eyes flicked toward me. "Welcome to Woodland High!"

I raised the side of my mouth in a smile, aiming for casual but likely landing among the stiff and uncomfortable. "Hi. Thanks."

"Are you interested in cheerleading?" Carrie asked. She reached up and tightened her ponytail.

"Oh, sorry, but no, thank you."

Now that she knew she didn't have to meander back to her own table, Carrie's body relaxed. "No biggie."

Stella Rose kicked her feet up on the table. "Freshman soccer is over there if you're interested." She tipped her head toward the other side of the gym.

"I'm not a freshman."

Now three faces were on me. Curious.

"Wait a second." Maisie held up her hand, and a friendly frown puckered her features. "You look familiar. Do you live at Bright Acres?"

I nodded. "I'm December. I moved in about five months ago, but it was so close to the end of the school year that I finished up at home."

"Cool sneakers," Carrie said. "What year are you?"

At the compliment, an unexpected glow of warmth spread through my chest. I expected to feel awkward here, standing with people who didn't know they were about to become my friends. "I'm a senior."

Maisie tossed a pen on the table. "Oh! Wow. Starting a new school senior year. That's tough."

"I'd never forgive my parents for pulling me from here," Stella Rose said, which was exactly the sort of thing someone who enjoyed school might say. Evan would love her.

"My parents want to move, but they're too terrified a new school would blow my chances for the Ivies," Carrie said. "Do you know anyone here yet?"

I nodded again. "I've met Nick Irving and Maverick Tate."

"Then you must know what Nick did this summer," Carrie said.

I twisted my hair behind my shoulders, an old habit from when I was a kid. "I do. I was there, actually."

Stella Rose's feet dropped to the floor. "You were *there*?"

Maisie sat back in her chair. "I thought I recognized you from the pool. We didn't go that much this summer." A small undercurrent passed between the three of them, as if they shared a secret. "But we did go right after Mr. Francis almost died."

(Maisie didn't usually go.)

(But Stella Rose was always drawn to attention.)

"What else should you know about Woodland High?" Carrie said. She gazed up to the ceiling and pursed her lips. The picture of thought. "Don't use the water fountain near the boys' locker room."

"Or the one by the football field exit," Stella Rose added.

"Homecoming!" Maisie said. "Our parents usually take pictures by the pond out in the back of our condos. Your family should totally come."

Evan. Right now, sitting with my grandmother, running his nostalgic fingertips over her age-spotted, wrinkled hands, talking about Fourth of July fireworks and her old jalapeño corn bread recipe.

"It's only me and my uncle," I said.

"Well, you're more than welcome," Maisie said. "Hey, do you want me to show you around?"

Cue one of those times I was caught off guard by what I felt. What Maisie offered me here was genuine. Polite, not even an invitation of friendship, but I knew deep within myself that this girl's heart was shiny and bright. I gestured over my shoulder. "I poked around a little bit, but why not?"

It turned out that the start of something new was more recognizable than I would have thought. It felt a lot like sunshine streaming across my shoulders, lifting my mood high above the high school gymnasium. It felt like a promise.

CHAPTER TWENTY

Nick

TOGETHER, MY PARENTS were the masters of clumsy hinting. They spent the last several weeks of summer dropping increasingly hefty comments about swimming and my lack of time spent practicing it. They left my goggles and cap in the chipped porcelain bowl that lived on the console by the door.

How's the water been these days?

Make any progress on your backstroke start?

When are you supposed to hear from the farm team, exactly?

Empty. Maybe. October?

Unlike school, swimming was something that had always come naturally to me. Thanks to my mom's side of the gene pool, I had the height and the awkward lankiness going on, so my shift into swimming for sport was sort of a natural progression. But after a summer spent with a tenuous relationship with the pool, I was definitely not in top shape.

The morning was full of seasonal whispers of homecoming and bonfires and see-your-breath drives to school, with pre-fall leaves flecking the surface of the water like dried-out boats. The oak and pine branches had webbed over the pool house roof, and the fallen golden needles clung like wet hair to the pool's liner. Clung like my worry over school starting.

Guilt for what I did to stay at Woodland High.

Regret over not being able to move my goddamn feet for Mr. Francis.

I slipped into the water, nailing my splashless descent, and dunked my conference swim cap—a red one with a giant white *W* on each side—in the pool. I adjusted my goggles and fit the cap over my head. Without my waterproof headphones, which had broken and were too expensive to replace, I was left alone with my thoughts. I sank forward, exhaling through my nose and propelling myself through water I knew wasn't warmer than the air but seemed to be, trying to push through side-effect guilt of something else.

The day we met, December had done me the most seriously solid favor anyone could. What if she hadn't been there? What if I'd frozen in place so long Mr. Francis died? I still couldn't understand why she was unwilling to set the record straight, but there in the pool, I could admit I was also not doing the best job to make up for it. Other than that day in the library, I'd neglected my promise to search for December's mom.

Besides, something kept drawing me to her. The way she toed her phone on the ER bed. The choice her mother made to abandon her two days after Christmas, when all I'd ever complained about was my parents being too on top of me. Her liquid brown eyes against the pool's blue, blue, blue. A drop of ice cream on her lip, her soft smile when examining old pictures of her mother, the wishing well figurine that stood, quiet but menacing, atop the journal on my desk.

Her long, curling hair, her aforementioned eyes. Nothing good comes from thinking about someone else's eyes.

I sliced through the water, keeping my palms flat, fingertips down, the way my coaches had always taught me. Pointing and flexing my feet. Stretching through my shoulder and elbow joints. I reached forward, pushing the water out of my way. Trying to warm up. Trying to outswim my own head.

Spectacularly failing.

Ever since that night at the hospital—or, really, ever since our first fated moments together—December had been on my mind. Dad always said that when something stays stuck in your head, it's for one of three reasons. You love it, you hate it, or you're not proud of how you handled it.

So what did that mean? Why couldn't I quit thinking about her?

I stopped at the block. My backstroke start nemesis. I have historically sucked at perfecting my start, which is bogus because the backstroke itself is my ideal stroke. You're supposed to dive your hands away from the block before you push with your legs, but I always push first, so my cut into the water was never clean.

I practiced a few times before swimming more laps, but I didn't need a stopwatch to know that my times were junk. I switched focus, working to elevate my hips and legs in the long, rectangular lane. Losing count of how many laps I'd completed, how many minutes I'd been in the water.

Mid-flip turn, I got all tangled up in my head and my body. I spun with a *whoosh* of water, a cramp knifing my rib cage.

Beneath the surface, a vibrating thread of panic beat in my chest, air bubbles bursting from my nose and tickling my face. My legs locked up—*Nick, move move move, Mr. Francis, Mr. Francis*—and every molecule in my body stiffened in fear. I wondered, almost idly, if this was what my future science teacher had experienced in this exact pool—the sensation of being without oxygen, and the all-encompassing fear of *what if this was it.*

Before I could fully form the thought, my body made this rolling

121

up-and-over motion and I broke into the cool morning air, macro-inhaling as much as I could.

I made my way to the pool's edge and hitched my torso on top of it, panting.

"Hey, hero." Behind her sunglasses, my boss squinted. She jingled the loop of keys in her hand.

"Please stop calling me that."

"I'll do that if you stop swimming alone. You know swim buddies are a thing for a reason." Concern washed over Trish's features. "You okay? You weren't swimming like yourself there. Something on your mind?"

I scraped the edge of my thumb along my mouth, rubbing it on my water-wrinkled lips, across the roughness of my new stubble.

Something. Someone. I met her eyes. "Sorta."

Trish nudged open the pool house door and reached in to hang her keys. "You've got a good head on your neck, kiddo. And talent. I'm sure you'll figure it out."

The water swirled around my calves. No matter how fast I tried to swim, I couldn't leave it behind. The guilt of not moving in time. The guilt of what I'd done before.

But even though there was nothing I could do to truly absolve myself of either of those things, there was one thing I could do. It was time to follow through on trying to solve the mystery of December's mom.

—

With that resolution, I sailed through my second-to-last shift of the summer. Filled with a renewed sense of purpose, I texted Mav, who immediately agreed to help (I THOUGHT YOU'D NEVER ASK, DUDE).

Plan in motion. I felt good.

That night, Mav and I holed up in my room with two giant bowls of popcorn Sophie had made for us—mine with Buffalo sauce, his with sugar and cinnamon. I dragged a dining room chair to my desk for Maverick, then fired up my computer.

"Okay. Fill me in," Mav said. "How much have you tried to search for her?"

I completed a slow turn in my desk chair. "Just that one day at the library?" I took in his look: eyebrows raised, one eye squinted, mouth half curled. "Easy, Mav. No shade."

"Eff you, Irving. All the shade." He dug into his popcorn. "You want to be the idea person or the computer person?"

I retreated from my spot in front of the computer. "By all means. Take it away."

He fished in his pocket and pulled out his glasses. "Excellent. You know I like to have control."

While he clicked and keyed in his search terms, I spread the travel journal and the pictures across the desk. ("No, I did not mean *Maura Jones,*" Mav muttered.) The wishing well figurine was smooth, heavier than it looked, and cool in my hand. It was intricately detailed, but the bottom was inexplicably thicker than I would have expected. I placed it above the other items.

"Whitepages!" Mav shouted, pumping his fist in the air. But then his face dropped. "Never mind. It's only her name and age she'd be now. Forty-four. Her last-known address is the Dorchester duplex December told us about."

I opened the journal. Inside was her old contact information— email address, phone number. "Try these," I said, reciting her info, my eyes catching on stray words detailing her travels, meals, weather. Nothing revolutionary. No glaring *I'm leaving my daughter to enter the Witness Protection Program* or *I've decided to join a cult* entries. I sighed.

"Nada here." Maverick's hands rippled over the keys.

I glanced up. "I don't know what they're called, but my dad has talked about these sites where you pay to find out information only if there's a hit. Can you find those?"

Mav punched in a few words. "Find and Connect? Where Am I?"

"Try 'em."

"'Search bears no results,'" Mav read. He tipped the chair back and braced his head in his hands. "Shit. I thought brain science was hard. Finding this woman feels impossible. She's a ghost online."

I ran my hand over the cover of the journal, thinking. Travel. Geography. "We don't know why she left."

"Obviously not."

"What if we figure out why she stayed away?"

Mav exaggerated his handclap. "Bravo. Mystery solved."

I rolled my eyes. "It's one thing to leave, but it has to be even harder to stay gone." I flexed my feet, thinking. "Clearly, it's not the same thing, but I once ran away from home for probably an hour because I was mad my parents were making me do my homework. I made it to the convenience store, realized I didn't have enough money for a bag of chips and that if I didn't leave soon, I'd miss swim practice, so I went home."

Mav laughed. "Yeah, it's not the same thing. But people stay gone because of all kinds of crap. Shame. Betrayals. Addiction, like we said before. Some legal reason, though I don't see a mug shot."

I cleared my throat. "She could be dead." Which could also be why December didn't want to join this whole thing. Pouring your heart into searching for someone, only to have the opportunity for making future memories fizzle away? It would hurt twice as much to find out you were abandoned and then lost for good.

"Well. Whatever the deal is with this woman, it kept her from her kid." Mav slid one of the pictures over. "What about custody . . . ?" He trailed off, typed something into the computer. "If she left and meant to return, then would she worry she wouldn't get December back or something? The law says 'reasonable provisions' have to be made. I don't know what kind of arrangement her mom had with December's uncle."

We sat in silence. I tossed the journal onto the desk in defeat. "Thanks for helping."

"December's situation reminds me of my cousin Jill's." Maverick's aunt—Jill's mom—had been in and out of their lives, fighting an opiate addiction for years. She was a big reason why he got into neuroscience. One of his hobbies was reading pre-prints on addiction, genetics versus environment, stuff like that. Mav used the heel of his palm to push his glasses up his nose. "I feel for her. For both of them."

"It's depressing."

"As hell. At least December seems, I don't know. Well-adjusted enough?"

"Our brain chemistry is a major factor in how we handle anything, bro." His face took on the look he wore when he talked about neuro stuff. Chin lifted, eyes bright, voice an octave lower and intense.

"Yeah? How so?"

He rummaged in the popcorn bowl. "There's a huge range in biological makeup. Some experiences produce hormones such as CRF and cortisol, which basically make an emotional imprint, or work to repress your memories." Mav's glasses glinted in the computer's glare. "They're like nature's yellow flag. One person in a train crash might ride a different one the next day, while someone else reading *about* that train crash might never travel again."

I stared at him. "Seriously?"

He wrinkled his nose and nodded. "It's more obvious in childhood stuff. If you experience something super traumatic, then the stress hormones that enter your amygdala can prevent your hippocampus from remembering that event perfectly. Memory gaps, sorta. The hormones actually screw with the way your brain processes stuff."

I was in awe of all this information, and a little jealous that Maverick knew exactly what he wanted to do in life already. "You're gonna change the world, Dr. Tate."

He laughed. "Brainpower. Just my party trick for impressing girls."

I gave him a look. "Oh, yeah? How's that working out for you?"

He frowned. "About as well as your detective career."

CHAPTER TWENTY-ONE
December

FIVE DAYS BEFORE school started, I rapped three quick knocks on Nick's front door. I wore an old landscaping tank top of my uncle's, basketball shorts, and my Adidas slides, my hair knotted on top of my head. I held a tray of blondies—my excuse for coming over.

The truth was, I wanted to see him. But I would keep that to myself.

Nick answered, barefoot and smelling like dryer sheets and deodorant, his hair wet from a recent shower. In his hand was a triangle-shaped calzone slice.

"I come bearing gifts," I said, holding up the treat. "My uncle's specialty." I'd baked them, but he didn't need to know that. "A belated thank-you for staying with me at the hospital."

He waved me inside, miming that his mouth was full. "How's your arm?" Nick asked once he swallowed.

"Healing." I stopped, taking in the scene before me: a misshapen but incredibly delicious-smelling homemade calzone on a tray atop the coffee table. Some epic battle scene paused on the television. "Sorry to interrupt your dinner."

"Oh. No problem. My dad made Sophie and me a broccoli-and-chicken calzone. The end of August is always an absent-parent time for me and Soph with them prepping for the school year." He collapsed backward on the couch.

"Your parents are teachers?"

"Mom's a principal in Woodland. Dad teaches law and ethics in Easton." He nudged the tray. "Want some?"

"I don't want to eat your sister's dinner."

"She already ate. Kid is hell-bent on 'fueling her body.' She's in her room."

I picked up a piece, feeling the bristle of flour dust beneath my fingertips, surprised by its hefty weight. I broke the calzone in half.

Nick took a bite of his slice, chewing. "Hey, I was thinking. If you wanted to meet people before school starts, you could come with Mav and me to Stella Rose's end-of-summer party."

A buzz of excitement booted its way through my stomach. I latched onto it. This. *This* is what I'd feel in this moment. No wonder people did wild things for love. "Oh," I said, trying to sound casual. "I actually met her and her friends the other day. Maisie Cabrera and Carrie Lee."

His face was unreadable. "I've known them my whole life. Maisie lives in Bright Acres, too."

Nick's sister sidled into the room, carrying a tablet. She halted when she saw me. "Hey, it's you! The Scrabble genius whose uncle plants all the flowers."

I waved. "I'm December."

"I know." Sophie tugged her ponytail.

"What trouble are you up to now?" Nick asked.

She made a face at him. "I'm trying a pirouette."

"Like a dance spin?" Nick tipped his head back and drank from his water bottle. I watched his Adam's apple work in tandem with the pulls of water.

She brushed an escaped strand of hair out of her eyes. "Yeah. Here." She tapped the tablet, which was paused on a YouTube video of a ballerina clad in a black leotard. "See?" She pressed the PLAY triangle, and we watched, absorbed, as Misty Copeland executed a flawless quadruple pirouette. She finished in a perfect lunge, her sculpted legs showcasing muscles that would make Olympic judges drool.

"Wow. If I tried that, I'd look like a water buffalo on ice skates." I had about as much grace as a block of wood.

"Why *are* you trying that?" Nick asked.

Sophie's sigh dripped with exasperation. "I can't run summer track my whole life."

"You're in fourth grade."

"Exactly. Jayla said if I want to make the competition team, I need to practice my turns."

"But you've only taken one dance class," Nick said.

"And?" Sophie laid the tablet on the coffee table, backed up a few steps, and then jerked herself around. Her body ricocheted, more Halloween skeleton than American Ballet Theatre.

I leaned forward, adjusting the playback to half speed. "Look," I said, gesturing toward the screen. "I think you have to bend more. Get a foundation for the turn. And press into the floor with your foot while you squeeze your legs."

She studied me. "How do you know?"

"Just a guess."

Sophie sighed. "I've been trying to teach myself from YouTube for the last few weeks."

Nick stood. "Like this?" Lithe and long, he spun, his arms somehow chasing his torso. Very giraffe in a tutu.

They took turns thoroughly embarrassing themselves. My cheeks hurt from laughter, my rib cage failing to contain this glowy feeling I'd never felt before.

"You try, December," Sophie said.

"No way."

"Too scared?" Nick asked, his grin spreading over the entire southern hemisphere of his face.

I jutted my chin in his general direction. "I don't want to show you up. That's all."

"Please. Be my guest."

"Oh, fine. But don't judge me." And in the time it took for me to flip through a fraction of the world's dance teachers shouting, *"Spot! Squeeze your core! Soften your elbows!"* I dipped into a ballerina's plié and willed my body to turn. My world kaleidoscoped, laughter bubbling in my core.

"Whoa, that's amaz—" Sophie cut herself off at my stumble. I almost caught myself, then tripped over the leg of the coffee table, bracing my uninjured arm on my lifeguard's shoulder.

He laughed, steadying me. I glanced up at him.

Until now, we'd only been this close—faces inches from each other close—while we were under some kind of duress. Saving Mr. Francis. The arm tourniquet at Pire's Dairy.

I trembled with the urge to keep touching him, but now was not the time.

"We have to stop meeting like this," Nick said.

"Thanks," I said, stepping back.

He cleared his throat, his voice a murmur. "Anytime."

CHAPTER TWENTY-TWO
Nick

"YOU TRY," MAVERICK said.

I handed him the brown-paper-wrapped package—a bottle of booze with gold flecks dancing inside, procured from Mav's barber cousin at a 200 percent markup—and lifted my hand, echoing his knock on the front door of Stella Rose's house. Nothing.

"Are you even supposed to knock for a party?"

I shrugged. "How would I know?"

"You go to parties."

"I go to swim team gatherings where there are approximately six people in a basement playing video games and eating hot Cheetos. You know, the ones you've come to with me?"

He sighed. "The parents are home at those."

"So we knock."

"Right."

"The parents are very much not home here."

"Also right."

We were quiet for a moment, listening to the house vibrate with the bass of the music. Mav leaned toward the door. "This song is a jam."

"A *jam*? What century are you from, the 1900s?" I paused. "Should we get out of here?"

"You're not going in because she didn't answer your knock?" He frowned. "What's going on with you?"

I rubbed my palms on my shorts. "I haven't seen most of these people since the time I *didn't* save Mr. Francis."

"Hey, dude? Sorry to burst your big worry bubble, but I don't think anyone here is going to care that you're here. I think they care about having fun, making out with other people, dancing, and establishing their social presence for the year."

I opened my mouth to respond, but the door swung open. "Nick! Maverick!" Stella Rose's smile left dimples in her cheeks. "You're here. You both know where everything is, of course. Grab anything you'd like."

"I've never been here," Mav said.

"I haven't been here since I was little." I stepped inside.

"You haven't?" Stella Rose's face puckered. "That's weird. I thought you'd been here with the swim team, but you know how summer goes."

We followed her through a wide-open foyer into a plushly carpeted living area with vaulted ceilings. Over the years, Stella Rose's back-to-school party had morphed from a parent-supervised pizza-and–T-shirt-decorating soiree to an all-night rager. The room was full of the yeasty smell of beer, the biting trace of liquor and chasers, the soft flip of cards and cups against the shouts and laughs of everyone there. Stella Rose led us out to her backyard through one of two sliding doors.

On one end of the massive expanse of yard was a firepit, several empty chairs and benches arranged around it in a circle. On the other was a detached garage, all three doors yanked open to reveal kids playing flip cup and beer pong.

"Games over there," Stella Rose said. "Everyone else is down-stairs. Follow me?"

In the darkened basement, we were greeted by a sea of red and white. I checked my own selection, which I'd put on with a massive sense of skepticism, but my white shirt and red shorts fit right in to Stella Rose's theme: Woodland's colors.

"We look like we're about to erupt into a full-party flash mob," Maverick muttered.

I thought of Sophie's antics in the living room the other night. "Or like an entire grade trying out as a dance crew."

Maverick pulled a red cup from the top of a stack. It rattled the others, knocking a few to the floor.

"Here," December said, materializing out of nowhere and picking them up.

Something was different about her. I couldn't put my finger on it. She wore this blousy white dress, and she'd worked whatever magic people do with hair tools to create a somehow both straight and curly effect, which tumbled in a waterfall over one shoulder. Her vibe was absolutely killer. I didn't have the words for it, but Mav did. "What's up, December?" he said. "Your look is fire tonight. All warrior prin-cess meets the heroine in a fantasy novel."

"Thanks. Too bad these sandals are murdering my feet." She wig-gled one gold-strapped foot. "This is some kind of place, huh?"

I made a show of looking around. "Yeah, seriously."

Homes like Stella Rose's were high-ceilinged and higher-moneyed. Bright Acres was the only condo complex in our bougie town, so our kind of shared-space living—even in separate units—was not under-stood by others. Mom and Dad worked long-ass hours for what we had. We didn't need a three-car garage. We didn't even have a one-car one, but we were all fine. Every single person I knew my age, except for Maisie and December, lived in stand-alone houses. Sometimes, especially when I had to draft brutally precise texts detailing where people had to park, followed by how to walk to our not-listed-on-Waze unit, I was jealous of this kind of ample-parking, easy-address life, but mostly, I felt like an outsider.

"Generational wealth," Maverick whispered. I hid a snort.

December shook her cup. "I need a refill. Do you guys want anything?"

"I'm hitting the dance floor," Mav said, slipping into the pack of writhing bodies.

"I'll join you," I said to December.

At the bar, she cracked open a can of seltzer with a crunchy hiss. She poured it into a cup, along with a tiny dash of vodka. "I'm not a big drinker."

"Oh, yeah?" I asked, trying to cycle back over the words she said and mash them up with how my brain felt.

"I don't like feeling out of control."

"I don't, either. My party experience is mostly limited to the off-season or victories after swim meets."

"You have a lot of those?" She tapped her cup against mine. "Swim team victories, I mean. Cheers."

"Cheers. I'm—" I stopped. Exhaled. Truth was truth, and part of me wanted to impress her. "We have enough wins, yeah." The air caught in my chest as if it were paused by my rib cage.

The music rose in volume, the crowd—my classmates of twelve years, my teammates, my friends and acquaintances—shrieking with delight. December ducked her head to my ear. "Why do you think it happened?" she shouted.

"What?" I asked, even though I knew precisely what.

She drew back and held my eyes with liquid ones. "Why you couldn't move that day."

That day. Everything came back to that day. I'd spent what felt like every still moment of my days since then trying to figure it out. Was it doubt in my abilities? Fear of failure? Some sort of biochemical interference? I shook my head. "I wish I knew."

"Me too. But even though it was awful, I'm glad it turned out okay. And at least I met someone before the year started." The lights in the basement glinted off her hair. "Want to go find Maverick on the dance floor?"

I joined her. Joined everyone. We danced until we were sweaty and laughing. Drinks splashed all over the place, soaking my sleeve at one point. But I didn't mind at all. Over the next hour or so, December proved herself to be a terrifically off-beat dancer. But the way she closed her eyes and tipped her head skyward, she either didn't know or didn't care.

And I found it adorable. I was slipping over the edge of a cliff I hadn't banked on going near. December laughed at one of Mav's ridiculous moves. I found myself analyzing every single one of her actions and reactions, not paying attention to Maisie or Carrie dancing beside her.

She slid her eyes in my direction, and *man*. It was like she was a sun, and I was a newcomer to her galaxy. I was something that didn't belong in space accidentally falling into orbit. The way she looked at me, I could almost imagine she felt it, too. And suddenly, more than anything else in the world, I had to know if she felt the same way.

What was *up* with me? Why was I so drawn to this girl—the one who'd saved my ass and then left me hanging?

She bit her lip, studying me. "Have you learned anything about my mom? Made any progress?"

I worked to relax the tension in my hands. I cracked my knuckles, the sound lost in the basement but the relief palpable. "Not yet, but I'm looking."

December nodded, then stilled. Her head swiveled toward the center of the dance floor.

I nudged her hand with mine. "Hey, what's wr—"

"Put me down!" The scream echoed above the beat.

The crowd paused. I stopped dancing, searching for the source of the shout. Someone muted the music; someone else turned on a corner lamp.

December's upturned face caught the glow of the light. She frowned, her eyebrows furrowed.

I followed her gaze. In the middle of the dance floor, Jake Dirks, the captain of the soccer team, had Carrie slung over one shoulder. She punched his back with her curled fists. Laughing, he released her. My shoulders drifted south, tension released.

"All good," he called, grinning. "We're good."

"Who's that?" December asked.

"Tall white kid?" I tilted my head toward him. "That's Jake Dirks."

"Do you like him?"

"Jake?" He had the sort of loud, jokey, impish vibe that teachers rolled their eyes at. "I don't know him enough to like him or dislike him. He's lived here as long as I have."

A thin, vertical line on her forehead deepened. She pressed her fingertips to her temple.

"What is it?"

"Carrie looks . . ." She let her words trail off. "I'll be back." She weaved her way through the crowd, took Carrie's hand, and vanished.

CHAPTER TWENTY-THREE
December

WHEN STELLA ROSE saw how upset Carrie was, she broke up the party, cutting the music and herding people out. We—Maisie, Carrie, and I—waited on a curved rattan bench in a sitting area accessible only through her parents' bedroom. The three of us were shoulder to shoulder, wrapped in an oversized caftan against the air-conditioning, listening to the crackle from the gas fireplace in front of us and the clang of empty cans being tossed into trash bags by Stella Rose, Nick, and Mav below.

I was angry. Ragey. White-hot lines crackled across my sightline, left over from looking into the fire for too long. I blinked to clear them away, searching my mind for what came next, an actress prompting her director for a forgotten line. "Hey, I know we don't know each other that well." I hesitated. "If you want me to go . . ." I let the sentence die out.

"No way," Carrie said. "You were the first person to ask what was up. You're good."

Even before Carrie explained between bitter hiccups what had happened between her and this boy earlier in the summer—at a party in the woods, he'd run his hand along her hip, drifting his fingertips along the waistband of her skirt; she had removed his hand three times before he gave up—I'd climbed both forward and backward.

Jake Dirks had been on my radar the same way everyone is. One soul bobbing in the endless sea. Carrie's explanation of what she was feeling in real time put a whole new layer on a cake frosted with the patriarchy.

I'd missed it. Courtesy of my Blank Spot. I'd taken that one moment to ask Nick about Mara Jones's whereabouts, and *boom*.

"When he put me down, his hand cupped my butt," Carrie said, breaking the silence. Her voice was low, clogged with tears. "I don't know if he did it on purpose—"

"When's the last time you grabbed someone's ass by accident?" Maisie took Carrie's hand. "I always thought he was so nice."

Carrie tipped her head onto Maisie's shoulder and relaxed. "Me too. It wasn't until last month that my internal alarm rang."

I bit down hard, top teeth meeting bottom teeth, jaw clenching. Jake Dirks wasn't a serial killer. He wasn't publicly crass or rude. He was observationally polite, even. I knew how terrible he was the same way I know how terrible a lot of people are, but now his actions had personal relevance to me.

Standing on the dance floor beside the boy who I wanted to fall in love with me already—because I knew what was coming,

(oh, did I know what was coming)

I'd taken the opportunity to climb, triggered by the look on Carrie's face.

And I didn't like what I saw about Jake Dirks one bit.

A wave of heat spread through me, starting in my gut and exploding from my ears to my feet. I shifted, the rattan bench groaning beneath me, desperate to figure out how I could help this miserable-looking Carrie.

The first time I succeeded in changing the future, I lost my mother.

I only knew that I'd done something—*something*—to make her go. I gained my Blank Spot.

The second time, I set myself on this path. Tipping the first domino to propel the death of this tragic lifeguard, who was currently jogging up the back staircase with Maverick and Stella Rose, on their way to see us.

"Headache?" Maisie asked.

"Huh?"

"You're pressing your temple."

"Oh." I smiled weakly. "Yeah."

"Squeeze here," Carrie said, pointing at the web of skin between her thumb and forefinger. "Acupressure spot for headaches. The Hegu point."

"You have to hold it till you're uncomfortable, right?" Maisie flashed a smile at Carrie.

Carrie rubbed her eyes. "Correct."

I obeyed, snaring my hand between my fingers the same way my brain was trapped in a puzzle.

You could try to throw a curveball into Jake Dirks's trajectory, said my thinking, rational brain.

My head ached with possibility. The future held its breath. Carrie had great things ahead of her, including a gorgeous love story sitting beside me, and I didn't want to jeopardize that.

But wait.

My organs felt out of place, like I was a giant shaken snow globe. My heart was stuck in the base of my throat, my stomach twisted in either worry or excitement. I'd failed to change so many events before. I had succeeded only twice. I'd spent so much of my childhood trying to prevent violent bank robberies and terrible things happening in my town and in my state and across the world, and the ocean readjusted itself every goddamn time that

I'd

given

up.

And now a swirling realization spread through me. Nothing worked—*except* the unspecific something with my mom, and the specific saving of Mr. Francis. Those were the only two that changed the course of events, because *they'd directly impacted me*. In major, life-changing ways. Not like the cut on my arm—I'd switched how I'd gotten it, from a trash can to a picnic bench's nail, sure, but I still had the scar to prove it.

Beneath the hem of my white dress, I dug my nails into my thighs. Was that it? Maybe I could change the big things after all, if I had a personal connection to them?

Just as this suspicion hardened to a tangible certainty, the door to Stella Rose's parents' room burst open. I released my hand and filed the thought away, resolving to return to it for further exploration, as Carrie peeled herself from Maisie.

"What's going on in here?" Stella Rose asked. "You okay, Car?"

"I'm fine." It was immediately clear to everyone in the room that she was not.

After an awkward pause, Nick cleared his throat. "Anyone else feel weird standing in someone's parents' bedroom?"

"Oh, don't worry," Stella Rose said. "My parents haven't slept in here together in probably two years." She punctuated her sentence by taking a sip of her drink. "Someone, anyone, change the subject?"

Maybe it was the desperate need to find relief after Carrie's incident with Jake Dirks, or to make sure the night wasn't a total lost cause, but suddenly, I was everyone's favorite interviewee. I answered questions about how we moved around, what life was like living with an uncle who adored craft beer we couldn't afford, video games, and flowers.

Along the way, we shifted. I slid to the floor, scooting ever so closer to Nick. Mav danced across the room two or three more times, Stella Rose snort-laughing. Carrie sprawled out, her head lolling on one of Maisie's folded thighs. We hung out there for another hour as the fire burned low, holding on to that dizzy feeling of bonding.

Stella Rose yawned, stretching her arms above her head. "Weird that I will forever now look at this fireplace and think of tonight."

Mav rose up on his knees. "Isn't that cool?"

"Cool?" Stella Rose repeated.

He nodded. "How your brain can make those sorts of associations."

"Mav here is a neuro wizard," Nick said.

"How so?" Maisie asked.

"Well, if this is your brain"—Maverick made a fist with his hand and held it so the bottom of his wrist was parallel to the floor—"then one of your nucleus accumbens would be roughly here." He pointed to the curled-up index finger with the tip of his beer bottle. "One of my professors—"

"Your *professors*?" Carrie interrupted.

"Summer classes," Mav said, shrugging. "Anyway, she studies the role the nucleus accumbens plays in processing rewards, among a bunch of other things scientists don't know. Long story short, if you form a good memory someplace, the brain remembers—and can take you back. Part of the rewards system."

"That must be why I love the picture of a table set for dinner," Maisie said. "There is absolutely nothing in the world that can compare to a holiday at my house. It's family. My mom. I'm not happy unless she is." She paused. "Which is maybe a problem?"

"I like the thrill of falling," Carrie said. "I'm a flier, in cheerleading. And toward the end of a lift, there's this quick dip when they're about to throw me, and my stomach drops, then my whole body sails in the air. I love it."

Me: *intimacy.* Feeling important to someone else. "Oreos and milk."

Stella Rose stood up. "Pizza makes me happy. I'm going to go make a frozen one. Anyone in?"

Maisie shook her head. "I think I'm going to bed."

"Me too," Carrie said.

I glanced at Nick. "Want to call a rideshare back to Bright Acres?"

———

Outside, the air was warm and lightly humid around us. It lifted the hair from my neck, away from my face. We walked in preoccupied silence; me nervous, him mulling.

"Wait," Nick said, halting us in place at the base of the driveway. "Tell me I'm not alone here."

My glance was sidelong. I worked to keep my voice steady. "I'm right next to you?"

He shook his head. "No. That's not what I mean." He drew in a breath and faced me. "Tell me you're feeling what I am. That my mind isn't playing tricks on me."

"Your mind isn't playing tricks on you," I murmured. That made one of us.

"And if it's true . . ." He stepped closer. "Tell me there's something between us and you feel it, too."

My heartbeat was everywhere but where it belonged. "I'm feeling something."

Closer.

"I like how it feels," I whispered.

His hand encircling my wrist was dry and hot. Or maybe my skin was.

(This, oh, this, it had finally come to this.)

One hand cupped my cheek; the other tilted my chin with a soft uptick toward him. His lashes were longer than I'd realized. His curls rustled in the breeze, making a bumpy, moving shadow in the pavement behind him, an adorable victim of the streetlight.

"Yes?" he asked. Permission.

I blinked, using my eyelids as a camera shutter so I could keep this memory for myself. The rosiest gumball.

"Yes," I whispered.

Had I known it was going to happen? Of course. But I was unprepared for the sensation. The cool surprise of his lips against mine, eager and soft, questioning and answering. ChapStick and spring water and predawn mint. An imaginary rope in my chest wanted to bind myself to this moment for all time. My hands rose to his shoulders, linked behind his neck; our noses brushed. A tightening, thrumming urge raced through me for more.

My mind split in half. One side flew, exalted; the other crashed, irreparably sad. Because what this kiss did was unzip me. Turned my feelings into reality. My desire for this emerging love.

It was here.

And with it came the crushing sense of dread at his death. The image of him on the ground, that orange shirt that played in the back of my mind, like static on a distant radio station.

If only I knew how it felt to have a mind like anyone else, to experience this kiss as the wax seal on the beginning of something new. Lost in his lips, focusing on the fingertips that traced tiny circles on my lower back, I allowed myself to pretend for one instant. Pretend my brain didn't whorl into other places in the world. Pretend I wasn't petrified to lose this lifeguard.

Pretend I was only a girl, living in her moment.

See, this kiss?

It was everything.

Everything.

CHAPTER TWENTY-FOUR
Nick

AND IN THAT moment, everything changed.

CHAPTER TWENTY-FIVE
December

(EVERYTHING.)

CHAPTER TWENTY-SIX

Nick

"ANOTHER ONE," DECEMBER said.

Her hair floated around her in the pool, brushing her bare shoulders like electric eels. She kept as much of her body underwater as she could because the day of my last shift of the summer was the picture of the iOS Weather app icon: sunny and seventy. Empty of swimmers, except for December.

Ducking, she blew bubbles on the surface, her butterfly lips forming an *O*. She threw me a plastic pool ring, and I tossed it into the shallow end, closer to my perch. Closer to me. Her mouth curved into a smile, and she dove.

We hadn't mentioned the fact that our lips had met two nights ago. Only a tiny hint via text.

Me: I had fun yesterday. You around today?
December: Visiting my grandma
December: ps I had fun, too 😍

I'd let my phone's reading app repeat the text out loud three times.

December surfaced beside where I sat with my feet dangling in the water. She shook the ring in the air, triumphant, then draped it over one of my ankles. I nudged my submerged calf against her arm, grateful I had the excuse to keep staring thanks to lifeguard duty. I pressed the GUARD-inscribed rescue tube against the lap of my bathing suit and swirled my feet in the warm water. "You're pretty."

"Thank you." She ducked her mouth below the water, trying to hide her smile, but I caught it.

Every time my dad told my mom she was beautiful, she balked. I loved that December didn't try to deflect the compliment.

"You ready for school tomorrow?" I asked.

She hiked her body out of the water, wrapped herself in her huge black towel, and settled next to me. "Anything I should know?"

I thought for a moment. "It's not like Stella Rose's party."

"Good," she said, shivering. She lowered her head. "Hey, I've been thinking."

"As you should be."

She rolled her eyes. "I don't think you should keep looking for my mom."

I stilled my feet. "What?"

She pulled the towel tighter and made a strange face. I couldn't decipher it. Relief? Fear? "Honestly, I'm pretty sure it's impossible. And now that we are . . . whatever we are, I'd rather spend time with you. You're here. She's not."

Something about her words—or her tone, maybe?—wasn't sitting well in my chest. "So that's it?"

"What?"

"You're just . . . giving up?"

"It's not that."

"But I haven't done everything I can do." I frowned. "It's not fair that she left, Dec."

"Lots of life isn't fair." She kicked her feet in the water. "But seriously. If she's meant to be in my family's life, then she'll come back on her own."

I frowned. "I mean, she's your mom, but . . ."

She smiled. "Great. It's settled. And about the newspaper, maybe we can—" She was interrupted by the buzzing whir of bicycle spokes, followed by a squeaky kickstand.

Sophie.

"No swimming right now," I called.

"You're not my boss." Sophie unhooked the gate. "Relax, brother. Hey, December."

"Hey, Sophie," December said. "You get that dance move yet?"

"Nailed it." Sophie produced a folded white envelope from her pocket and tossed it to me. I plucked it out of the air just before it landed in the pool.

"Mom's doing her massive *the school year is starting, let's pretend we're organized* purge," Sophie said. "She's tackling the mail pile now. I said I'd give you this and ran before she made me get rid of all my too-small clothes."

"What is it?"

"How should I know? It's a federal offense to open someone else's mail."

December laughed. "How do you know that?"

Sophie scratched her ear. "Sometimes I stay up and watch documentaries with my dad."

I eased my finger beneath the flap. Nondescript town return address and thick paper. Call it suspicion or call it premonition or call it whatever you'd like, but my stomach twisted with nerves. December shifted closer and put her hand on my shoulder.

"Are you okay?" she murmured. "You're all tense."

I glanced at my sister. Her arms were crossed, one eyebrow raised in the creepy way she did. "Someone has a giiiiirlfriend," she said.

"Shut it, Soph." I unfolded the letter. "'From the office of Mayor William Stephens,'" I read.

The words jumped and wriggled all over the page. I couldn't focus on them except for my name and *congratulations* and *thank you*. I handed it to December.

"'Dear Nicholas Irving,'" she read. "'Congratulations on your recent heroic act of bravery in saving the life of fellow resident Mr. Ronaldo J. Francis. This act is a true demonstration of valor and quick thinking. The entire community benefits from having upstanding young citizens like yourself working to protect lives.'"

I groaned. "This is out of hand."

"There's more," December said. She bent her head. "'To honor this measure of lifesaving achievement, I would be thrilled to invite you to the annual Thanksgiving celebration, where I hope you will accept an official key to the city. This ornamental award symbolizes our trust in you and gratitude for your actions. I expect you will do good things in the world, Mr. Irving, and we are proud your origins will be here in Woodland.'"

"Woodland's a *town*," Sophie said, shedding her swimsuit cover-up. "Why would they give you a key to the city? That makes zero sense."

My throat was dry. I swallowed. "It's the name of the award."

"It's a bad name." She backed up a few steps and grinned at me. I made a weary motion with my hand, and she sprinted toward the pool, showering us with her cannonball's splash.

As soon as she was out of earshot, I turned to December. "I can't accept a freaking key to the city for an 'act of bravery' I didn't even commit."

"Hey. The act of being a lifeguard at all is brave. Trying out for that farm team? Brave." She dropped her voice. "Being vulnerable about what you're feeling? Drumroll, please. Brave."

I picked up the discarded rings, whipping them into the pool for Soph to collect. "Don't you think it's time to go to Joe DiPietro? Tell him the truth?"

"Wait." December frowned. "Was this why?" Her voice sounded strange. Quaky.

"Why what?"

She waited for Sophie to dive back underwater, leaving me suspended in impatient agony. "Why you kissed me. To try and get closer to me? To get me to change my mind about coming forward about Mr. Francis?" She moved away from me, and my bare arm prickled at the loss of her body heat in the September air.

I recoiled. "Is that what you think?"

She hesitated. "I mean, what changed? I knew . . . *know* we've spent more time together. And the driveway two nights ago meant something to me." She gestured between the two of us. "I'm feeling things I never have. I'm not sure it's the same for you, and I want to know . . . is this real for you? Or are you trying to get out of this fake-hero thing?" December drew her knees to her chest and stood.

In front of us, Sophie tossed another ring onto the growing pile beside the pool. Leaving a path of wet footprints in her wake, December moved to the lounge chair where she'd dropped her stuff—her bag, sweatshirt, headphones, her mom's floppy black-and-white hat.

"December, wait." I grunted with frustration, waiting for Sophie to dunk again. "Please don't leave me at this pool again. I have to watch my sister in the water."

December paused. Came back over and sat. Her hair dripped, leaving a ring on the neck of her sweatshirt.

"I'm into you," I said. Which I *was*. An excited buzz swept through me because this moment was so *real*, the high only slightly dampened by the fact that I had to keep my focus on my swimming sister.

I cleared my throat and continued. "That kiss meant something to me, too. Something big. Tons of stuff in my life is confusing, December. But what I'm feeling right now isn't."

Her smile was slow but strong. She inched closer to me again. "All right. If you feel like it's gone on long enough, want to go to the newspaper office together? We can clear everything up." She wrinkled her nose. "Though I can't say I'm looking forward to the attention."

I shaded my eyes with my palm, squinting in the sun. I thought back to our first moments together—her saving Mr. Francis, and the fallout since. The inaccurate article. My determination to find her mother.

Everyone kept letting me out of things without knowing they were letting me out of things, and if I had any chance of proving that I didn't have to doubt everything about myself for the rest of my life, then I needed to follow through on something for once in my life. I *could* keep going and look for December's mom—she didn't have to know about it. And once I found her, *if* I found her, then we could set the record straight together. A sudden gift of resolve soared through me.

"Nah, not yet," I said. "Maybe once all this dies down."

Her mouth quirked. She squinted at me. "You sure?"

"Are you two gonna kiss again?" Sophie interrupted, bobbing close to my perch.

I stared at her. "How did you know?"

Sophie's laugh was a cackle. "I didn't. But I guessed. And now you told me."

CHAPTER TWENTY-SEVEN
December

THIS YEAR, MY first day of school jitters were nonexistent, thanks to the early strings of friendships taking root and a someday-soon boyfriend. I pretended to bumble my way around the high school campus as if I had difficulty navigating someplace unfamiliar.

After lunch, I was the first to arrive in the biology classroom. I slid into my seat at a table meant for three. Mr. Francis, now in his last year of teaching, had the most-decorated classroom I'd been in all day. Bio-joke posters lined the walls. (*Did you hear the teacher's humerus joke? I think it was pretty cornea*—the words written in graphics designed to look like bones, alongside a winking eyeball. A cartoon cell holding a selfie stick, captioned *These genes look great on me. I think I'll take a cell-fie.*)

In the doorway, Nick caught sight of me and waved. Candle smoke heat curled through my veins. A yellowed piece of paper tacked above the open door read:

BIOLOGY, NOUN. THE STUDY OF LIVING ORGANISMS.

Nick, in the doorway. A living organism.
Alive. Not dead.
All the light in my body snuffed out.

In chaos theory, the butterfly effect is when one small change results in large differences later. A hiccup in the beat of a butterfly's wings culminating in a tornado weeks thereafter.

Now those butterflies shriveled into chrysalides and glommed onto my nerve endings.

Tock. Time. Tick.

I kept waiting for what would help me figure out how to save Nick's life. He made his way to my table, face split open by a smile, completely unaware that every night, visions of his death danced in my head.

(the shirt, the blood, his startled, scared eyes)

My nerves crackling, I tapped the pen against my table's lacquered top, poring over my options for the thousandth time. I'd had no knowledge of Nick's impending death until I broke character, exercised my free will, and saved Mr. Francis's life.

That small action—saving the life of this broad, grinning man who sat at the helm of the classroom with cheeks like ruddy apple skin and salt-and-pepper hair—had cost me everything but had given me a chance to fall in love.

I pressed the pen so hard into the table that it bent in half. Every time I considered my choices, I came up with zilch.

Nick slid into the seat beside me, Maverick at his heels. "It appears we have a class together."

"Correction," Maverick said. "We have the *best* class together."

Maisie, Stella Rose, and Carrie trickled in, claiming the table in front of us. "Happy first day," I said. I squinted at my schedule. *Elective: Human Studies*, it read.

"I've been looking forward to this class forever," Maisie said.

"She gets it," Maverick said.

"I thought Mr. Francis taught biology?"

"I do," Mr. Francis said. "Don't tell the administration, but Human Studies is my favorite." He winked. "Here, we'll study a complex idea: what it means to be human. As you know, I'm the biology teacher here, and to be human correlates nicely with that, don't you think?" Mumbles of assent from around the room. "So enthusiastic," he said, rubbing his hands together. "No tests in this class. One or two at-home projects each term. Instead, we chat. We listen. We ask questions." He paused. "We empathize. Acknowledge our biases and flaws. Make progress. Move onward."

I leaned into the back of my chair, settling into the good energy that radiated from this man, bracing myself for what he was about to do.

He cleared his throat right on cue. "Before we jump in, I can't let the opportunity go by." He picked up a stack of papers from his desk and held them above this head like Rafiki lifting Simba on Pride Rock. "Because we're in 'The Great Age of Necks Bent Like Coat Hangers,' named because you crick your necks down and glue your eyeballs to your phones with organic adhesive, you already know my summer was more exciting than yours." Mr. Francis's eyes skimmed the room, settling on Nick.

I exhaled. I knew what Mr. Francis held, and I knew how Nick would react. A pang of sympathy caught my insides. I resisted the urge to put my hand somewhere on Nick—his shoulder, his thigh, his sleeve.

Nick shrank beside me. "Here we go," he muttered.

Mr. Francis beamed. "The lifeguard among us did his job. The rescue of a lifetime—*my* lifetime, at least."

"Thank God!" Maverick punched his fist in the air. "I've been looking forward to this class since freshman year."

"He'll get through this quick," I whispered. I gave Nick what I hoped was a reassuring smile and grazed my knuckles against the side of his thigh.

Mr. Francis walked to our table and dropped the packet in front of Nick. "Thank-you notes from my grandkids." He rapped his fingertips on the table. "Thanks again for saving my life, sir."

The class gave an obligatory round of applause.

"Now!" Mr. Francis jogged to the front of the class. "Brothers, sisters, cousins—I'm calling you that because along with all of life on earth, we're all descendants of the same thing! A bacteria-like little bugger we call LUCA, the Last Universal Common Ancestor." He grinned. "Ready to learn?"

—

We left school after the last bell. Outside, Nick's hand bumped against my own twice before his fingers hooked into mine and my heart grew, not unlike the Grinch's, with a hysterical kind of glee. The sun shone from our backs, so our double shadow—linked in the middle—walked in front of us.

Beneath my camel-colored suede fall booties, so soft and velvety you wanted to lay your cheek on them, the fallen leaves crunched. The trees swished in the wind with a comforting kind of white static noise, their leaves riotous with color. Even the taste in my mouth was extra, blasting my sinuses and my throat with the cool, clean peppermint of a Crest commercial.

Nick's hand squeezed mine, catching one of my heartbeats in his palm. My pulse carried on and on and on, agonizing over what bloomed between us, over what could possibly end before I knew it. I'd been preoccupied with school starting, so I dipped into the events of the afternoon ahead, frowning when I saw Nick sitting at his desk, the vision nearly graying out, when I was interrupted by something whipping across my face. A Frisbee. Painless but off-putting. I rubbed my cheek, annoyed.

A figure darted in front of us and held up his palm. "Sorry about that."

Jake Dirks. The jerk from Stella Rose's party.

He turned to fling the disc at someone else. I stared at the back of his neck. He'd gotten a haircut this weekend, along with 247 out of 289 members of my new graduating class. The barber—Maverick's cousin, small town, after all—had nicked the back of his neck, the buzzer leaving behind a scrape that resembled fork tines.

My mouth filled with disgust, which, I've learned over time, tastes different for everyone. My brand was a mix of actual sour grapes— the overripe ones—and anise cookies.

Before the world could keep turning, before Nick blinked, before I took my next breath, I absorbed what I'd already learned about Jake Dirks from my first launch into his timeline at Stella Rose's party, and focused deeper. Student council, soccer team, yearbook editor—Jake didn't seem like the type of guy who would do anything wrong. But future rapists don't preregister with the National Sex Offender Registry or put roofies on wholesale. They fester.

(Sometimes it's power. Sometimes it's sickness. Control. It's years ago, forever back, all the way back, and years ahead. But different. In the *now*, it's finally talked about.)

(Sometimes.)

Jake's behavior did not pass the Subjective December Test. My climb revealed uncomfortably long hugs, lingering palms, a too-firm grip on the bicep of a date. I was fairly fluent in body language at this point, but it would be easy for anyone to see his actions were about as welcome as a virus.

157

(Behind the snack shack, at a party at a football player's house. But the movements were all the same—pushing away, shrinking into oneself, folding. Carrie.)

And in the future. Oh, the future.

Cajoling,

pleading,

whining,

until girls give in.

Until one girl, two hours past midnight the night after Halloween, after a bar and in her dorm room, did not.

A helpless kind of anger was a worm in my chest. This was the part of this gift that flat-out sucked. I could view all the things of the world, back and forward, from pendulum to pendulum, and yet there was so little I could do to change any of it. Future memories don't come with phone numbers to call your representative, or longitude and latitude points. I was left with nothing to offer saucer-eyed children hungry for meals, to save the lives of people in yoga studios or schools or malls or concerts, to do everything except be in over my head.

I kicked some of the leaves out of my way, furious that even in these moments of quiet flirtation, I was still me. I carried the wounds and weight of everything, alive and injured.

And then the barely aged memory of the rattan bench in front of the fireplace returned to me, whispering that I'd made a resolution. I'd seen a pattern. *When it was personal, I could change things.*

I'd been thinking so hard about how to save Nick, and every time I thought I'd found the key—like bleeding all over his death shirt— none of the future events had shifted in any substantial way, meaning that his death was still coming. The boy whose death I desperately wanted to prevent. But if I could figure out how, maybe I'd succeed.

And because Jake Dirks had been aggressive toward my friend, maybe I could change this.

The shred of a plan clicked into place, and the ocean did its small shudder. *It's okay, December.*

I tugged Nick's hand. "Hey, you know that homecoming dance next month?"

"Yeah?"

I gripped harder, pretending I was simply a girl outside a brick school in the early New England fall. "You want to go with me?"

CHAPTER TWENTY-EIGHT
Nick

THREE DAYS AFTER December asked me to homecoming, I opened my laptop and put on a Netflix documentary so Sophie and my parents wouldn't bother me, then sprawled belly-down on my bed. Trying to stomp the blip of excitement and possibility in my chest, I opened Mara Jones's journal, bypassing her defunct contact info. She'd filled out probably half the pages with a handful of sentences on each.

Not overly verbose. Got it.

I thumbed to the first page and traced the words with my smartpen.

SAN DIEGO | June 1999

Everyone claimed fish tacos were amazing here + they were not wrong. Mom said San Diego had the most beautiful weather she'd ever experienced, but for whatever reason, it's been gray and humid. Canvassed as req—great downtown, busy streets.

"'Canvassed as required'?" I muttered, checking the date: 1999. I rolled over and swiped the stack of pictures, picking up the oldest one. Scrawled on its back was *May 1999*. Right before she'd started this thing.

Compared to the later photos, Mara's cheeks were fuller in this one. She wore a Red Sox hat—one they'd rereleased as "vintage" now, fresh off the rack then. Her resemblance to December was uncanny. Deep brown eyes, wild-beautiful hair.

LAS CRUCES | June 1999

What. A. Day. There's an enchilada festival here in October that's supposed to be amazing, but the green chile one here now is bomb. Gorgeous snowcapped mountains + striking powder.

The town is quiet. I wouldn't mind coming back here. Pauls been twice. Hiking trails, wide streets, friendly people. Was going to work the P/Us, but too tired.

The what? I frowned, thinking of what P/U could be. Pick up? What was she too tired to pick up?

I flipped forward, skimming the entries for Kansas City and Raleigh. December's uncle had said her mom was *flighty*—but this was an epic trip that spanned June and July of 1999.

ATLANTA | July 1999

One of the last stops. Tons of activity near the aquarium. Had a cup of clam chowder outside. Regrettable.

Her mother's handwriting was partly cursive, which was easier for me to decipher, but harder for the audio pen. I read for the better part of a half hour, stopping when a listening headache made itself comfortable in my skull.

I pressed my fingertips to my temples, applying pressure in tiny circles. December was mostly right. The entries were useless. Fluff. Why did people bother keeping these kinds of diaries? There was nothing in here about how she feels or why she was in these places.

No lamenting over emotions or crushes or fears or embarrassing moments or something.

I paged back to the Las Cruces entry and hovered over the only person's name in here other than December's grandmother. *Paul.*

The year 1999 was way before December was born, way before Mara disappeared for good. But one thing I didn't know much about was December's dad. She'd shrugged off my only real mention of him. Could he be Paul?

I threw the journal aside and rubbed my eyes. My stomach rumbled. I pictured Mav scolding me for LBSing—his mom was the queen of feeding us to prevent low blood sugar.

In the kitchen, I found two-day-old cinnamon rolls Mom had wrapped in tinfoil and stashed above the toaster oven. I poured milk into a frosted glass and dunked a roll in.

"That's *disgusting.*"

"Aaahh!" I whipped around to find my sister sitting like a cat on the counter. "What the heck. You scared the sh—crap out of me."

Sophie wrinkled her nose. "I was right here the whole time."

"I didn't see you."

"Why are you dipping a cinnamon roll in milk?"

I stared at the pastry. "I dunno. I saw Dad do it once."

"He does that in coffee, not milk."

"Huh." I dunked it again, then shoved the entire roll in my mouth.

"You're going to choke," Sophie said cheerfully. "Do you know if you pour a dish of milk, dot in food coloring, and drizzle it with dish soap, it explodes with color? Kinda like fireworks."

I did know that. Junior year chemistry, day one. The dish soap and the milk broke down the surface tension of the milk, and the dye illustrated the chemical reaction in tie-dye Technicolor. I swallowed. "Yeah? How do you know that?"

"I saw it on Mom's Pinterest page."

"Why are you on Mom's Pinterest page?"

"Because she pins what she's buying us for our birthdays. And I don't like surprises." Sophie bit into a cookie, then leaned back against the cabinet. "Pretty cool that you can put together things that don't go together and something happens, huh?"

"Science," I said around a mouthful of the second roll.

I grabbed my phone, opened my message thread to December, then hit the microphone button. "Do you have any bread question mark."

"You need bread?" Sophie asked. "I have the whole loaf here. And peanut butter. And Nutella."

Me: Do Hugh have any bread?

Annoyance shot through my fingertips. I jabbed the keys, corrected it, then pressed SEND.

December: Um.

A selfie of December wearing a confused expression popped up on my screen. I grinned.

December: Are you going to make a joke about my buns?
Me: Your buns are no joke. I mean real, actual bread
December: We have some. Why?
Me: I knead it. 🙃
December: Groan
Me: Have you been to the pond at the back of the complex?

163

December: No, but I know where it is

Me: Meet me there tomorrow afternoon? 3pm?

December: *Butter* make it 3:30. Evan and I are finishing our uncle-niece movie aft school

Me: Don't forget the 📖 🦆 🦆 🦆

December: Hey . . . What are you doing now?

Me: Waiting for you to come over, Jones

My parents fawned over December. I could hardly blame them.

My mother over-complimented her hair—its length, color, and (apparently high) degree of shine. It was true that her hair was like something out of a movie, I guess. I know it smelled of sunlight and something herbal, like basil. My father kept asking December questions about her uncle's favorite gardening hacks (??), feigning interest.

A new ice age happened, a thousand children shouted *are we there yet?* from their parents' back seats, hell froze over, and finally, we were alone.

Our condo was big enough for the four of us Irvings, but it wasn't abundant in privacy. My parents' bedroom was in our loft, which took open concept to a whole new level. I don't know how they got any sleep—a giant shade-free skylight hung over their bed. Facing east.

Tonight, they had graciously "gone to bed" in Sophie's room to let us hang out. My sister was sleeping over Trista's, probably trying to convince her friend the dance team was useless. And here I was, my leg sidled alongside December's, jean to jean but somehow burning together on our microfiber couch, trying as hard as I could to focus on the movie in front of us.

December poked me. "Remember when you didn't like me?"

I pretended to flinch at her touch. "What makes you say that?"

"Just thinking." She pulled the blanket to her shoulders and snuggled into my shoulder. Her head rested there, inches away from my heart, which had picked up tempo.

What do I do here? I put my arm around her shoulders and sort of squeezed.

She sighed what I hoped to be a contented sigh. "Are you watching this?"

"Barely. But let's keep it on." *So my parents couldn't hear us*, I didn't say.

"Hey, what were you doing earlier today?"

Trying to secretly find your mom. Why? "Hung out. Watched a Netflix doc."

"Oh. Huh."

"Why?"

"Just wondering, I guess." She bit her lip, then shook her head. "Oh. And why the bread?"

"It's a surprise."

She wrinkled her nose. Her nose wrinkles were even cute. "Wanna play a game?"

"What game?"

"We say a thing, then we either say *love* or *dislike*. Ready?"

"Why not *love* or *hate*?" I asked, stretching my arms above my head.

"Evan doesn't like the word *hate*."

"Okay. Pancakes," I said.

She smiled. "Love."

"Not me. Dislike." On the television, Will Ferrell waved frantically at a man coming down an escalator.

"Who doesn't love pancakes?" She shook her head in mock disbelief. "Chicken piccata."

"Is this all supposed to be food? I've never had it, so pass."

"Ugh. Love."

"Night or day?"

"Incorrect way to play the game much? Though I love the stars. And how people feel braver after dark. So, night."

Sun. SPF. The swish of the water in the lanes. "Day for me. Okay, back on track. Uh. Pumpkins?"

Her eyes leveled me with a look I couldn't measure. "Dislike. I don't like the color orange."

I nudged her shoulder. "My favorite shirt is orange! But light orange."

"That sherbet-orange monstrosity?" Her smile was syrupy. "I mean I love it so much."

I mimed a dagger going into my chest. "Ouch."

She slipped her pinkie over mine. "Holding hands," she whispered.

Her skin was so soft. Impossibly soft.

I swallowed. "Love." I shifted so my body faced hers. "What about one quick kiss?"

"Dislike," she said, her voice low. "I prefer long ones. Endless ones. Especially first ones in a driveway."

"Those are pretty great, too."

Right before the end of the movie, December fell asleep. Her head lolled on my shoulder, her eyelashes dark fringes against her cheeks. The remote fell off the couch, but I stayed as still as I could through rolling credits, through the start of the late show, until she woke and smiled sleepily and let me walk her home.

CHAPTER TWENTY-NINE
December

THE NEXT AFTERNOON brought me twenty feet up in the air, tucked like the little spoon against a big spoon tree. Not so fun for someone who wasn't thrilled about heights. My foreknowledge of this stretch of time was hazy and dappled, so I'd assumed we'd discuss my mom, which was confusing, because we'd agreed that whole thing was over.

Beside me, Nick gripped the tree branch above him and did a partial pull-up. His arm muscles tensed, and so did my insides. His perch was far more precarious than my own.

Fear of heights isn't rare, but mine was extra irrational. Even though I knew with my usual certainty that nothing bad would come of this—I had plenty of my own gumballs ahead of me, so it wasn't like I was moments away from dying by a fall from this tree—this knowledge did not stop my body from revolting. My muscles took turns clenching involuntarily. Every time I looked down, my fingers tightened in pain, as if someone had wound dental floss around them and pulled tight with a minty green twang.

I took a deep breath and focused on the scene before me to steady myself. The sun was a yolk, the sky a brittle blue. A small, quiet pond, encircled with oaks and pines and cumulus clouds. Blues and grays and greens, sugared whites. Emerald-headed mallard ducks skimmed the surface of the pond, dipping their heads and flapping their wings.

"I was hoping you could fill in some blanks for me," Nick said.

"What kind of blanks?"

"Wait. First, you bring the bread?"

I shook my head. "I brought oat-and-birdseed balls."

He raised his eyebrows. "Come again? How'd you know?"

"Three duck emojis and a loaf of bread?" I forced a laugh. "Not super subtle. Bread makes duck bellies hurt. And it can kill fish. *And* it can lead to toxic algae."

"Seriously?"

"Dead serious."

"Uh. Oops. Where'd you learn that?"

"Evan," I lied.

His headshake was slow. "'Kay. Moving on. You know what we've never really talked about?"

"What?" I took out a few balls and threw him the bag.

"Your dad."

"What about him?" My tone was cautious.

He checked my face for my reaction. "Is he someone you mind talking about? You know, like how talking about your mom makes you upset?"

(Tired. Drained. One little girl, one mom, one Cam, one uncle. Us against the world. No. Yes. No.)

I was able to see some dim past knowledge of my dad, if I climbed hard enough—but everything that intersected with my mom had clouded, like an ink drawing over pencil erasure smudges. He was just a guy. Someone I'd pass at CVS or Duane Reade and not think of ever again. Other than contributing 50 percent of my DNA, my dad wasn't much to me.

Sure, there were times in my childhood when his absence reared up like a screaming nose zit on school picture day. Back-to-class nights, father-daughter dances, and once, falling off the monkey bars at the playground. I didn't know why. I wasn't proud of it. But I've never dissolved into tears while missing my dad, or worried it over in my mind until the worry was polished smooth with time.

The truth was that to me, my uncle was worth a thousand dads. But although he would never admit it, I was a burden to him. I was his reason to make sacrifices, and sacrifices were by definition giving up something of value.

My feelings about my father were opposite from the way I felt about my mother. Every day, I longed for her. I ached for her. The urge to sprawl my legs across her lap and watch a movie or nestle against her knees while she fastened my hair into a ponytail crushed my throat and clawed into my insides.

"I don't mind talking about my dad. But . . ." The oat ball crumbled in my hand, bringing me back to now. "How often do you talk about people you've never met? It's hard to miss something you never even had."

"Okay, but outside all that, do you know anything about him?" Nick flushed. "Could your mom have run away to be with him or something?"

"I don't think so. All I know is that she met him at her work gym. And I only know that because I overheard Cam and Evan arguing about it after she left." When the static began.

"Was his name Paul?"

I shook my head. "Why Paul?"

"That name was in her journal."

I plucked at the hem of my shorts. The branch swayed beneath me, tightening my imaginary dental-floss-wrapped fingertips. "His name's Lucas."

He sagged. "So your mom didn't leave for some long-lost love?"

"Not to my knowledge, but weren't we going to stop the search?"

"I thought with everything going on with Cam right now . . ." He chucked a ball into the water to finish his sentence, then handed me one.

Relief loosened my chest. "Oh. I'm actually starting to think that it wouldn't help anyone if she came back right now. It might frighten or confuse Cam, and I know Evan's so angry with my mother that it might make dealing with Cam's—" I swallowed. "With you know, losing Cam. Having my mom here could make everything worse."

"All right," Nick said. "If you ever want to talk about it, or resume the search, I'm yours."

"That means a lot. Thanks." I crushed the ball in my fist before sprinkling it into the water like cheese on pasta. The birdseed scattered, spiraling in the air, landing splashless and soundless below. Lured in by the silent siren melody, the ducks whisked through the water toward us. Yet before they got there, dozens—no, *hundreds*, at least—of thin silver fish darted, as if they were conjured from the water itself. The sunlight sparkled on the water, turning it sapphire blue, and I was so overwhelmed by the beauty of this moment that tears pricked the edges of my eyes and I forgot, forgot, forgot what it was like not to know something so breathtaking.

"Wow," I whispered. A single word with a sole syllable. People without foreknowledge were so lucky to be caught in these kinds of moments all the time. Without my mother's disappearance and broken part of my gift, I wouldn't have this, either. I inhaled the clean oxygen through my nose. "This is gorgeous. It's like looking at molten silver."

"Right?" Nick tossed another oat ball in, this time for the ducks. "Isn't it weird to think that at some point in time, none of this was here?" He swept his arm across the scene, indicating the pond, the trees, the lake.

I pressed my back against the tree. "Yeah, I mean. Twenty-five thousand years ago, Massachusetts was covered in ice."

He crumpled the bag in his fist. "Amazing to think about. All these trees started as one spot. Maybe the pond itself was carved out when all that ice melted."

The pond was the result of a team of seven rotating construction workers and a crapload of John Deere equipment in the mid-1980s, but Nick didn't have to know that. He tucked his lower lip against his teeth and released it—his big tell that he was lost in thought.

"Maybe," I said finally. Maybe.

Maybe I'd figure out how to change the future. Save his life.

CHAPTER THIRTY

Inside the Blank Spot

IN THE SCHEME of the world, it wasn't all that long ago. Not even ten years. The girl wasn't always sure, since memories of her mother were shrouded in static, hidden like riddles in a scavenger hunt.

In what seemed to be the blackest hours of the night, the child and her mother lay in the mama's bed, the window propped open, the radiator hissing, choking, breathing heat without fire. The mama rubbed her daughter's back, trying to lull the child into her resting place. The place where she wasn't bothered by all the Bad in the world. The mother grazed her palm, open flat and mostly steady, between the dark-haired child's shoulder blades, which stood like a pair of winged, bony bridges on her back.

The longer the girl—December, we know it's December—stayed awake, the fiercer the pressure from the mother's hand.

—Sleep, the mama's hand would've said.

Tell me a story, Mama.

—Count your breaths, December. Quiet your head. Relax your toes.

Please. I'm so tired. A story will help me sleep.

A pause while the mama exhaled and stretched her body alongside her daughter's. Her ankles crackled; her knees popped.

—Have I told you the story of the boulder on the beach?

A rustle from the pillow while the girl shook her head. The mama's hand stilled.

—There was once this sprawling stretch of beach in the smallest state in our country. One that enjoyed a short-lived spike in attendance each summer of families dragging coolers and no sunscreen, because this was before sunscreen. They sprawled moth-eaten sheets on the sand and covered their heads with parasols or straw hats. Each morning from Memorial Day to Labor Day, a wooden gate opened to buggy cars lined up like ants on sugar. You'd only see the bathing suits in a history book today. They were long-sleeved.

One of my bathing suits is long-sleeved.

—True, but these were long-sleeved because of the patriarchy, not because of skin cancer. Though I suppose in some ways, patriarchy and cancer are the same thing. But that's for another time. For this story, people ate sandwiches from tin lunch pails and bodysurfed, then went home, sunburned and spent, right before the wooden gate closed.

Is this the beach we go to sometimes, Mama?

—You'll recognize it in a moment. Close your eyes, sweets.

The child obeyed. Her mother continued.

—On one hot July morning, people piled out of the cars and were greeted by something they hadn't seen the day before, or the day before that.

The child sat up. *What was it?*

—A boulder. A magnificent boulder, almost all the way up the beach. Where you'd find a lifeguard chair if you went today. It sat smack in the middle of the sunbaked khaki-colored sand, blocking the view of the ocean from the road.

A boulder.

—A boulder.

How big was it?

—So big that when a toddler wandered up to it and put her palms against it—flat, like this—she couldn't even reach where the boulder curved upward. As big as a house.

How'd it get there?

—Well, that's the mystery, isn't it? The tide never went up that high, and even if it had, it would've taken a tsunami wave to bring that ashore. There were homes overlooking the ocean, even in those days, and they were undamaged. There were no jetties in a reasonable distance. It was as if the sky opened, dropped a ball of rock, and let the sand cradle it for its own. Or perhaps the sand had split in two and birthed this house-sized rock for the beach.

None of that makes sense.

—Not everything does, sweets.

Why not?

—I don't know. But either way, the reporters came and wrote stories about it. Wondered if it was from another world, or a joke. But people were angry about it, December.

Why would someone be cross with a rock?

—Well, the surface problem was petty. The rock took up so much space, you see, that unless you got there very early in the morning, most of the beachgoers had to head to a different beach. But the real problem was that the people were afraid of the rock.

Afraid?

—Since the beginning of time, history tells the same truths. In this story, no one knew where the rock came from, and that scared them. In most stories, people are afraid of what they don't understand.

CHAPTER THIRTY-ONE
Nick

MY PARENTS HAVE a standing deal where Dad cooks if Mom buys the groceries. Ever since I was maybe ten, my mother and I have competed in timed runs through the store. I start in the first aisle while she takes the last, and we work our way to the middle. The first person to aisle 6—aka the treat aisle—with all their required groceries picks dessert. Year-round, Mom goes for these terrible gingerbread people. I'm partial to Swiss cake rolls, unless it's fall, at which point I head straight for the cinnamon cider doughnuts.

Now I careened around the back end of aisle 5, my mouth full of a sample slice of a new apple hybrid—HoneyLaden Guru—and headphones crammed in my ears, blasting the newest episode of *Mystery Buff*. I'd been right about last week's crime clues, where the culprit had stolen a DNA kit from someone's mailbox and sprinkled it at the scene of his crime.

I was annoyed with myself for only grabbing a basket instead of a cart. Dad's chili recipe was aisle-1-through-5 heavy—green peppers, jalapeños, onions, and cans upon cans—three kinds of beans, two of diced tomatoes.

I was sure Mom had beat me to aisle 6. And as I rounded the endcap piled high with store-brand corn chips and spotted her brown ponytail and long sweater, all I thought was *Goddamn gingerbread cookies again.*

But what I was not prepared for was the sight of her talking to Mrs. Dovetail, my history teacher from last year. The teacher I deliberately avoided in my daily sojourn through the halls at Woodland High.

I swallowed the apple sample, which had been the kind of delicious you can't replicate. Crisp, smooth, sweet. Fantastic. For the rest of my life, I'd probably associate the taste with the bristly stroke of guilt.

Mom glanced in my direction and waved. I forced my feet to listen to my brain and plod over to her. Funny how they listened *now.*

"There he is," Mom said. She slung an arm over my shoulders.

"I haven't seen you around this fall, Nick," Mrs. Dovetail said. "Everything going well senior year?"

Perfect. Beautiful. I'm purposefully lying to 90 percent of my loved ones and batting one hundred for lies of omission. "Great. Thank you."

"I was telling your mom how proud I am of your final grade last term."

I yanked the corners of my mouth into a jack-o-lantern's grin. "Thanks, Mrs. Dovetail."

Mom squeezed my shoulder. "We're thrilled. We're also waiting to see if he gets onto an elite swim team, which might help his chances for making a college team, too." Her voice oozed with pride, choking me.

"Well, at some point before you go off into the world, you'll have to tell me how you solved navigating your test-taking by healing your dyslexia." Mrs. Dovetail pulled a box of cookies from the shelf and added them to her cart. "I wasn't aware it could be cured."

Oh, shit.

I squinted against the fluorescent lighting. Behind us, someone slammed the poultry freezer door, sending a cold gust of manufactured air our way. My skin puckered with goosebumps.

Mom straightened, assuming her *advocate of all advocates* posturing. "Nancy, as an educator, you know dyslexia isn't *cured*. Nor is it something *to* cure. It's something that needs to be taught toward."

A wheeze I was sure would be audible escaped my throat. Mrs. Dovetail touched her fingers to her neck. "Of course. That's why I was so confused."

Mom pulled her sweater tightly around her waist and frowned. "About what?"

"Mom, this is heavy. We'd better get it up front." I hoisted the basket.

"You don't have to hold it, honey. Put it down for a second."

"Maverick says that twenty-six percent of shoes have *C. diff* bacteria on them," I said. "You really want me to put all our food on the floor?"

Mrs. Dovetail and Mom both stared at me. I wished for the ability to melt into the grimy tile. I would happily lick the *C. diff* from the floor to ditch this moment.

"My kids are waiting in the car." Mrs. Dovetail eased her cart around us and fluttered her hand in a wave. "Great to see you both."

"What was that all about?" Mom shifted a loaf of French bread into the crook of her elbow.

"Nothing."

"I hardly think that was about nothing." Her face was troubled, which squeezed my stomach in a vise. I was so proud of my mom. Never wanted to let her down. I'd sworn after what I did last spring, I'd never let myself go back to being a scum-of-the-earth son. My heart raced, palms slick and tingly.

"Honey? Is there something you want to tell me?"

Together, we walked to the front of the store. Only one spot in line for the self-checkout lane. Without conferring, we both headed for it. "No," I said finally. Not a lie. There was nothing I wanted to tell her, expect maybe that December was with me to save Mr. Francis, but I couldn't even bring myself to do that.

"She said your dyslexia was *cured*." Disgust crowded her features. I'd spent a lifetime growing up thinking she was the prettiest person in the world. I hated seeing her like this. She dumped the groceries on the table next to self-checkout and scanned them, one by one, while I bagged. She handed me a can of black beans. "As if it's something to heal."

I crushed my rising nausea with a mental fist. "So?"

"So . . ." And she did the parent thing where she let silence take a seat between us.

Well. Wiggle in and get comfortable, silence. But I was nothing if not a hypocrite, so after less than fifteen seconds, I opened my mouth to confess a partial truth. "I took my history final without accommodations."

Saying those words out loud was supposed to make me feel better. I'd nearly voiced them thousands of times since last May, and I'd wondered over and over again how it would feel to lift up that piece of myself and hand it to my parents.

My lie had hardened my insides into a giant oak tree trunk of deceit. I figured confessing all this would strip me down, bark or leaves or whatever peeling away, crinkled and then forgotten. I thought I'd feel lighter. And maybe I would, once I got through this. But for now, I felt worse.

Mom's hand hovered over the scanner, full of a triangular hunk of Parmesan cheese. "You *what*? But at that IEP meeting last year, didn't you say most of Mrs. Dovetail's tests were fill-in-the-blank? Why would you do that?"

I had said that. Mrs. Dovetail had explained her preference for that format, saying with a half smile that they were handy to *reduce or eliminate* students guessing. I fought back tears, suddenly no longer caring that the entirety of the Woodland Grocer could hear our argument. "Why not? You think your own son is too stupid to take a test without someone reading the questions to me?"

"You know I don't. I *never* said that." The color left her lips and went into her cheeks. "Nicholas Irving. How *dare* you."

I shoved the French bread into the bag, cracking the loaf in half. "I'll catch you at home," I said, hating myself. "I'm out of here."

CHAPTER THIRTY-TWO
December

WHILE NICK WENT to the grocery store with his mom,

(Wince. Wince. Utter wince.)

I stood outside the high school, my phone screen open and set on the rideshare app to act as my prop.

"December! What are you doing out here?" Maisie hitched the second strap of her backpack over her shoulder as she quick-stepped down the sprawling stairway.

I held up my phone. "Calling a ride," I lied.

"You should've texted me." Her face adopted a look of admonition. "We live in the same place. Come on."

"Thanks," I said, smiling. "I didn't know if you had debate practice," I lied again. "Plus, I'm not going home. I'm going to Wisteria Hills."

"The nursing home?" At my nod, she smiled. "Hop in."

—

"What are you doing at the nursing home?" Maisie asked, turning on the windshield wipers against the newly falling rain.

"Visiting my grandmother."

"Aw. Is she in the assisted living section, or the patient unit?"

"Alzheimer's wing."

Maisie's mouth twisted. "Yikes. That sucks."

"Sucks indeed."

"Were you two close?"

"The closest." I leaned forward. "You can turn—"

Maisie waved my hand away and sipped the Café Cubano she'd chosen during our drive-through run—dark roast, undiluted with cream, milk, or sugar. Effortlessly cool. "I volunteered there all during middle school. I know the way." Her eyes slid to me. "How're you liking Woodland High?"

I tapped my chin, pretending to think. "Oh, I'm not sure what I like better. Cake decorating? Puppy petting? Eyebrow threading lessons?" I grinned. "Joking, obviously. But my uncle and I moved around kind of a lot. I've been to school in thirteen different towns. Woodland High seems better than most."

"I bet being with the guy who saved the world's favorite teacher makes it a little better than the other schools." Maisie's tone left the thought sort of . . . lingering. She tipped back her head, finishing her espresso.

"Doesn't hurt."

"Yeah. I mean, I've known him for most of my life. We've always lived in the same spot. And now he's suddenly the most interesting guy in town." Maisie flicked the turn signal. "Nick Irving. Who would've thought? Bright Acres's finest. It's strange how someone can be in your world, but you don't even know them."

(Jake Dirks Jake Dirks Jake Dirks)

"Totally," I murmured. Her hands resettled on the steering wheel. Maisie always had her nails done. Today, they were painted in a shiny, subtle ombre, streaming from pale aqua to medium blue along her hand. "Hey, your nails look so cool," I said, but then I clamped my mouth shut when a series of seemingly unimportant gumballs popped into my brain. Maisie stripping high-end labels from jeans that didn't fit and sewing them onto her own; cutting the tops of conditioner, lotion, and makeup to eke out the last drops. With her neon tips, stripes, and flawless lacquer, I'd assumed she always had her nails done professionally, but Maisie and her mother did their nails in their kitchen. I saw Maisie saying, *Who needs a salon?* to her mother and then crying in her room and writing in her diary that she was ashamed she felt the need to cover up not having the kind of money most of the kids in town did.

A grin broke her face open. "Really? Thank you so much." She hesitated. "I painted them myself."

"Seriously? You're talented. When I do my own nails, I look like the victim of a kindergarten art class."

She laughed. "Yeah. It's either that or car insurance, and, well." Maisie shrugged. "I don't even know why I'm telling you that."

"It's cool," I assured her, holding up my hand. "I've never had mine done."

"Want me to do them sometime?"

A flutter in my chest, warmth in my belly. "Sure. That sounds awesome."

When we pulled up to the U-shaped drop-off zone, my chest tightened with the anticipation of seeing my grandmother. "Thanks for saving me from a rideshare driver's incessant yakking and either cheap or expensive cologne. Which I can't tell the difference between, by the way."

"No one can. The scent industry is a bewildering place." Maisie handed me my latte. "Oh! Let's go shopping this weekend for homecoming. I'll get Stella Rose and Carrie, too."

If I analyzed myself as hard as I did everyone else, I'd have to admit I didn't jump into this social circle to find friends. Which, in hindsight, was crappy. I talked to these girls on our first meeting so it wouldn't be weird when I showed up to Stella Rose's party, because I knew my night would be made of driveway kisses, moonlight, and the warm, satisfied glow of slipping into something new for the first time.

But now these girls were becoming actual friends. This feeling was a tiny spark of hope. A perk.

A feeling that, for the first time in pretty much ever, I belonged. In more ways than one.

"It's a date," I said, grinning.

—

It was ironic that I was a sieve for all the world's past and future memories, yet my favorite woman in the world was unwillingly losing hers. Piece by piece. After her diagnosis, she'd mourned her waning short-term memory. She began confusing me for my mother, sobbing because, someday, she'd forget me completely.

I couldn't prevent it. I steered her into taking supplements and eating only omega-3-loaded foods, which may or may not have held it off, or made her decline more gradual. Invisible to us, Cam's brain essentially performed CTRL ALT DELETE, only made concrete when she began putting the fruit basket in the linen closet, or calling Evan's notebook a *paper word holder*, and making gargantuan purchases of exercise equipment and telemarketing products.

(me, a little girl in one half of the duplex, sharing food-truck fish tacos with Cam and knowing, knowing, knowing)

I dropped into the seat beside Cam, her face slack with sleep. Today, someone had taken care to brush her hair and wind it into a loose bun atop the pillow, and my eyes welled with tears at the kindness of the gesture. I tried to make it a habit of not feeling sorry for myself, but at this moment in time, I broke this self-imposed rule faster than an American politician flipped sides. I rubbed my jaw, attempting to loosen the tension that had gathered there, finally exhaling when I remembered at least *some* good would come out of today's visit.

I took Cam's hand, shocked at how bony and weightless it was. She used to be so strong. Wisteria Hills sponsored yoga every month or so, and one time when we lived nearby, I joined her, my awkward body contorted on a mat in the back corner of the room like this Christmas ornament we'd always had—a nutcracker who did a jerky little jig if you pulled the string woven into his back.

Cam moved through each pose, a lithe, nimble warrior. She got so into it that she didn't notice when one of her breasts popped out of the neckline of her top. I tried to get her attention through an entire sun salutation. And failed. When she finally noticed, she let out this whoop, followed by an *oh, shit!* We fell into the kind of giggles that chase each other, hiccupping and clamoring for attention. We'd had to leave the class.

I dug my fingertips into the arms of the chair, thinking of the last time I was here. Remembering Evan, sitting in the precise spot I sat in now, encouraging me. *Why don't you say something?*

(a gumball not too far from now: Cam's bed, empty)

I rolled my neck. Applied minute pressure to Cam's hand, trying to infuse her with some of my warmth. "Cam, I met someone," I began, clearing my throat and looking around the room. The clock, the framed family picture on the wall, the TV routinely turned on from ten to eleven in the morning and six to seven at night. "And he's *amazing*." Something released inside me, my words coming easier, finding their home. "Everything started so strangely. He's a lifeguard.

And I was at the pool when something big happened. I helped him save someone." I dropped my voice to a whisper. "I know you don't know what I'm like. Not like Evan does. But I did something that changed everything, and the way he looks at me . . ." I trailed off and wiped my eyes before my words sped up, a summer-afternoon downpour. "He looks at me like I'm the first person he's ever seen. I won't bore you with all the gory details on the off chance that there's a consciousness locked in there doctors haven't yet discovered, but dang, is he a good kisser." My sample size was tiny with no control group, but still.

I pressed my lips against her hand as two quick raps came from the doorway. "Here to take Cam's vitals," the intern said, stepping in. "Hey, wait. I recognize you!"

I watched my hospital hero, Sim, take in the scar on my arm. "Good job with the stitches."

"You're . . ." He snapped his fingers. "November. No. December!"

"Bingo. This is my grandmother Cam." I glanced at the empty doorframe. "What are you doing here?" I asked to be polite.

(Because when you knew how things went, sometimes you did what you were told, even though you weren't sure who—who?—was doing the telling.)

"I work per diem," Sim explained. "One day here, another day there."

"December! Sorry I'm late," my uncle said, bursting into the room. His hair was matted from his shower. He turned his attention to Sim. "Wait. Have we met?"

I watched Sim's eyes flicker on my uncle's frame, a sensation of relief filling my entire body. Because yes, *yes*, now Evan was here to stay. He could settle down. I climbed to the not-so-distant future

(Evan and Sim, a quiet wedding)

But then lost in my future memory, and completely full of bliss at what was to be between this intern and this landscaper, at the floating joy that had come from telling my grandmother all about a boy, a sharp, completely unmistakable stir of guilt dove into my stomach.

I frowned.

I had nothing to feel guilty about.

What was—

(Grocery store. Aisle 6. Gingerbread cookies.)

My palms dampened with sweat, my breath coming in shortened hitches. *This was not my guilt.*

I bowed my head, trying to hide my panic.

In all my seventeen years of being alive, in all my 6,430 days of orbiting the sun, of foreknowledge and forethought and anticipation, this had never happened. The only rule break was my Blank Spot.

This was not my guilt.

All my life, I'd been living behind a one-way glass. I knew everything that was happening around me, and I could anticipate how those experiences might feel. But now somehow, the tables had more than turned—they'd flipped and shattered. I itched and wriggled, uncomfortable with my inability to control my nerve endings, my arm aching with the weight of another family's canned goods.

I was experiencing the sensations Nick felt.

And I had no idea why.

CHAPTER THIRTY-THREE

Nick

Mystery Buff Episode 65: a Game of Clue

INTRO MUSIC PLAYS.
All right, Buffys. Did you solve last week's crime?

INTERLUDE MUSIC FADES IN.
Was it the butcher, the baker, or the candlestick maker?
Who kidnapped twenty-six-year-old Mariesa Dunley?

INTERLUDE MUSIC SPEEDS UP.
If you picked the chef at Bistro Chic, you were right. And
as for today's mystery?

CYMBAL SOUND EFFECT.

From behind me, the doorknob rattled. Sophie barged into my room, clad in the running sweatbands and wristbands she'd worn during her summer race series, a pair of my old athletic shorts, and look of sheer dejection.

I removed my earbuds and shook my head free of *Mystery Buff*. "What's wrong, Soph?" I asked, closing December's mom's journal.

It had been open on my lap for half an hour, a sorry attempt at reading. Multitasking was not my superpower.

Her lower lip wobbled for a moment before righting itself. "I didn't make the dance team."

"People don't generally get placed on competitive teams without . . ." Knowing the sport? "Uh, learning for a bit?"

She crossed her arms. "I'm good. You saw me with the pirouette."

Exactly. "I know." I sighed. It was hopeless. "I'm sorry you didn't make it."

Footsteps sounded from down the hall. I tensed. *Mom?* Since yesterday's trip to the grocery store, we'd circled each other, polite but wary. I didn't know what she thought of the whole *Nick took the test without his fail-safe equipment!* thing, and I didn't know if she'd told my dad yet. In their marriage, it was not a matter of if she'd tell, but when. In sum, it was an anvil she held over my head, waiting to strike. She was bold like that.

But when Mav appeared in the doorway, my shoulders melted. "What's shakin'?" he said by way of greeting. We clapped hands.

Sophie brightened. "Oh, yeah. Mom said to tell you Maverick was here."

"In the flesh." He pointed to the journal. "You solve the mystery yet?"

"A mystery?" Sophie's voice was full of glee. "What mystery?"

"Nick's trying to figure out where December's mom is," Mav said.

"Where her *mom* is?" Sophie repeated. Her eyes widened, and a cloudy look came over her face. "December doesn't know where her mom is?"

"Not everyone lives with their mom, Soph."

"I know that. But I guess I didn't know . . ." She trailed off, reminding me, for one quick moment, how much of a kid she still was. "I never thought about people not knowing where their moms are before. How are you looking for her?"

"Trying to puzzle out her life." I pointed to my desk, which held the contents of Mara Jones's life: her journal, the wishing well, a handful of photographs.

Sophie frowned. "This is not how you find someone."

"What do you know about finding someone?"

"You know. Like on TV." She gestured to my bedroom wall. "On *Homeland*?"

My best friend and I stared at her. She tried again. "*Criminal Minds*? *SVU*?"

"Aren't you nine?" I muttered. But Sophie had a point. I'd cycled back and forth, through hours of frustration and days of procrastination trying to solve this riddle. I took a deep breath, trying to steady myself.

"I'd think you'd have the whiteboard going, that's all." Sophie shrugged. "Anyway, I'm gonna go do some sprints." My sister sailed from the room.

"Nothing like getting called out by an elementary schooler." Mav snapped his gum. "Really puts things into perspective." He picked up the journal. "What's in here, anyway?"

I groaned. "Nothing that makes any kind of sense. It's like a travel journal. Weather. Food. Sightseeing." I paused. "Plus, a bunch of these notes that she seems to reference as either trials or accomplishments, but I can't make out what they are. It's from 1999."

"Challenge accepted," Mav said.

While he paged through the journal, I rolled the old whiteboard out from its forgotten spot in my closet. Mom had brought it home after the kindergarten got iPads, and Sophie had demanded we play "school" with it for years. I scrubbed the dust and old markings with my sleeve, then taped the pictures of December's mom along the side.

"Sometimes, when I'm trying to figure out science stuff, I think about what info I have, and how it might relate." Mav tapped the journal. "I think you've got to transform the unclear stuff that's here. Like, what's this?" he asked, pointing.

I leaned over. "Which part?"

"'Not much to report from Denver, Dallas, and San Antonio. Barely saw the cities. I'm so wiped out—fiiiiinally hit the 12:29 (4) in the 6LAP!'" Maverick read. "There are five *i*'s in *finally*. Why do people do that?" He shook his head and kept reading. "'Mom would disown me if I skipped Graceland. This is a city of blues. But by 11:30, my sole's screaming!'" He sighed. "Feet are among the hardest-working parts of the human body. Impractical footwear is a leading cause of foot problems."

"Foot problems? What are you even talking about?"

He pointed at the last sentence. "Right here."

I leaned closer. When my audio pen had read the entry, I'd heard it as if her *soul* was screaming, which I'd chalked up to being a dramatized diary overreaction.

Sole. Her *foot* was screaming? "That makes no sense," I muttered.

"There are about a million cities in this." Maverick glanced at the whiteboard. "I'll tag the stuff in here that's not straightforward. You map out the places?"

On the whiteboard, I drew a big freehand picture of the contiguous United States. I was decent with the shapes of general geography. When I was done, Mav and I starred the places Mara Jones mentioned. San Diego, Denver, Dallas, San Antonio. Kansas City, Memphis, Mobile, Atlanta. "What do you think?" I asked.

"Let me put up the questionable stuff on the board." Maverick palmed the marker in one hand and paged through the journal with the other, scrawling along the corner of the whiteboard. When he was done, we both stepped back and stared in silence.

S/U: 50 (6)

300 – > 52.9 (7)

P/U: 34 (6)

6LAP: 12:29 (4) (1.5mi)

I tried to find the connection point, but even though I had that buzzy, let's-solve-a-mystery feeling in my gut, and I knew there must be a pattern, my brain felt like a bowl of wet spaghetti. "Any clue?"

"A map. A bunch of stars. Gibberish. An objectively hot nineties future mom."

I sank onto the end of my bed. "This is all I've got, man."

Maverick flopped beside me. He reclined on my bed, rubbing the bridge of his nose. "I'm pretty sure we've got jack here."

I gestured toward the whiteboard. "Obviously."

"I'm gonna ask you this one time." Mav averted his gaze, staring at the ceiling. "Are you doing this because of your messed-up moral scale, or are you trying to impress a girl?" His tone reminded me of a thousand other memories with him. *Is there anything I can say about your grandmother to make you feel better? George was a great dog. Are you positive we should sneak out your window?*

I kicked my foot against the wooden post of my bed. I had always worked my academic ass off only to feel a half step behind everyone else, even when I was ahead. I used to assume I was disappointing my parents when they'd swear I wasn't. Call it worry, name it anxiety, give it whatever kind of definition you'd like—I spent so much of my childhood preoccupied with what other people thought instead of how I felt. Life was made of all these moments where I was helped or pitied or accoladed or *anything*, and at some point, it occurred to me that no matter how my day went, I was still lucky enough to put my head down on a pillow and start the next day anew, and that it was up to me to live life in worthwhile ways. I'd done that, with two exceptions: last May's test, and my failure to save Mr. Francis. "My moral scale is not off."

"You can't keep track of good and bad actions. Just live life like a good person who makes mistakes. What's that called?" He snapped his fingers. "Right. Being human."

I made a face. "Yeah, yeah. And also, yes. I really, really, really want to impress December."

"You're too far gone." He tossed a wad of gum into the trash and pulled out a pack of Trident.

"Whoa!" I was impressed. "To what do I owe this pleasure?"

He made a face. "Scientific research," he muttered.

"But you always say this gum is nothing like smoking," I said, shaking my head when he offered me a stick.

He pocketed the rest. "It isn't. And I'm not gonna preach about nicotine and brains, but I was reading an article in the new issue of *New England Journal of Medicine* on different effects of drugs on organ function, and, well. I rate it five yikes."

"Sounds legit."

"Pretty depressing, to be honest."

"Agreed." I dropped everything back on my desk. I knew December wasn't expecting anything from me. The opposite, actually. But I wanted so, so badly to make up for my mistakes this year, both from last May and Mr. Francis.

Mav was wrong. My moral scale wasn't what was off.

It was me.

CHAPTER THIRTY-FOUR
December

"TRY ON THE gold," I said, perching on a velvet footstool in the dressing room of our twelfth boutique.

Maisie's brow furrowed. "Gold? You think so?"

"Trust me." It was the one she was going to wear. The gold was radiant against Maisie's brown skin.

Carrie pivoted in the fitting room mirror, wearing the jewel green I'd coaxed her into. "Obsessed."

When you already know what you'll buy and wear from here to eternity, shopping becomes a chore. "You should get it."

I was still deeply unsettled about the way my body had seemingly experienced what Nick had when I was at Cam's bedside. I'd spent the last day not listening when Evan spoke, taking twice as long to do my homework, even forcing smiles around Nick. There I was, swimming in the joy of knowing my uncle had found the guy who was all in—cling-on niece and all. Hiding the joyful secret of Evan and Sim before they became *Evan + Sim* as they regarded each other next to Cam. Neither one of them knew what lay before them.

(Caribbean timeshares, dinner parties, and Sunday-afternoon movie traditions)

When *boom*. I'd been catapulted into a pool of ice water.

I shifted on the velvet and hid a frown.

No question: The best part of my gift was that I got to anticipate the happy moments in advance. Because I knew I'd fall in love with Nick, I could savor every morsel of interaction we had leading up to being together. Every crinkle of his eyes, the seriousness in his face while lifeguarding.

The bad? Obvious. Not being able to prevent the ugly.

But what happened at Cam's was *different*, and I was at a major loss as to why. Never had I ever been wrenched away from my own feelings like that. It was as if my stomach had been extracted from my insides and reinserted upside down. My mind was my own, but my body was not. I could almost feel the cool air of the grocery store, the heft of Nick's basket. And I had no idea what any of it meant. All I knew was it had stayed with me, like a nail stuck in a tire.

If my gift could change, what else might happen?

I sucked in a breath, dipping into whatever Nick was doing now: headphones and an episode of *Mystery Buff*. I smiled.

Stella Rose leaned against the wall. "I can't decide."

What I wanted to say: *Go get the first red one you tried on and save us all time!*

What I said: "Wanna go grab a table at Tea Melee so you can think about it?"

—

Laden with shopping bags and iced teas of varying flavors, we crowded into a booth. "Did you see that guy in front of us when we were in line?" Stella Rose asked. She moved on without waiting for an answer. "That's the cousin of that Soton Prep guy I used to talk to." She rolled her eyes for emphasis. "Anyway, he"—she tipped her head toward the prep school kid's cousin, a white kid who wore his sunglasses inside— "is such a piece of crap."

I'd climbed a bit while waiting for my tropical tea. The kid in line in front of us was doing some unsavory stuff now, including dealing drugs at his school. But as walking proof that decent people do bad things, he would also discover an inexpensive way to manufacture blood pressure medicine in a dozen years or so, saving hundreds, if not thousands, of future lives. "There are pros and cons to almost everyone."

"What do you mean?" Her voice was curious. "You don't know him."

"Do you?"

Stella Rose reached into the little tray of honey and sugar, stacking the packets neatly in their slots. "I don't exactly want to?"

I sipped my tea. My mouth flooded with whatever hibiscus and rose hips were. "I don't think people who do rotten things are always, like, baseline bad. I think people are all capable of doing bad things, which they either do or they don't, depending on their own experiences. Plus, there are a ton of things that impact those. Their socioeconomic situation, systemic racism, toxic masculinity. You name it."

Maisie leaned against the waxy material of the booth. "That is ultimate debate team goodness."

"What do you think, debate queen?" Stella Rose tossed a packet of honey her way.

"I think even the phrase *bad things* is malleable. There's a huge difference between robbing a bank to become rich versus robbing a grocery store to feed your kids. Neither is right, but one is done by necessity. The world is complicated."

My mind wandered back to Nick. For a moment, the image blurred and righted itself. *I really, really, really want to impress December*, he said, now hanging with Maverick.

I covered a smile with the dregs of my iced tea. "Okay. Hypothetical," I said, casting my words out slowly. Thinking *Jake Dirks, Jake Dirks, Jake Dirks.* "Let's say you knew someone was going to do something bad."

"How do you know?" Carrie interrupted.

"It doesn't matter."

But it did. Maisie leaned forward. "Of *course* it matters."

"No, it—" I paused, taking a fraction of a moment to remind myself what I said next. "Fine. You're given two envelopes with your name on it. On the paper inside it, someone's written the next thing that will happen to you—a blue jay will squawk above you, or something."

"And?" Stella Rose prompted.

"And then a blue jay squawks above you." I glanced at my friends, their eyes trained on me. "You open the other envelope. The message says that, in the future, someone you know is going to assault someone you don't know. A stranger."

The table was quiet. Motionless, but for the three pairs of eyes on me. Their lack of chatter opened my eardrums for everything else. The click of the Tea Melee cashier's fake nails on the register. The hissing and boiling and simmering steep of teas. Someone with the audacity not to silence the individual keyboard strokes on their phone, their taps popping like bubbles. Through the mall plexiglass, the distant bark of a horn's honk, tires crunching on wet pavement outside.

Stella Rose was the first to break. "The first thing happens, so you believe the second." Her hands stilled on the sugar packets. "Okay. Brilliant."

I nodded. "And what's *supposed* to happen is written down for you. Not stopping this person means this assault happens."

Carrie exhaled. "You stop the person. Unquestionably."

I focused on her, hoping my smile was encouraging and not sad. "Stopping them will save the girl's pain in the future, which is worth it. Right? Unless you consider the other consequences. What if stopping this creates some massive ripple effect and everything else falls apart if you save her?"

"But not stopping them means the assault happens," Carrie echoed. "And if you somehow can, in this miracle scenario, then you do."

"You'd absolutely *try*. It's unforgivable." I pulled the sugar packet tray over. "Pretend this is how things have been set up for us. Each of these packets represents one event. But then . . ." I spread out a napkin, tore open a baby blue packet, and dumped it out. I fished my lemon out of my tea and held it up. "This lemon is you trying to change the order of events." I squeezed it, releasing leftover tea and citric acid on the snowy white mound. We watched the liquid eat the sugar, dissolving it until there was nothing left. I matted the empty wrapper on top of the soggy mess. "This is what *could* happen if you try to change things."

"You try anyway. To change things," Maisie said, repeating my words. She inched closer to Carrie. "To save that girl from the experience."

"Even if it risks this mess?" I spread my hands out before me.

"In this case, I think so," Carrie said. "But don't watch that *Butterfly Effect* movie beforehand. Otherwise, you'd change your mind because you'd get a third envelope telling you that, instead, the guy will murder someone. And it's you."

Stella Rose had been uncharacteristically quiet. She was the sort of person who viewed things from every angle, a literature student desperate for a unique thesis statement. "I don't know."

"Explain," I said.

Stella Rose jiggled her cup in her hand, the ice crunching together. "I guess I've always thought of myself as the *everything happens for a reason* type. Unless you have some magical envelopes we don't know about?" She poked my side. "There are too many what-ifs here. What if solving it changed things, like Carrie said? What if stopping this particular horror show makes this guy turn around and assault two girls? Or twenty? I don't know that I would disrupt everything or risk everything I had to do so." Stella Rose chewed on an ice cube. "But, on the other hand, if I was handed this envelope and had the ability to stop it, then I'd assume I was meant to do so. And if there was a third envelope, maybe there was supposed to be three in the first place."

I smiled. "You're a predeterminist."

"A *what*?" Maisie asked.

"Someone who thinks things are determined ahead of time," I said, tossing my iced tea in the trash can. "People who believe events have been preestablished, and human actions can't change outcomes. Essentially, they think everything's a chain, no matter what. There is no butterfly effect." I turned to Stella Rose. "There's no free will."

(Mr. Francis. The beat of the song. Chest compressions to *stayin' alliiiive* . . .)

Carrie cupped her chin in her hands. "That's depressing."

"How so?" Maisie licked the edge of her straw.

She shrugged. "What's the point? If all our actions are

predetermined, then things will be how they are. And in this scenario, this girl gets assaulted. She suffers."

"Unless having the envelope—knowing what was going to happen—was meant to prompt her into action," I said.

"But how would you *know*?" Carrie shook her head. "This stuff is so heavy."

I nodded. "This example was. But it doesn't have to be."

"How so?" Maisie asked.

"For instance, we *all* know Stella Rose is going back for that red long-sleeved lace dress."

Stella Rose gave me a wry smile. "How do you know?"

Do you really want to know? "First, you looked hot in it; second, you felt good in it; and third, we all gave you compliments on it."

Maisie stared at her. "Are you?"

"I *was* planning on it," Stella Rose said. "So?"

I lifted one shoulder, let it fall. "So, you're the type of person who wants to see what else is out there. And now that you've seen there's nothing else you like, you'll go for it."

"The dress is my destiny," Stella Rose intoned. "Bring it, homecoming."

Destiny. I turned the word over in my mouth, tasting the lemony tea. Changing destinies. I imagined the loud flap of a million butterfly wings. It was the sound of possibility. I didn't know how to do something as big as saving Nick's life *yet*, but I might be able to change someone else's—Jake Dirks's—saving others in the meantime.

I glanced around the table, feeling lighter than I had in a while. Anyone walking by would see four friends slurping teas, plastic shopping bags piled at their feet, and two fancy dresses draped over the back of the booth.

I tried to lean into that vibe, but there was the smallest sliver of something heavy sitting in my gut. I worked to shake it off, to right my balance, wondering, stricken, if the concept of friendship was so alien that I couldn't even sit at a café with people my own age without trying to ruin it.

CHAPTER THIRTY-FIVE

Nick

CHOPPED GREEN PEPPERS and onions. Six cans of beans and diced tomatoes from the fateful grocery store trip. Dad's screw-top spices, caps strewn across the counter. A giant silver pot. A growling stomach.

The day after Mav and I made zero progress on finding December's mom, I slid onto the counter stool. "Chili?" I asked my dad.

He turned off the sink. Used a dish towel to dry his favorite chopping knife, which he slid back into the wooden holder with a soft *snick*. He flipped the towel over his shoulder and turned to me.

And I knew.

He knew.

His face was passive, but his eyes held the kind of resolve they did when he explained why he turns the heat down to sixty-four at night in the winter.

We stood there, both of us in front of the same ingredients, my dad so kind-eyed and big-shouldered with brown hair that curled like mine. Breathing the same space, surveying the same ingredients.

One disappointed in the other.

The other disappointed in himself.

"Chili," my dad finally confirmed. His voice was light, as I knew it would be. "Anything you want to tell me, Nick?"

I never planned to cheat. I didn't wake up that morning, haul myself from my wooden loft bed onto the clean-but-stained carpet, and say to myself: *Screw this test. I'm copying.*

Nope. I stayed up all night, at first tucked at the desk beneath my elevated bed, greenish light from my banker's lamp casting a nauseating shadow over my notes. The more I looked at the US involvement in World War I, the less I looked at it, if that made sense. Sure, I could walk into a pub and play trivia with my parents, but how much of this was learning instead of memorization?

But then whenever my eyes strayed from the page, all I could hear was Principal Morehouse's admonition when he'd called me into his office the week before. *Listen, kid. I know you're trying. But I think summer school will be good for you, you know? Get prepped for senior year. At your own pace.*

Translation: You can't keep up with everyone else. And he didn't even know about the other school my parents had wanted me to go to.

All that night, I tried every trick to work through the material. I stood the way Mom had shown me to try and get the information into my brain a different way. *Triple Entente*, I said, lifting three fingers in front of me. *French Republic. British Empire. Russian Empire.*

The origin of the word dogfight *stems from the sound of pilots restarting their engines in midair.* I jumped across the room, mimicking a jumpstart, thinking about the O'Malleys' dog, which snarled at anyone who walked by.

I drew a square in the air. Square. Sophie. Square. My sister. *Sophie, Duchess of Hohenberg, is the name of Franz Ferdinand's wife. Historians often call his assassination the start of the war, forgetting Sophie died alongside him.*

I tried to do anything I could to associate the material with things I knew. And then I'd return to the desk, write the answers, and royally mess them up. I had slammed my palm on the desk, bruising the heel of my hand.

When the sky grew rosy, I shut my shades. They were meant to be blackout ones, but they were too small. The dawn light bordered them in a long rectangle. Three sides illuminated, the top one snuffed out.

I climbed the loft bed and sprawled facedown, my stomach churning, trying to remember the facts attached to the jerky dance I'd done all night long. Before long, the worn cotton of my pillow was labeled with my tears.

A handful of hours later, I sat in the third seat of the third row, behind Mav. I tapped my fingers against the cardboard cup of my coffee, which had long gone lukewarm.

He turned around. "Yo. Why are you in here?"

I shrugged. "I'm taking my final. Why are *you* in here?"

Mav's jaw worked around a wad of gum. "You know what I mean, dude."

"I'm taking the same test you are, aren't I?"

"Yeah, but—"

"Nick? You heading to the AC?" Mrs. Dovetail called from her perch on her desk.

"I'm good," I said, unable to look her in the face.

She came over to my desk. "You sure?"

I gave her a tight nod. My leg jerked up and down, pumping the brake on some imaginary bicycle.

Mav crossed his arms, then checked to see if the muscles he strove after were popping out. "Dude, summer school?"

Summer school meant the entire lifeguard certification I'd just gone through would be shot to shit, because it would cut my shift availability to weekends only. Dad's income—given his ten-month contract—was nil during July and August. Summer school meant next-to-zero spending money for me—no movies, no ice creams, no beach parking or sneakers or new phone if mine broke all the way. My screen had been cracked for six months. I shook my head. "I studied all night."

He popped his gum. "It's your summer, I guess."

A flare of anger sliced through my anxiety. My exhaustion evaporated, as if I'd gotten a clean eight hours the night before. Why was it so impossible for my best friend to believe I knew the answers? "And yours, too, bro," I said, nearly breathing the words.

When the exam landed on my desk, I almost stood up and took Mrs. Dovetail's offer. I'd taken dozens of tests in the AC, dictating my answers to a bored teacher's aide who barely listened to my oral explanations on the process of meiosis or the themes in *The Hate U Give*. My grades were almost always the same. B. C. B. D.

But I'd taken a year's worth of US history tests in there, and yet I still couldn't swing above a D. And part of it . . . it was the principle of the thing, you know? I'd leave the brightly lit AC, full of beanbags and dictation computers and squeeze balls for anxiety and join my friends in the cafeteria, them already halfway through their lunches, their backpacks lying at their feet. I felt torn in half between wanting to speak up for the help I needed and the person who'd be in summer school if he failed another test. Part of me knew I was being ableist toward myself. The other part of me struggled to perform to the standards by which acceptable curriculum indicated were . . . well, acceptable, and resented that.

I wanted to be the sort of person who didn't spiral into despair when given something every other kid in my class was given. My parents, my sister, and Maverick had always celebrated me for me. Why couldn't school?

I stared at the questions on the ivory page, the black letters swimming and wriggling, ants marching along.

To my right, Sara-Beth Seaborn scribbled on her page.

Sara-Beth Seaborn didn't fail things.

I licked my lips. Stared at my paper.

What was the name of the luxury passenger liner sunk by German U-boats that helped prompt the United States to enter World War I?

No matter what I did, I could not summon the boat's name, even though I remembered the rhythm of its five syllables. I knew it had taken eighteen minutes to sink, and that local Irish fishermen helped to rescue and recover its victims. I dug my pen into the paper.

And finally, my eyes betrayed my brain. I glanced to my right. I made out the word *Lusitania* about a third of the way down Sara-Beth's paper, her handwriting as perfect as a computer font.

You're not a cheater, I had shouted at myself. I thought about hitting the chest of my shirt. The one I hadn't bothered changing out of before school.

In truth, I expected to get caught. Maybe a part of me *hoped* to. At her desk, Mrs. Dovetail used a stylus to zip through her iPad.

The Lusitania, I penned, guilt clanging into my spine. My leg stopped pumping, stilling in place like poured concrete.

I didn't realize it until later, but the worst part of the whole thing was that other than Maverick, who was clearly concerned about my choice, and maybe Mrs. Dovetail, not a soul cared that I stayed in the room. It was me. I was the one who worried what everyone else thought, when it didn't bother anyone else that I usually left for tests. *I* was the one judging myself.

Forty-eight minutes after the test began, I left with Mav, my backpack slung over my shoulder. In the cafeteria, I started my lunch at the same time as him, forcing my way through half of my turkey sandwich before I went to the bathroom and puked it up.

—

I told my father everything.

Between scrapes of the chopped vegetables into the pot, I spilled about Sara-Beth Seaborn, about the word *Lusitania*. About the pops of my best friend's gum. Dad and I worked side by side, dumping ingredients and not looking at each other, Dad making small *mm-hmm*s and *Oh, Nick*s and *why*s. Outside our window, it was cool and rainy and fallish, but my mind was stuck in last spring.

"You know, I wish you'd come to me, buddy," he said when I finished.

The steam was spicy, and it twisted in my throat. "I *did* come to you. I told you I didn't want to switch schools."

Dad was quiet for a moment. "I guess we should have listened to you a little more, huh?"

"Might've been helpful. Yeah."

"Well. Look." He slid the cutting board into the sink and squirted dish soap on top, then turned to face me. "I talked to your mother. We suspected something might have happened, after you two ran into Mrs. Dovetail."

I lowered my head. A tear found its way down the slope of my nose, dripping onto my palm. I stared at the perfect round circle. "I'm sorry."

Dad wiped off the can opener and dried it. He washed his hands before he spoke again. "Do you know what the hardest part of changing jobs was for me?"

I shook my head, watching him. "You've always said it was the easiest choice you ever made."

"It was. But even easy choices can be complex." He stared out the window, the picture of someone lost in thought. "Money aside, quitting law meant knowing I was giving up an important piece of myself. A piece that could help people who have been wronged. All my life, I'd wanted to help others, and when I got there, when I got to that point of actually making a difference, it became really clear really fast that by giving myself to everyone else, I was missing out on life. On you guys." He cleared his throat. "What I needed was a balance. So now I teach the kids who might make that difference in the future. That helps me stay true to myself until I decide whether or not to return again after you have grown and flown." He pulled the dish towel from his shoulder, folded it into quarters, and turned to meet my eyes. "Do you think you stayed true to yourself there?"

The rain fell harder, washing a dead leaf from the window. "No," I whispered. I glanced at my bare feet, hot against the freezing floor. "Dad, I've regretted it every single day. I'm not a cheater."

"I would hope not. But it appears that at least for a moment, you were someone who cheated."

The sadness on his face was what did it. Torpedo. Stomach to floor. My eyes filled with more tears. "Dad . . ."

My father held up a palm. His watch, a vintage one from his father, glinted on his wrist. "We've seen a change in you, kiddo. I know how much it's affected you."

"I can't even tell you how guilty I feel—"

"And that feeling sucks. But cheating got you what you wanted, didn't it?"

"What do you mean?"

Dad splayed his hands on the counter. "You stayed in the same school."

My vision blurred. I'd gotten to stay at Woodland High, sure. But in another sense, there was no way to get what I really wanted. I gritted my teeth. "Well, yeah, but it's not fair," I burst out.

"What?"

"The whole thing. The way we're tested." I put the knife on the counter with a savage clang. "I couldn't have studied any harder than I did, but that test? The fill-in-the-blanks? The way it's set up might make sense for the majority, but I'm almost guaranteed to fail it."

"I see what you're saying."

"Do I wish I didn't cheat? Yes. But is the rule even fair? Doesn't it matter at all that I get the boat's significance? That it was this huge inciting moment for that point in history? That it became a launching point for more people to join the effort, for countries to take the threat seriously?"

"Nick—"

"What matters," I continued, "is that I understand its significance and how it relates to the world. Not how it's spelled or that I couldn't find its name in my head, even after I studied all night long." I scraped the back of my hand beneath my eyes. "Tell me how that's fair."

"Why would I do that, when it's not?"

I blinked. "What?"

He sighed. "I know you didn't want to leave Woodland High. And I get it. I do. But don't you remember why we thought you should?"

I swallowed, my chest full of that familiar sinking feeling. *A grades-free atmosphere. No standardized testing. Accessible curriculum.*

"You leaving WHS was not to punish you. It's because my personal belief is that grades don't define your self-worth. I know you studied your tail off, and I get why you're feeling the way you are—about the guilt and about the test, especially because Mom and I are so big on honesty."

I dropped my elbows on the counter and put my chin in my hands. "I can't win."

A slow nod. "This does resemble what we ethics nerds would call a no-win situation. So here's the deal. You get to decide what happens from here. You can be your own personal justice system." He glanced at the ceiling. "I better not regret this," he muttered.

I wasn't sure what I felt. Relief? Worry? "I—Are you serious?"

He rubbed his beard. "I am. We'll let you decide the right thing to do. You're not in trouble with us either way. You can choose whether or not you approach the school and tell them what happened. On your own volition."

Me? Decide? "Is this you guilting me into telling on myself?"

"No." He shook his head to emphasize. "Nope. You're old enough and mature enough to determine what makes sense for consequences. Especially given how brave you were in saving Mr. Francis this summer, this feels like the right thing to do."

No. No no no.

Brave. I was anything but. Shock rooted me to the floor, the spoon hovering over the simmering pot.

There was no better time to come clean.

There was no possible way to come clean.

It was as if gravity took on water. My shoulders hunched under the weight of the hulking monster of guilt who'd made a comfy home on my vertebrae.

"Your grades are technically final, so I want you to consider what

makes the most sense. After all, we're not under a ticking clock here."
My father sniffed the chili. "Did you add jalapeño? Oh!" He raised
his arm, hunting in the open cabinet shelf where we keep the cook-
books. He slid out one. "This book! It's for adults with dyslexia, so
you might not be ready for it yet."

I plunged the wooden spoon in the vat, barely feeling when small
dots of the burning liquid scalded my hand. "Thanks," I muttered.

Dad nodded. "Has some good tips. More on the kinesthetic learning, some stuff about navigating careers."

"Thanks," I said, glancing at the title. *The Dyslexia Road Map:
Driving Success in Adults.*

ROAD MAP.

The letters were big and red and sort of curvy against the white
backdrop. I stared at them, blurring the image over the vat of chili.
The image fit into place in my head, overlapping something else like
tracing paper over a comic.

The starred cities across the whiteboard.

I inhaled.

What if Mara Jones's travel journal wasn't about the places she
had been, but about the path that she had traveled?

CHAPTER THIRTY-SIX

December

I HALF RECLINED in my uncle's armchair, colored pencils clinking gently in my lap, my biology homework propped against my thighs. A sunshine-yellow pencil wiggled in my hand, a cerulean-blue one shoved in the crook of my ear.

My assignment was to shade in the stages of mitosis versus meiosis, which was fine. Simple. Though scientists would change their opinions on these stages in a few decades, I could do what my teacher wanted.

But what he wanted was a simple color breakdown of these stages, not what my fingers itched to do. I thought of the old artwork Evan had found when we moved in here, shoved into a manila folder, and stored in the back of his closet. All my landscapes.

My fingers wanted to shade. Add verve. Change the shape to something I pictured in greater depth, thanks to all of what I knew. I jammed the yellow pencil into a sharpener, breathing in the scent of freshly cut cedar, mixed with . . . cumin and garlic? I inhaled again, recognizing chili pepper and that whiff of natural gas that comes before the flicker of a burner flame. My stomach rumbled, and I settled comfortably into my uncle's chair before I realized it.

No one in my home was cooking.

I sat up.

It was happening again.

And it was stronger.

Only this time, it was a release.

Again, I was flooded with someone else's feelings—Nick's. Regret and guilt. Anger, metal-flavored and heavy enough to sink a six-foot lifeguard through a fake hardwood floor, followed by love and devotion, cloudy as milk, light as spun sugar on a cone.

My heart staggering in my chest, I absorbed Nick telling his dad about the test he'd cheated on. Nick held tight to a sheer confidence that his dad would always love him, and I clung to the ends of it.

What was that like?

(My mother. My father. Two shadows in another place, tangled together for a moment before a gentle dissolution. Then me.)

I imagined what it might be like to love a father. One who would protect me and guide me and play video games with me and cook with me and

and

and

and nothing. I did not have a father. I never had one. I had Evan. But . . .

Is this what it felt like to know your father would love you no matter what? One who cared deep from the marrow of his bones?

(unconditional love)

I didn't know if this was different from what my uncle and I had: a chosen trust and love and family. I knew I felt that way toward Evan, but it was impossible to know if he felt that way about me on his own or if he felt like he had to. Me, the burden that changed his life.

I ground my teeth together, catching a taste bud between them. Pain nicked my mouth, warring with the scents in someone else's kitchen. I mashed my fist against the halfway-shaded-in cell on my homework sheet, fighting the intrusion of Nick's feelings in my nerve endings. Was it the proximity that made it stronger? I tried to inhale and slow my racing heart, but it only sped up, each frantic beat reminding me I had no idea why this was happening.

And then it was a held-up book, white with red letters, and a *whoosh*, and his feelings were gone, leaving me with one thought: Nick's death, which I held in my hand, a cool, glassy marble nestled among my gumballs.

(Time was running out.)

Desperate to cast myself back into whatever he was doing, I closed my eyes to climb to where he was.

Door.

I couldn't get there. The colored pencils clattered to the floor, and my insides trembled with a mix of fear, worry, and wonder.

Nick was grayed out. That could only mean one thing.

My mother.

CHAPTER THIRTY-SEVEN

Nick

ROAD MAP.

The bubbling scent of chili filled my room. I stared at the white-board, rubbing my jaw. I slid my phone from my pocket and clicked the microphone button.

"US Interstate road map," I said into the speaker.

"Where can I direct you to?" my phone answered.

"C'mon," I muttered, punching the buttons in myself. After approximately two eternities, the search populated, and I clicked on the first image that came up. The major highways unfurled like veins and blood vessels, and the map of the contiguous United States was their body.

My eyes flicked from my phone to the whiteboard. All the places she'd gone were connected by major highways.

I used a red marker and filled them in, watching an image come together. The lines were a constellation. A rake. From west to east, they started narrow, and then sprawled, exponentially reaching across the states.

But what did that mean? Did it mean *anything*?

I paced. *There's not one way to read*, I remember my mom saying when I was ten and my head was buried on my folded arms to hide my sobs after one gruff teacher demanded I read out loud on the first day of school.

I flipped open the journal, scanning my audio pen across the page, listening to the city names and the weather and tacos and *my sole's screaming*.

The pictures. In the most recent ones, December's mother appeared to have gotten *buff*. Her legs were crossed, one calf muscle a mountain ridge. Her biceps were visible, too, shadows appearing above and below them, where they weren't in the first picture. I frowned. She was toned. So what?

I had all the pieces in front of me. The *Mystery Buff* host always warned the Buffys not to discount anything.

But this was different from working out the broken alibi, or the science behind a DNA analysis, or incongruent witness accounts. There was something so satisfying about being presented with a story and reading what the Buffys did on the forums to piece together the solution.

I caught my lip in my teeth and bit hard. This wasn't an episode of *Mystery Buff*. This was real life. This was December's life.

It wasn't only that. Every episode of *Mystery Buff* was someone's life. Real people's lives. I had known this before, but there was something unsettling about experiencing a mystery and the shock and grief that came with it firsthand. I knew that everyone involved with these cases agreed to go on the show, and donating its ad revenue to missing persons organizations and other charities seemed like a solid move, but still. It was all more voyeuristic than I'd realized.

I snapped a picture of the whiteboard and dropped it into my biggest text thread.

Maverick: EPIC ROAD TRIP?

Me: Can't explain it, but I just have this feeling. It's something to do with why she went to those specific cities in that specific order

I tossed everything on my desk. Sat down. Rubbed my jaw again, which had started to . . . burn? A glance in the full-length mirror on the back of my closet door revealed a red stripe of skin right where I'd been rubbing. I checked my fingertips. They were warm. Dark pink in color.

My stomach bottomed out. Sometimes, hotter peppers—habaneros, for instance—snuck into the collection of jalapeños at the grocery store. And when your not-thinking son slammed through the aisle to try and avoid gingerbread cookies for dessert, he might've not thought to double-check. I'd washed my hands right after cutting, so my fingers had been mostly saved, but I must've swiped at my face at some point.

"Well, shit," I said in the mirror. My face prickling, I jogged to the kitchen. Sophie was perched cross-legged on top of the counter. She crammed a gluten-free chocolate-chip cookie into her mouth. "What are you doing?" she asked, wiping crumbs from her lips. "Ugh. Yuck. These are garbage."

"Burned my jaw."

"On what?"

"Pepper oil, I think." While I scrabbled through the cabinet above the sink for burn cream, knocks came from the front door. Sophie hopped off the counter to answer, muttering.

My right eye watered, and I squinted against the sting. Tylenol, gauze, baby aspirin. No burn cream. I groaned.

"What's up?" December asked, Sophie trailing behind her.

"He rubbed peppers on his face," Sophie said.

"Did not." I pointed to my jaw. "Sous chef side effect. Pepper oil."

"Oh!" December pulled milk from the refrigerator.

"He burns himself and the first thing you do is have a glass of milk?" Sophie shook her head. "You're weird."

"Weird is good," December said. "And no. I read you're supposed to put it on there to help it stop burning."

My feet stuck to the cool floor, so different from the hot cement of the pool deck that got me into this mess. The skin on my jaw burning, burning, burning. "Go for it, Dr. Jones."

She palmed a clean kitchen rag, soaked it with milk, and pressed it to my cheek. I closed my eyes against the immediate relief. Coolness flooded my skin, chasing the heat from the leftover oil. "Ow."

"This hurts?"

I raised my eyelid. "No. I'm remembering what it felt like two seconds ago. This is heaven."

She hesitated, then smiled. "Good." She lifted the rag from my skin and inspected my jaw. The pain returned like a warm draft.

"Put it back," I said, my voice coming out in a beg. "I might bathe in this."

"That's aggressive." She sighed. "What a bummer."

"What?"

"I'm not making out with this."

I mock-jutted my lower lip. "This doesn't do it for you, huh?"

"Not one bit," she said, trailing a kiss on my forehead.

—

A few days later, I parked Dad's car in the condo lot after dropping December off. We'd seen a truly horrible movie, full of plot holes and overacted to the point where the audience laughed at moments that were supposed to be serious. We left when some guy threw his bag of popcorn at the screen. On our way home, we picked up fries from the diner and split them on the ride.

Outside my front door, my phone lit up. I paused.

Maverick: WAIT. THAT MAP PIC.
Me: Yeah?
Maverick: . . .
Maverick: HOLD UP. I'M DRAFTING SOME
SUPPLEMENTAL QUESTIONS FOR COLLEGE, AND I WAS
GOING THROUGH MY OLD RESEARCH ABOUT WHY
CERTAIN PARTS OF THE COUNTRY ARE MORE DRAWN
TO SOME DRUG TYPES THAN OTHERS
Me: depressing
Maverick: VERY. BUT CHECK THIS

He shared a link to a map of the United States that looked a hell of a lot like my whiteboard one. Except his had a title:

Drug Flow and Opioid Overdose Pathways in the United States, 1996 to 2022

The bottom of the map had a button that toggled to each year. I slid the lever to 1996. Pockets of the United States, close to the areas where Mara Jones traveled in 1999, were shaded peach to indicate overdose deaths, with arrows that looked suspiciously similar to the whiteboard rake to indicate the flow of opiates across the country.

"No effing way," I breathed. I slammed my hip into the screen door and ran to my room, my phone held up.

The lines were nearly identical. My stomach sank. I wasn't sure what it meant, but the visual was close to proof that I was right about one thing: The travel journal was a record of a road map. And Mara Jones had traveled the same path that opiates had across the country.

I moved my thumb across the lever, watching the years unfurl and the map explode with color. Areas that were shaded peach to suggest "mild activity" deepened to a salmon pink, then a crude cranberry red. Over two decades, the mostly-gray-and-slightly-peach drug-activity map mutated into a Doppler radar. Little of the map was left untouched, except for areas in the middle, where maybe the drug of choice wasn't an opioid.

I had that helpless feeling I sometimes got when I thought about all The Bad Shit in the world that I was not involved in, but that exists nonetheless, bringing millions of families to their knees. It was exhausting and sad, and I wished I had some way to fix everything. Especially because this might be December's mom.

I answered Maverick's FaceTime. The phone was *thisclose* to his face. "Yo, Irving. You check out that map?"

"It's a horror story."

He shook his head. "Show me the whiteboard again. I want to see if it matches up."

"I checked. It does." I thought for a moment. "What if *P/U* is *pickup*? And maybe the other acronyms are code names for heroin or something."

Maverick whistled. "Damn."

We were both quiet for a moment. I broke the silence. "I don't get it."

"I do."

I sat on my floor, leaning my back against the wall. "What? How?"

"Science. Drugs start off by fooling you into thinking you're your best self. They bug all your head circuits out by playing in the pleasure part of your brain, messing with your neurons and making you feel like you ate the best meal of your life, laughed harder than you ever have, felt warm and cozy and confident. Until, suddenly, they rob you of any kind of pleasure and make your body think you need them only to not feel anxious and depressed and sick and desperate for relief, which becomes a vicious cycle."

"So feeling like your best self isn't worth becoming your worst self, essentially."

"Yeah, but at that point, a lot of people are addicted. It's too late. It's like trying to get protection from the mafia." Maverick shook his head. "People do things they would have sworn they'd never do all the time. People leave their kids. It's far from unheard of."

"So what we're saying is that this is a possible outcome of Mara Jones?"

"Yes. A probable one, even, if she went to those cities."

Out in the hall, someone flicked on the hall light, flooding my bedroom. I hadn't realized how dark it had been in there until that moment. My shades were drawn, but it was already getting dark out. It was amazing how quickly the sun went from lighting grilled dinners and football games to hitting the road at four thirty in the afternoon. "Dude, if we're right . . ."

"Yeah?"

"How can I possibly tell December this?"

CHAPTER THIRTY-EIGHT
December

A FEW YEARS ago, Evan and I lived in an apartment building above a laundromat. The laundry exhaust was vented in several spots around our kitchen window, and when the dryers ran in the colder months, you couldn't see a thing outside. All things ordinary went on behind the wall of cloudy steam—birds carrying twigs for the nest in the nearby oak tree, snow or rain or sun—but out this one particular window, curls of pulverized vapor hid what was outside, at least during business hours.

At first, it had been a cool spot. The house held this manufactured clean smell all the time, even when it was messy, the effect something like smelling hot chocolate while biting into a Brussels sprout. Evan would look out the bathroom window and say, *Sunny day out there. Could be beach weather.* I'd peer out the kitchen one while washing my cereal bowl and call back, *Are you sure? Because it looks like the apocalypse is imminent.*

But soon, a chemical in the fabric softener started itching our throats. I'd foreseen that prior to moving in, but as was my basic life pattern, I hadn't realized how much it would bother me. The sensation was needle pricks in my lungs, spiders crawling in my throat. We moved out quickly after that.

Now, as summer became a distant memory and autumn took up residence, secrets rose between Nick and me like that dryer steam.

I cheated on a test and lied about it.
I'm hiding something about your mother.

I can see the past, present, and future. Usually.
You're going to die, and I haven't figured out how to stop it.

—

I plunged the carving knife into the thick orange flesh of a pumpkin, sawing a rough circle around the stem.

Nick winced. "Careful."

"Are you judging my expert carving skills?" I wiped my hand against my jeans. I'd meant for the words to come out as a tease, a trail, a game, but they hadn't. They were flattened by my fear of whatever it was Nick was doing concerning my mother.

We sat on the back porch beside newspapers strewn with pumpkin guts, dressed in hoodies to guard ourselves against the first truly cool afternoon. It was a day of muted colors: gray sky, olive grass, khaki trees. Leaves stuffed into brown bags lined the edge of the porch, raked that morning by my uncle. The pumpkins were so bright they were almost hard to look at.

"Certainly not," he said. Then he grinned. "This must be your first jack-o'-lantern."

I made a face at him. "Funny."

He handed me the ladle he'd used to scoop out the insides handle-first—the way kids are taught to carry scissors. I scraped it along the inside of my pumpkin, bringing up soggy tangerine-colored guts and slippery white-pale seeds. "This is disgusting. And colder than I thought they'd be."

"Make sure you save the seeds." He passed me the silver mixing bowl we'd brought out for this purpose. "My sister loves roasted ones."

"What do you put on them?"

He bent over, absorbed in stenciling in the most standard carved pumpkin ever: triangle eyes, toothy grin.

"Earth to Nick."

"Hmm?"

"What's gotten into you?" It was funny, sort of, how I talked this big talk about how I'd love to just be me, and think about me, and not know things, and then the one thing I didn't know sent me flying into the universe, stomping my foot like a toddler. I'd practically climbed to Everest, trying so hard to see whatever had touched Nick's mood over the course of the last few days, and trying even harder to see what it was he was hiding.

He stared at me for a moment, then looked away. "Nothing."

I seethed. It was something. "You can tell me, you know."

"There's nothing to tell."

He was *lying*.

I knew by the way he shifted his eyes. The way he wouldn't look at me. The way his shoulders hunched, almost imperceptible, unless you knew what to look for. Like I did.

But in that same way I knew he was lying, I also knew I wouldn't call him on it.

Because I *didn't*.

What I wanted to say:

Do you know something about my mother?

How can I stop you from dying?

What is the worst thing you've ever done? What are all your

opinions? What is it like to soar through the water the way a bird does in the air? What do you want to be when you grow up? Why do you like me?

(Why are you lying why are you lying why are you lying?)

Could I? Sure. No one was stopping me from presenting those words to him, spitting the question *why are you lying* into the mixing bowl of pumpkin seeds.

(But it just

wasn't

what would happen,

which is why this gift was such a goddamn white elephant.)

I squashed the growl in my throat. "Mm," I said finally. I almost laughed. After all that.

He met my eyes, fidgeting with the stem of his pumpkin. "Is this our first fight?" ·

"Don't you remember asking me to come clean, and me refusing, and you running away from my doorstep?"

"But that was before we knew each other. I mean our first fight since we . . ." He flipped his finger back and forth between the two of us.

I crossed my arms. "Since we what?"

He blushed. "You know. Got together."

"Are you trying to weasel out of this cross-examination, Nicholas Irving?"

"Not hard enough, apparently." He flipped his pumpkin over. "Let me try again. Has anyone ever told you that you're *gourd*-geous?"

I groaned. "Pun game on point, at least."

He stood and brushed off his jeans. His cheeks were ruddy from the cold. My insides loosened, forgiving but not forgetting his evasiveness.

For the moment, at least.

"Be right back." He swooped down, brushing a kiss on my nose. "I'm going to get some water. Want anything?"

"Wait!" I stood up, planting my palm on his chest. "You can't go in there."

Confusion on his face. I couldn't blame him. "What? Why not?"

"My uncle's getting ready for a date."

"So?"

"*So*, his date's about to be here, and I want them to have a moment." I flushed. "You know? Like a *hey, you look great* kind of thing. And then . . ." I trailed off.

Nick gave me a strange look. "Okay? You're doing the thing again."

"What thing?"

"The thing where you think ahead so much. It's . . ." He tucked a strand behind my ear. "Pretty endearing."

I wrinkled my nose. "Endearing? Thanks, Grandpa." I circled around him, nudging the slider open with my foot. "But come on. I hear Evan's date."

Nick frowned. "I thought you said you wanted them to have a moment."

"I did. They've had one."

"Are you sure? I didn't hear anything."

"You're too distracted by my *gourd*-geousness, remember, Gramps? Let's go."

———

Inside, my uncle's date look was on point. A button-down with rolled sleeves, dark-washed jeans, smelling only slightly of soapy pine. Sim stood in the entryway, hands in his pockets.

"Hey, I didn't know interns did house calls now." I pointed to my arm.

Sim's eyes darted from my uncle to me. "Oh! December," he said. "I'm not here for. Uh. Your arm. I—"

I smiled. "I'm joking. Hope you guys have fun."

"Yeah, enjoy yourselves." Nick waved at my uncle and Sim.

Evan's eyes narrowed in our direction. "You two stay outside," he said. "No significant others in the house when I'm not home."

Before my uncle had finished speaking, Nick had already started walking backward toward the porch. "Message received," he said. "See ya."

I rolled my eyes at him. At everyone. "Sure. Places to be. Instagram stories to update. Pumpkins to carve."

I left them, joining Nick on the porch. He'd cleared the pumpkin refuse off, tying everything in a trash bag. "Your uncle's dating the intern from the hospital?"

I nodded. "They met again at my grandma's nursing home."

"Makes sense. I was gonna say the hospital wasn't the most romantic setting."

"Hardly." I rubbed my arms. "I'm cold. The pumpkins are done. Want to go inside?"

Nick shook his head. "No way. Did you hear your uncle?"

"Hard not to."

"The guy looks like a YouTube exercise coach. I think I'll listen to him." He checked his phone. "Besides, I have a swim team meeting with coaches and parents tonight. I better go."

"If you don't come inside, you'll have to walk all the way around four or five units," I pointed out. "It would be a lot faster for you to cut through my house." I leaned my butt against the siding. "And make out with me for five minutes or so."

226

Color rose in his cheeks again. His Adam's apple bobbed. "When you put it that way . . ."

I opened the slider and stepped inside, where for a few minutes, I wouldn't think about how to save this boy, how much I missed my mom, how I'd orchestrated this whole goddamn thing. I'd lose myself in my fingertips atop the warm skin on his back, the muscles stretched and long, his shoulder blades ridged, carved and firm.

He followed.

CHAPTER THIRTY-NINE

Nick

I'D HEARD THAT in other towns, everyone skipped school the day of homecoming. But here in Woodland, attendance at one was required for attendance at the other, which is maybe why the hallways at Woodland High teemed with more friction than usual. Even for a half day.

It was the second Friday in October. I made my way through the halls, lined with the same old lockers the size and shape of my rescue tube, decorated with streamers and other student-council-sponsored crap.

Everyone talked about what they were wearing—the size and cut of the suits, how many buttons their dads recommended buttoning; the color, fabric, detail, skirt length of dresses. Three kids in my gym class refused to participate, claiming they'd sweat too much. Unlike a typical school day, most of the girls wore makeup-free faces, sweatpants, and button-down shirts (because apparently, when they'd get their hair done later, they couldn't take off a shirt with a T-shirt neck, according to Carrie and Maisie).

All I ever did was shower and pull on clothes. Was I doing something wrong?

I averted my eyes when I passed the principal's office. Ever since last week, when Dad had taken his hands off the wheel of my morality barometer, I'd been at a complete loss as to what to do. I'd changed my mind a hundred times, flipping back and forth like one of those Newton's cradle things we learned about in physics. They're those small, decorative-looking devices that sit on office desks everywhere—five steel balls suspended between two bars. You lift one end ball and release it, and when it returns to its lineup with an audible clack, the force expelled through the stationary balls sends the steel ball on the opposite end swinging. They ticked back and forth in rhythm with my decision-making skills.

Tell.

Don't tell.

Tell.

Don't tell.

"My dude," Maverick said, meeting me in front of the computer lab and shattering my thought spiral with a clap on the shoulder. "You ready for tonight?"

"Sure." For the first time, I was amped for one of these. My mom was out of control, charging her camera battery and asking my dad how many pictures "the cloud" could hold.

"Hey, listen. I'm not sure if my mom and I will make it over beforehand."

My stomach dipped. "Oh, Mav. You can still come with me and December."

"Right on. But that's not it."

"Then what is it?"

"Stella Rose wants me over early."

I did a double take. "You? Why?"

Maverick winked, and I noticed his fresh cut. "We're going together.

As friends," he added. "But still. Since Maisie and Carrie are going together now—"

"They are?"

"Where the hell have you been?"

"They're going together? Like, *together* together?"

"Yep. Leaving Stella Rose going solo." He grinned, his teeth whiter than usual. "Till now, of course."

I elbowed him. "Did you switch to teeth-whitening gum?"

He beamed, pleased. "I guess it's working." We stopped at his locker. "Hey, you talk to December yet? About what we think about her mom?"

I pressed my tongue against my eyetooth, grounding myself in the small prick of near pain. *Tell. Don't tell. Tell. Don't tell.*

There was something stopping me from telling her. It was more than fear of hurting her; it was something impalpable, something I could not trace. I felt about as useful as the sludge inside the pool filter. Besides, I'd wanted to surprise her with good news, not bad. I wanted one more piece of the puzzle to fall into place. "Not yet."

We rounded the corner and found December, ignoring the school policy about not using phones in the hallway. She leaned against the cream-painted cinder blocks, her backpack abandoned at her feet. Down the hall, I spotted Maisie and Carrie, walking with their arms brushing, and Jake Dirks talking to a girl I vaguely recognized as a sophomore field hockey player.

We stopped by December, who was frowning. "Hey, are you okay?" I asked.

"What?" Her expression was dazed. "Oh. Hey. Yeah. You guys ready for tonight?" She grinned at Maverick. "Heard you've got a hot date."

Last block of the day: Human Studies. Mr. Francis wore a red bow tie in honor of homecoming, because that was one of the ingredients of being the town's favorite teacher. "Okay, you dancing fools," he said. "Human connection. What makes you feel connected to those around you?"

My classmates weren't shy about revealing the kinds of things that made them tick. Eye contact while talking. Parents buying kids their favorite snacks. The satisfied feeling of making someone laugh versus the physical sensation of laughing. Joining together to protest something, fighting for various social justices. I leaned onto the back two legs of the chair, thinking about my sister and her sweatbands and her cookie cramming and her well-meaning but inconsistent commitment to dedication.

Mr. Francis smiled, spread his hands wide. "Human connection. It's why we're all here, isn't it? Why we put in our time and energy into others?" He paced the front of the room, trailing his fingertips along the front tables. "Two people from opposing sides can bond over a shared experience. Think of opponents on two basketball teams. Maybe rival towns. Throwing insults at each other, on and off court, before learning in the locker room that they'd both experienced the death of a sibling. Or, heck, that both of them volunteer at an animal shelter." He paused. "Sometimes, when things don't appear to go together, they do."

I rocked forward, the two front legs of my chair clattering against the floor. Something kept rising to the surface of my brain, poking, insistent, reminding me of another time when a combination of things came together in a way I did not expect:

Sophie's Pinterest experiment with the milk, soap, and food coloring. P/U. 300. 6LAP. S/U.

Maverick and I had made serious progress with the journal, the whiteboard, the map. I was sure of it. But we hadn't nailed the acronyms or shorthand yet.

My heart picked up speed. I'd searched for each one separately, but what if I put them together? Would it change what I'd concluded about December's mother?

As casually as I could, I slid my phone from the zippered pocket of my backpack. December sat at the table in front of me, and I kept my eyes on the length of her hair. I straightened, settling my phone in my lap, and retrieved the photo I'd taken of the acronyms and the numbers beside them.

While Mr. Francis jotted an assignment on the board, I pretended to scribble it down, but I copied Mara Jones's shorthand instead.

S/U: 50 (6)

300 − > 52.9 (7)

P/U: 34 (6)

6LAP: 12:29 (4) (1.5mi)

Mr. Francis uncapped another marker, and December whipped around. She squinted one eye. "What are you doing?" she breathed.

Having my podcast moment. Maybe, just maybe, solving this case, cracking it wide open. "Nothing."

"December?" Mr. Francis asked.

She flipped back to the front, her ears pinking. "Sorry," she murmured.

Slowly, surreptitiously, I keyed in the acronyms and numbers, sitting as still as I possibly could. My body flared with heat, sweat creeping along the back of my neck. I held my breath and thumbed the SEARCH key.

Jackpot.

On the first link, I made out the words *PFT CHECK-IN* before the rest of them jiggled and ran together. I navigated to my accessibility app and tried a different dyslexia-friendly font, then shut my eyes and focused on the red darkness behind my eyelids, an old trick of my mom's. Inhale, exhale, and open, resolving to read slower.

I checked the source. Federal Soup, a forum for people entering government jobs.

Just what I needed. Another confusing phrase.

But this one was spelled out for me.

Gotta earn more than 12 points to pass the test, but it's a lot less nerve-racking if you score some extras along the way, someone with the handle **ciYAY736** wrote.

Q1Tco2004 replied:

> Here's a copy/paste of the PFT pulled from the site,
> **FBIhopeful3498**:
> The PFT test consists of four mandatory events that are
> administered in the following order with no more than
> five minutes of rest in between each event. There is a
> strictly defined scoring scale and protocol for each event.
> 1. Maximum number of sit-ups in one minute
> 2. Timed 300-meter sprint
> 3. Maximum number of continuous push-ups (untimed)
> 4. Timed one and one-half mile (1.5 mile) run

My eyes ran the length of the post, matching acronyms to terms I finally recognized.

S/U. Sit-ups.

300—> a 300-meter sprint.

P/U. Push-ups.

One point five miles . . . in six laps.

6LAP.

There in Mr. Francis's Human Studies class, the wall posters with their terrible jokes, the clock on the wall with a nearly imperceptible clicking second hand, my peers with hellfire opinions. My chest bloomed with certainty.

December's mother's mountain ridge calves. Her jacked-up arms. Easy smile.

FBI Physical Fitness Test.

Beyond, basically, the fact that my parents loved me and that I was a decent swimmer, there'd been so few things in my life I'd been ironclad sure of. Usually, things happened, and I went with them. Life was a series of small surprises, like diving from the block into the lane, convinced your body's about to be shocked by cool water only to be immersed into sauna-like temperatures.

But those kinds of times are easy to rectify. Assess. Adapt. Move on.

This was one of those times. My brain whirred, recalibrating. I glanced back at the board, where I met Mr. Francis's eyes. He made a gentle motion with his head, as if to say *put your phone away*.

I dropped it into my bag, blood rushing to my ears. I glanced at December, bent over her notebook, hair in her eyes, pen flying across the page.

I folded my arms, satisfied. I couldn't believe that here in Human Studies, sitting right behind her back, I'd figured everything out.

December's mother hadn't been using drugs. Or selling them.

She'd been training for the FBI, trying to stop them.

CHAPTER FORTY

December

I WASN'T PREPARED for how magical homecoming would feel. Stepping through the threshold of the double-sized doors of Thames Barn, a gorgeous, seasonally rustic space on acres of conservation land, I took it all in: the arcing beams, the thousands of twinkling lights, trays of sugar cookies, and cups of room-temperature seltzer. The solid warmth of Nick's large hand wrapped around my small one. The selfies and pictures and the bouquet of out-of-season peonies from Nick. Evan had beamed about them before placing the fluffy flowers in a glass vase of Cam's.

My bones ached with the beauty of everything before me, but my belly was on fire with the anticipation of what was to come during the dance.

Stella Rose sidled up beside me, tugging my arm. "Pictures," she demanded, lacing her fingers with mine.

"More pictures?" I protested.

"Are there ever enough?"

We joined Carrie and Maisie against a backdrop emblazoned with the words *A Night to Remember*.

I smiled. One to remember indeed.

I settled at the end of the group, keeping one hand in Stella Rose's and the other on her shoulder. Carrie scooted against Maisie, sharing an adorable *is this good?* look that Maisie answered with a one-sided smile. We crowded together while Nick snapped our picture.

"Look at them." Stella Rose squeezed my hand and tipped her head toward Carrie and Maisie. "We're third and fourth wheels now, Jones." She turned to Nick and Maverick. "Guys, get in!"

"I'll take it for you," a voice offered. I stiffened, knowing whose it was.

"Thanks, Jake," Stella Rose said.

Jake took Nick's phone and waited while we rearranged ourselves. Stella Rose linked her arm through Maverick's. I melted against Nick's warm limbs, trying to still my staccato heart rate.

It was remarkable how handsome Jake was. His hair was this squid-ink black, and he had what I can only describe as a strong nose. Arresting blue eyes. This late in the fall, his face still carried a summer tan. On the scale of one to surface charm, I could see why girls entered his orbit. A lot of them wanted his touches—some might even welcome them. But others . . . I didn't know why they stayed.

That wasn't right. I know why they stayed. They didn't know how to leave. He was toxic, and his victims didn't have the antidote to his poison.

Jake lifted Nick's phone. "Say cheese," he said.

—

The night passed at light speed in trips to the open dance floor, in picture taking, in avoiding these massive taxidermy animals in the hallway out back. In jumping as one unified body so hard we shook the barn floor, in making song requests and in those moments

(This was why. This, from the beginning.)

where I could feel Nick pulling me closer. Tightening his arms around my waist. Smiling his lips into that half-moon curve just for me.

During the evening's obligatory last slow song, I took a deep breath, ready to break with the gumballs of time. At our table, I popped open my clutch to ensure my phone was on. Step one in starting the plan I'd hatched. A plan that was so opposite to what the universe dictated that I was possibly bound for a lifetime of cosmic detention.

Already, like the universe knew what I was up to, it became more difficult to move. My brain felt dizzy, dehydrated; my insides clanged with the urge to turn off my phone. Turn this whole thing off.

Instead, I shut my bag and found my way back to Nick, where I looped my hands around his neck. He was so tall that I hung on him like a human wreath. I rested my head—weighted with approximately a hundred thousand pounds of gumballs—on the wall of his chest, trying not to shake against the frantic beat of the universe's drum.

I shifted so I could look at his face. "Hey, remember how I changed my mind and offered to go with you to the newspaper office?"

His back tensed for a moment, then relaxed. "Yeah?"

"Offer still stands, you know."

Nick was quiet for a moment. "Thanks. I'm thinking about it." His ribs contracted with his breath.

I sighed. He carried the weight of an old ship destroyed by a torpedo. "Okay."

His suit had hung in the hallway off the kitchen for the last three days and had magically soaked up everything Irving. Lemon cleaner, oregano from pizza night, and . . . peppermint, from breath spray Sophie had sprayed on his suit.

I was so tired, so terrifically zapped, and if things went according to plan—*my* plan, the unforeseen one, this time, the way things were not supposed to go—it was only about to get worse.

"What time is it?" I asked, waiting for him to say 9:57. Dread beat through my temples.

He craned his neck to the giant clock hung above the entrance. "9:57."

It was time.

A chain reaction of lights joined the strings of twinkling bulbs over the dance floor. The room was pockmarked with glowing phones, held aloft by people dancing. Notifications shone through suit pockets and in hands. The room turned into the after version of a citywide power outage, phones twinkling on when the electricity came back.

"That's weird," Nick said, because it was noticeable even to those who didn't know what had happened. Which, of course, was everyone except me.

Because at this minute in time, every single person at the dance had been tagged in a series of Instagram comments beneath a prescheduled post.

A post by the handle @dontbeaDirk featured a video clip of one very recognizable blue-eyed, black-haired soccer all-star crowding a field hockey standout sophomore named Ava Prey, her face obscured, in the hallway earlier this same morning, skimming his hand on her hip.

And her shoving it away.

Instead of stepping back,

instead of apologizing

storm clouds crossed his face.

The words *I'm sorry* did not pass his lips.

Hence my clever caption: **when Prey owns her Predator**.

I braced myself against my lifeguard, taking the opportunity to slip into the rabbit hole of my brain as billions of changed gumballs rolled into place. My skull throbbed. The dance floor lost its shouts and chatter. Whispers and gaping mouths becoming the bass drum of the song playing. Somewhere in the room, Jake Dirks's arrogance flamed away like a smoking candlewick.

Nick and I stopped our slow movement. "What do you think is up?" he asked.

"No idea," I lied.

We broke apart and found our phones—mine in the small gold clutch I'd brought, Nick's in his pocket. He frowned when he saw the tag, then opened the notification.

I navigated to the web version of Instagram—not the app, which had my usual account. I selected the option to delete my account, then tapped CONFIRM.

The post vanished. After almost everyone had seen it. Those who wouldn't see it would hear about it, and I wouldn't get caught.

"Did you see?" Nick asked, showing me the screen. With his eyes off it, the screen refreshed, vanishing.

I nodded. "But—it's gone."

"What?" He glanced again. "This is so weird."

I did this for everyone here. So I could show people like Billy Dawson, whom I'd never talked to and never would talk to, who held doors for women as his mother had taught him but kept a rating log of how he thought girls' butts looked when they wore a skirt. One he passed around to his buddies.

For Jake's friends, yes, but for everyone else in the room. It would affect their futures, too. Shame him in front of people whose opinions mattered to him.

I did this for a girl I'd never meet. One who was at the movies with her friends six states over right now, brushing salted popcorn off her lap. One who had no idea that a person who was going to assault her had received his first dose of public shaming.

It wasn't enough to get him in trouble—hence the deletion. Any stray screenshots wouldn't show the video in its entirety. Getting in trouble would have made him angry.

I'd reasoned if there was something I could do to affect his Now, then maybe he'd learn how to think in the Later. Learn that consent was something we were all entitled to. Too many people thought it was fight or flight, and if they started a little something and it wasn't pushed away, then it was welcomed.

They ignored the third one. Fight. Flight. *Freeze.*

I waited, nerves in my gut, while the ocean of my knowledge shifted, ebbed, swirled. Righted itself. I worried it would settle in a more drastic way, the way it had when I'd saved Mr. Francis, leading to a huge change.

Falling in love.

Nick dying.

Or even the real first time, when I'd done some unknown thing to make my mom leave.

But other than a handful of scattered changes in Jake Dirks's path, nothing massive changed in my own. Nick and I, in love and happy, until, boom. His death.

Yet something else clicked into place. A thought. A piece of knowledge. A fact. A villain that shook up all my atoms and spit them out.

It was in front of me this entire time.

See, there was a difference between having knowledge and under-standing it. And for the first time,

(please not the last, please not the last)

I understood it.

My head pulsed. I dropped my phone.

"Easy," Nick said, laughing. He picked up the phone and handed it to me before taking in the expression on my face. "Whoa. Are you okay?"

I took the phone. "I need to see Cam."

"Is—" He paled. "Is she . . . ?"

I shook my head. "She's alive. I just need to go."

"I'll drive you. I wasn't going to talk to you about it tonight, but I have something I need to tell you, anyway."

"No. I—I gotta go." I stumbled back, unable to look at him. Unable to face him with the truth that had been in the palm of my hand for our entire story.

I ran.

CHAPTER FORTY-ONE

Nick

11:48 PM

Me: I don't feel right about you leaving

11:53 PM

Me: . . .
Me: Did I do something?

11:57 PM

Me: It can't be visiting hours at the nursing home
right now
Me: Please tell me if you're okay
Me: And it's okay if you're not okay
Me: Just tell me if you're safe

—

Stella Rose's basement. Same movie, different day. Gone was the end-of-summer red-and-white school spiritedness of the back-to-school party. Gone was the girl in the white dress, dancing with her new friends, kissing me at the bottom of the driveway.

In her place was a strong feeling of unsettlement.

It was not how I'd imagined the after-party of the evening. I'd thought December and I would leave Stella Rose's later on tonight, and I'd be able to kiss her beneath that same streetlight, and we'd have a small *remember when* moment, because we were falling into the rhythm and cadence of a couple who had remember-whens.

My fists clenched. I attempted to loosen my fingers. I sat on the edge of the pool table tucked in the corner, a nearly full red plastic cup of beer balanced between my legs. My phone was faceup on the pool table's ledge. The screen dark.

"Nicky!" Stella Rose weaved through the throng of people sporting loosened ties and oversized blazers over formal dresses and pants.

"Huh?" I asked, my voice too loud. I stretched my lips into what I hoped was a smile. "Since when do you call me Nicky?"

"Since right now, I guess." She held up her cup for a silent *cheers*.

I raised mine to hers, tapping it with the lightest of clinks.

"Where's our girl?" Stella Rose asked.

I glanced down. Dark screen. "I'm not sure."

She nudged her hip in the direction of Carrie and Maisie, who were standing in the corner, not physically touching but totally enthralled with each other. "I think you two have been usurped as Woodland High's most adorable new couple. You'd think one of them was the new girl at school."

"Fine by me."

"You know something? Last year, I don't think I would've put myself out there and tried to be friends with December. I had my friends, and life has always felt so narrow here, you know?" Stella Rose waved her hand and made a *can you believe it?* expression. "But I'm trying to be different. Our whole lives are about to open next year. Meeting new people and all that." She shrugged. "My parents are splitting up. Ever since they told me, things feel different now. Kinda . . . less and more important, if that makes sense."

"I hear you." I cast my eyes around the basement, lined with pictures. One of her dad with the mayor, another of her mom proudly leading a horse around a stable. I refocused on Stella Rose. "And that sucks. I'm sorry to hear it."

Her mouth twisted. "Thanks. I don't even know why I'm talking about that now. They've been together since high school, and I sort of used to think that's how it would be for me, too." She laughed. "Y'know, I bet if all this happened last year, I would've gone for you. Especially with the whole rescue thing."

I frowned. "What do you mean?"

"For the record, this is not me flirting. This is me being straight-up honest." She waved her hand. "Heroism is, I don't know. Attractive. Intriguing. That's all."

I covered my frown with a sip of beer. The sear of bubbles popped against my throat. I gripped the edges of the table. Beneath my fingertips, the wood was as smooth as the surface of a frozen lake. I exhaled. "What if I told you I didn't do it?"

She raised her eyebrows. "Didn't do what?"

"I didn't save Mr. Francis." The admission was my own red rescue tube, floating me safely away from letters from the mayor. I clung on to the relief it brought as if it would save me, giddy with its release. Holy shit. Wow.

I felt good, until I took in my dark phone screen.

"What on earth are you talking about?"

I met her eyes. "December is the one who saved Mr. Francis. She did CPR on him. It's how we met."

"No kidding?" A new song came on, louder than the one before. Stella Rose leaned closer. "Why didn't you say so?"

I'm an ass. That's why. "I should have!" I shouted, grinning. I held up my phone. "I'm gonna go find her," I said.

"You don't know where she *is*?" Stella Rose stepped back. "Maybe you should call her uncle?"

I opened my mouth to reply, but my phone lit up. A text.

12:09 AM

December: I'm safe. I'll see you tomorrow.

CHAPTER FORTY-TWO
December

HERE WAS WHAT I realized during homecoming, when the world fell apart in my head and Jake Dirks's did in real time:

The vision of Nick's death was a future event, yes. A gumball the brackish color of decayed leaves.

But it was *my* gumball. It was not the detached rewind and fast-forward of my other foreknowledge. It was witnessed through the binocular lens of my own two eyes.

And the fact that it was *mine* could only mean one thing. I had to choose.

Fulfilling my own selfish destiny—maybe, according to my current view of future history, my only chance of ever feeling this kind of love. My only chance to be dizzy happy, strung together by joy shaped like charms on a bracelet.

My own fulfilled happiness, or Nick's life.

Because maybe if I wasn't there to spectate his death, it wouldn't happen. And when you put it that way, how was it even a choice?

Love or loss.

Life or death.

It was no question.

I had to leave him to save him.

—

Of course, the next time I saw him, he was doing something selfless.

It was the day after homecoming. Nick's face was flushed and sweaty, his hair sticking to his neck in damp curls. He raked the leaves that had fallen overnight into baggable piles, small blips on a lawn's radar. I watched him for a moment, the leaves rustling against the grass so emerald dazzling and rich in hue it almost hurt.

"What are you doing?" I asked.

No answer. I waited for him to notice me—he had earbuds in. *Mystery Buff.* I fidgeted with the button on top of my plaid flannel. The October sun was warm, borderline hot, but the air was cool. Perfect New England fall day.

Great day for a breakup.

He turned, took in the fact that I was there, and met me with a smile. He pulled a bud from his ear. "Hey!" Nick set the rake down perpendicular to the sidewalk and came over to greet me with a kiss.

"Hey," I echoed, letting myself receive the smallest of kisses. ChapStick and coffee. Because why not? It was the last one I'd ever get. "Why are you raking leaves?" I heard the warble in my voice. He didn't seem to.

It was my uncle's job to rake leaves. He was doing something nice for my friggin' family even though I was going to break his friggin' heart because it meant I would leave him with his friggin' life intact.

But all he said was: "Just something to do."

I pushed my sunglasses back up my nose. I'd worn my oversized ones. "Do you have a few minutes to talk?"

"That doesn't sound good." But the loopy, ridiculous smile stayed on his face.

I said nothing. Bristled against his tone. Light. Teasing.

He shaded his eyes. "Wait, are you serious? What's got you so down?"

"I don't think I can do this anymore."

Nick's smile dissolved. "You can't do *what* anymore?"

I wasn't prepared. Massively unprepared, in fact, for how much his eyes welling with tears would slay me. "This. Us."

"What are you saying, December?" he whispered.

What I was saying was a lie. I stared at him, thinking of the coconut sunscreen he wore at work, sweet summer ice-cream cones and homecoming shopping and watching a movie with a shared blanket.

I thought of what it means to be a partner. One of two. Fifty percent stakeholder. I considered his hair, his eyes, the line of his neck and the broad paint strokes of his shoulders. His clean arc through a pool's lane, arms rippling with his fumbling backstroke start. Someone who asked about your days and your goals and your dreams and listened to the answers.

I'd spent a lifetime thinking about the holes in my life—Cam, my mother, maybe even my father. Plus this unwanted gift. How different I was.

And that brought me back to the start. *Our* start. If I was right, then he wouldn't die if he wasn't with me. After all, my presence in his life is what changed the trajectory of his.

I squared my shoulders. "I'm saying we need to break up."

"I was able to get that," he said slowly. "But can you help me understand why?"

"My feelings changed," I lied. "I think . . ." I trailed off, bracing myself for the slam of the Irvings' door.

"Hey, December!" Nick's dad tossed a roll of yard waste bags onto the grass. "Want to join us for the game? I'm making grilled pizzas."

Nick's eyes closed for the briefest of beats. His face contorted, and he set his jaw, trying to control it. "She can't," he muttered.

I cleared my throat. "Thanks, Mr. Irving. Maybe another time."

Nick's dad took a step backward. "O . . . kay," he said. "I'll be in the house if you guys need anything."

We waited in agonized silence until the door closed again.

"So why?" Nick swiped the back of his hand across his eyes. "Help me understand, Dec."

"The newness has worn off," I lied.

"I need to concentrate on me," I lied.

"I don't want to hurt you, so being with you isn't fair." Two lies and a truth.

"None of this tells me why." His voice was small but thick.

My heart broke in half, a melon dropped on a grocery floor. "I thought about our beginning, and I wasn't fair to you." I reached beneath my sunglasses and pressed the corners of my eyes. "I'll tell everyone the truth about what happened with Mr. Francis."

"I told you, that's not . . ." He sucked in a breath. My Nick. "I already told Stella Rose, anyway."

I know.

"All that doesn't matter like it used to. Plus, I found out—"

I held up my hand and stepped back once, twice, three times. "Please think about if you want me to do anything about all the Mr. Francis stuff. I'll see you around, okay?"

Nick swallowed and said nothing. His nod was curt, sharp.

I turned and cut through the unit behind Nick's, keeping my neck long and shoulders pressed back, walking with all the confidence in the world I did not feel.

When I rounded the corner, I slumped against a decorative rock wall, waiting for my one good thing.

Waiting for the gumball ocean shift.

Waiting for the world to adjust, for Nick's path to change.

But the change never came.

CHAPTER FORTY-THREE

Nick

SUNDAY

A day in bed. Comforter drawn up to my chin, sheets wrapped around my feet. Music on, then off. Dimness. Quiet. Phone left for dead.

—

MONDAY

I told Mom I was sick.

I know she didn't believe me, but she let me stay home anyway, which gave me all the time in the day to ruminate over what had happened. I dwelled in a horizontal cave of existential bummed-outness, wondering why December had cut things off with us. What I'd done. Wondering what to do with what I'd figured out about her mom.

The afternoon light streamed around the edges of the defunct blackout shades. I shut my eyes, wishing away everything I knew about December's mom, imagining it shrinking into an avocado pit in my gut, left to be cast aside into someone's trash.

—

I'd met December three months ago. I'd only dated her for two. I repeated the same mantra the entire school day: I shouldn't be as upset as I was.

All that hard-core resolve melted when I got back to school, though.

"You look like shit, man," Maverick said. He shifted his weight, hiking his backpack higher on his shoulder.

I glanced at him from my perch on the swim-annex locker room bench. The nylon of my bathing suit was extra crinkly, having been balled in my swim locker unused for the last couple of days. The swim season was three weeks away. I'd been so busy, either with December or looking for her mother, I'd barely been in the pool. My team was lucky I wasn't captain.

I hooked goggles around my neck. "Ouch. Don't you know everything about the brain? Isn't there some magical way for you to make me feel better, instead of piling it on?"

"The same parts of your brain that interpret physical pain also experience emotional pain." Maverick sighed. "Both are important. The magical way to get over a breakup is to process all your shit and work it out. Not to pretend it didn't happen."

"I'm not pretending it didn't happen."

"You walked the hallways today like an extra on *ZombiePocalypse 2052*."

"What's *ZombiePocalypse 2052*?"

"The screenplay I'm working on."

My laugh was hollow. I gathered my swim cap in my hands and squeezed.

"Besides," Maverick continued, "sometimes breakups are the best things to ever happen to us. Look at me and Holly."

"You were upset about Holly."

"I was. But then I got over it." He hesitated. "You and December . . . you were real. I don't want to take that away from you. But you won't always feel this way."

The door leading out to the pool opened, a waft of hot, damp air bringing in two sophomore swimmers. I stood up. "I'm gonna go work out."

"Great endorphin boost," Maverick said. "Work that mental health."

I weakly pumped my fist in the air.

"But remember. People change. Look at me. I went from handsome genius who chews nicotine gum to handsome genius who chews whitening gum." He wiggled his jaw. "Minty fresh."

—

I swam a record time for my personal worst. Being in these long, rectangular lanes of water was strange: like hearing a cover of a song you heard long ago, your brain chasing the notes that line up in front of you. Recognizable but different.

I'd been here before. A totally different person. Nick Irving, non-cheater, non-lifeguard, non-boyfriend, non-hero.

Reach. Stroke. Breathe. Repeat.

The air was as warm as a bath, but my body was so rusty. I hit my peak activity level, my blood pumping and my body sweating—much harder to recognize underwater, by the way, but still there, salty and metallic and unmistakable. I slowed to a breaststroke, thinking.

I didn't understand why December had ended things, and I had no idea how to find out why, short of leaving notes in her locker and pining for her while listening to angry music at night.

I blew bubbles into the water. Nope. Not gonna happen. I one hundred percent refused to bug her for my own sense of closure.

—

TUESDAY NIGHT

8:44 PM

Me: Hey, sorry to bother you, but
Me: Can we meet up?

9:43 PM

December: Sure. When?
Me: Now. If you can. I know it's late.

9:50 PM

December: What's this about?
Me: I want to talk a few things through with you. No pressure, it can wait
December: I'm good now—where?
Me: I can borrow my dad's car. Pick you up?
December: Sounds good

CHAPTER FORTY-FOUR

December

EVERY MINUTE OF every day since I broke up with Nick, I'd checked in with the world to see if it had changed. I was so sure that removing myself from his life would ultimately save him that when the plan didn't immediately work, I was surprised.

Maybe now, if I haven't talked to him in twelve hours and the universe thinks our breakup is real.

Maybe now, at twenty-four.

Now? Forty-eight.

Not that I kept track.

I didn't understand what was happening. Our breakup was free will. Not foretold. It was one that would change the course of destiny for someone I loved.

But it didn't work.

Instead, I'd wallowed in Nick's agony, bound together by some invisible tethered rope of emotion, and I still had no idea why. If anything, it had intensified. His despair cloaked my insides, sadness and confusion mirroring themselves in my gut. It was pretty freaking unfair that my gift made my breakup pain a double load.

For the first time in my life, I was the one walking away from someone I loved. I couldn't help but wonder if any of these things I was feeling—sadness, loss, despair, the uncertainty of being right or wrong—were any of the same things my mother carried so many years before, when she left me with my uncle.

—

I slid into Nick's car, my face scrubbed clean of makeup and a thermos of tea clutched in my hands. At the sight of him, my lips twitched. "Hey."

He gave me a smile with half of his mouth. "Hey, Jones."

The night was brisk. Sweatshirt weather. I nestled against the cool leather, silent and waiting. Heat blasting, we drove with the windows down, music playing too loud to talk. I fisted my hands in my lap, warning them not to reach for his. I'd given that up.

After a few minutes, Nick coasted along Main Street, cutting the engine in front of town hall. "Want to go for a walk?" Nick asked, pointing. "Maverick and I used to sit on the ledges for the holiday tree lighting every year. It's a cool spot."

The building was grand and impressive, standing over the center of Main Street with gorgeous large archways. "Sure."

We breathed in the silence of six flights of stairs, our feet making trudging *pat-pat* sounds on each step. Nick had an old beach towel hooked over his arm that he would soon spread over the cold marble of the building to keep our butts warm.

See? This guy thought of everything.

We arranged ourselves in the southernmost archway, our backs braced against opposing walls. The beach towel was a thin shield between comfort and discomfort.

Nick hitched himself straighter. Looked me square in the face. "I miss you."

"I miss you." My mouth was a traitor.

"So why not . . . why not see what happens?"

In front of us, the town was silent and still, streetlights lighting the way for stray cars. I picked at the beach towel, trying to remember what it might have been like to reveal the threads of myself to my family once upon a time, and now vowing to peel myself apart and lay my insides on a broken platter and hand it to the boy I loved, because nothing I had done had changed his future.

"The *Lusitania*," I blurted before my courage steamrolled itself. The name of that sunken ship fell between us, clanking into the darkness of the night. The words were a dare. A risk.

Nick's face transformed, his eyes hardening in their sockets. "How—" he managed to choke out. "How could you know about that?" He raked a hand through his hair. Color bloomed on his cheeks, right below where those football-player-sunburn-streaks were so long ago. His fingers folded together, splayed apart. "Almost no one knows. Who told you?"

"No one told me."

"What do you mean no one told you?"

I bit my lip and released it. "Do you trust me?"

His gaze was wary. He answered how I knew he would, but the pause before it still hurt. "I do."

"The way I think . . . it's not exactly the standard." I traced my fingertips along my chin. "It—I—" I cut myself off. Deep breath, December. "Everything that you've felt so far . . . it's real. And everything I've felt so far is also real."

He stared at me, silent.

"But here's the thing." Inhale, exhale. "I knew all this was going to happen."

"I don't understand. You planned this breakup?"

I shook my head. "From the moment right after I saved Mr. Francis,

I knew *we* were going to happen. You and me. I know *everything* that's going to happen."

His eyebrows found a new home under the brim of his hat. "You what, now?"

I don't know what I thought would happen when I told Nick about my gift. Whoever granted it to me to fall out of the clouds and slap my wrist? The air between us to electrify? My heart was a smashing cymbal; my ability to breathe a ghost. An avalanche of an explanation fell from my mouth marked with key words like *foreknowledge* and *precognition.*

"Come on," Nick said when I finished.

I stared at him, waiting.

"You've always been intense, December, but this is a weird one." The streetlamp lit his disbelief in profile. "This is like a Marvel movie plotline. You're joking, right?"

(But there was more.)

Door door door

(I'm trying to save you.)

(I don't want you to die.)

He stared straight ahead.

"I'm not." I took a moment to climb, my eyes flitting closed, open. "Do you subscribe to Breaking News? You do. Check your phone. There's about to be a robbery at the twenty-four-hour Citizens Bank right off the highway."

He unlocked the screen, but his eyes were still skeptical.

Until the Breaking News icon flashed. His eyes widened, but he said nothing.

"The next car that will drive by? Red. The one after that? Pickup. Dusty black."

We waited a beat, two, three. Then: Zip. Zoom.

His expression morphed into something else. Fright. "What is happening right now?" he whispered.

"Nothing has changed," I said. "I'm me. This is how it's always been, but you haven't known. Almost no one has."

"Tell me."

I did, watching his face darken, fold into itself, as I told him things defied explanation all the time, and I was one of them. His eyebrows betrayed what he must have felt, furrowing and leaping up to his hair-line, wondering if this was the truth. Wondering how it could be.

CHAPTER FORTY-FIVE

Nick

IT WAS FUNNY: I was able to comprehend every word December said, but together they made no sense. Her explanation defied the logic and order of my world. I swallowed a nervous laugh, jiggling my knee up and down.

It was as if she had pointed to the sky and said, *What a great boat*, or suddenly levitated. I ran my hands through the curls poking out from beneath my hat, struggling to reconcile the two images I had. Logic and order versus a magnum-sized rule break.

"So you're what, then?" I asked when she finished. "Some kind of psychic?" I paused, thinking of Maverick's scientific breakdown of the brain, wondering if I'd fallen and hit my head. "Are you *sure* this conversation is real?"

Her gaze was unyielding. "I'm me. A person. Just someone who happens to know past and future events."

"Okay. Let's pretend this is true for one second." A light breeze blew over us.

"It *is* true." She tightened her hoodie.

"I can't believe this," I said. "I mean I actually can't believe this. How can it be real?"

"I don't know," December said miserably. "I've never had to

cold-explain this to anyone before. My family figured it out over a long time."

"Try again."

So she did. I listened, warring with my internal skeptic's thermometer, while she listed three more car colors that would drive by right before they did. She pointed to a streetlamp and said it was about to go out. When the light faded, my stomach contracted. She closed her eyes and rattled off world events—an earthquake in Japan, a strange power outage in New York City, both immediately confirmed again by my Breaking News app. She said she could tell me the way the latest season of *Mystery Buff* ends, even though only three episodes have been released so far.

"This is out of control," I said. "I feel weird. Like I'm not in my own head."

Her laugh was bitter. "Tell me about it."

"So you knew everything about us before we'd even met?"

She hesitated. "I knew you'd have trouble saving Mr. Francis—but all I knew was that I'd be there to see it happen."

"Did you know that I'd flake out?"

"I did . . . ," she hedged.

"What?"

"I didn't know how I would *feel* in that moment." She blew out a breath. "You know those marionette puppets? I felt like someone handed me a bunch of strings, but instead of yanking one and making someone jerk their leg, sitting there and doing nothing meant I tossed them aside. I felt helpless. I didn't like it." December paused. "So when that was happening, I acted against what I knew. I had no idea that action would bind us together and change everything. I saved him, but you were supposed to."

"Me? But I couldn't move."

"You were going to, but he wasn't going to be saved entirely. He'd live but never fully recover." She adjusted a bobby pin in her hair. "That was going to destroy you, Nick. Because of the way you doubt yourself." Her voice grew stubborn, insistent. "You shouldn't, you know. I love the way you see the world."

My chest slipped into itself, uncertainty worming through my rib cage. I gave it a mental shove. "Let me get this straight. You were able to butterfly-effect the future?"

"I usually can't," she whispered. "But I was able to then. And it changed everything that came next." She paused. "That kind of became a pattern."

"Oh." The lights of a passing car illuminated her face, turning it a yellow-orange. "*Oh*. You knew we'd fall in love."

"Fall in love," she repeated. She covered her mouth with her hand, then pulled it away, a small smile tugging at the corners of her lips.

"Yeah. Is that okay to say I fell in love with you?" My voice was hoarse.

She tilted her head. "It is. I fell in love with you, too, you know. I did." She gathered the beach towel into her palms and clenched. "We were never going to, until I changed everything."

I leaned against the ledge. "How could any of this be valid?"

"It is. To both of us." She touched my forearm. I wished that I could bottle the warmth my entire arm felt when our skin met. "You have to believe me."

"But basically, what you're telling me is we would have never been an us."

"Yeah."

"So you didn't fall in love with me for me. You basically did what you were told."

"I learned we *would* fall in love. And then I felt it happen, bit by bit, day by day, until nothing had ever felt as good as being around you." She shook her head. "That's the difference."

I exhaled, staring in the direction of the unlit streetlamp. "If you can see everything, then why did you have me try to find your mom?"

She sat up straight, using her hands to describe a strange rule about this so-called gift: her mother being a blank spot.

"She's total static?"

"Yep."

"This whole time?"

"Yup. Since she left."

That meant she had no idea what I'd figured out. I swallowed. She wasn't the only person hiding something. "December—"

"I wanted, more than anything, to experience us," she interrupted softly. "To feel real joy. Excitement. Live life in ways I had never lived it before." December dragged her knuckles over her temples and frowned. "Ow. Whatever this gift is, I don't understand its malfunction. But no matter what, I always knew you'd never find her."

"You *what*?" The back of my neck prickled with unease.

"I was desperate to keep you around me. Letting you search was—" She shook her head. "I was selfish. Right in front of me, for the first time in my life, there was love." She paused. "And before I even knew what was happening, I found myself craving it. *You*. The chance to have that glow that spreads from your brain to your chest and wiggles in your stomach when a person inhabits the same space as you. *I wanted that, Nick.*"

"You put yourself in physical pain for *me*?" I shook my head. "I don't like that. You shouldn't have done that."

She shook her head. "You have to promise me something."

"Me?"

"The shirt you wore to Pire's Dairy Bar. The one that's the color of one of their Creamsicles. Don't wear it anymore."

Everything I'd ever known felt upside down, but I couldn't take my eyes off her. Her face was, in my estimation, perfect. Skin smooth, so alive and probably scientifically one hundred percent symmetrical, which Mr. Francis claimed was a supposed biochemical indicator of beauty in nature. And if I hadn't been staring so intently, I might've missed it: her eyes darting up and to the left, a twitch of her eyebrows. She was hiding something.

"Why?" I pressed my tongue against the roof of my mouth, hard, to focus, as my thoughts ran like a freight train.

"Just promise me."

I took a deep breath, calculating. "Fine. If you promise me something in return."

It was her turn to frown. She blinked, long and slow and sleepy and frustrating and gorgeous.

"Promise you won't hate me when I tell you that I never stopped looking. I know what happened to your mother."

CHAPTER FORTY-SIX

December

DREAD SWELLED IN my lungs. *No.*

That wasn't what happened. This was not what I had seen.

Pain drummed in my temples, rising to a pitch I'd never felt before. It felt like something more than pain. It felt like a warning.

I pictured my mother, tilting her head back in laughter, the black-and-white hat falling to the soft sand of a beach. I remembered every room I'd called my bedroom since she left, the nights I spent staring at the ceiling and trying to imagine what I could have done to make her leave. Image after image of myself, alone and young and then alone and growing up, without my mother but with her memory. Sadness exploded someplace behind my eyes, moving through my body in a languid ocean wave. "What are you talking about?" I croaked.

He jumped from the ledge and held out his hand. "C'mon. It's getting late, and this is long. I'll tell you on the way back to Bright Acres."

In the car, he detailed his search, filling my Blank Spot in with all the moments I'd missed. My heart fluttered. She was out there somewhere. Was she out there somewhere?

"And then I figured it out. I searched all the acronyms together instead of one by one. And everything sort of clicked into the FBI Physical Fitness Test." He paused. "Your mom joined the FBI,

December. Or at least, it's clear from her journal that she was training for the test."

The instant he said it, I knew it was true. In my mouth, the tea held a medicinal tang; in my head, my brain's door rattled. Things were shifting in ways they never had before, changing rapidly, gaining speed and trajectory that made me feel wild and out of control. I pressed my fingers to my temples, thinking of all the times everything had gone hazy.

When I was shopping with my friends and he was lounging with Maverick. That feeling of disquiet that had nudged me deep in my core, one I'd ultimately shoved aside.

The colored pencils and the biology assignment.

I'd known he was hiding *something*, but every time I checked in on—okay, *snooped* on him—I had figured he was listening to a podcast or watching a documentary, not trying to surprise his girlfriend with her missing mother. "When did you put all this together?"

He drummed his fingers on the steering wheel. "Actually, it was in Human Studies class."

Of course. A loophole. I was *right there*. Which meant I'd never dip into his life to find out what he was doing. "I was in the room." I hadn't climbed for this, hadn't gone looking for this missing gumball. I'd sat there, chewing on a gumball of my own.

He nodded. "And then I read more about it, and it makes sense that she'd leave if she thought her line of work was too dangerous." He cleared his throat. "Maybe she imagined leaving would protect you."

Grief—a beast I'd tried to tame my entire life—reared inside me, raging with the sort of heavy despair reserved for those with profound loss. I fisted my hand and pressed it to my heart, blinking away tears. Even if Nick was right, and she'd left for the FBI—presumably, fearing her family was at risk—she was still a thief, but in a different coat. The crime? Abandoning me.

Nick parked in the condo parking near the pool, dark and silent and empty. "I'm sorry she left you," he said quietly.

"Me too." I leaned my skull into the headrest, staring at the diamonds of the pool fence. "Do you know where she is now?"

He shook his head. "I wanted to fill you in first. She's not internet-searchable, but you might be able to talk to a government office or something."

My brain was a sticky collage of images and events, and I wasn't sure what was memory and what was the future. The dull ache that had been vibrating in my temples ever since Nick told me about my mother wrapped to the base of my skull. Desperate to feel something tangible, something solid, I ran my fingertip along the steel of my thermos, pressing until my skin glowed white in the dark, wondering how I could get out of this mess.

Because no matter what I do,

you

keep

dying.

Blood pounded in my ears, dropping a curl of nausea into my stomach. "Hey, Nick? I don't feel so good. I'm so, so tired. Do you mind dropping me off?"

"No problem." He shifted into drive and steered up my lane, parallel to his family's.

My throat was dry, my mouth devoid of moisture. I worked to part my lips. "We can talk more tomorrow, 'kay?" I worked to unbuckle my seat belt, the button seeming miles deep. It was only at that point that I began to worry.

"Sure. Are you okay?"

No. "Yes."

"December? Wait."

I turned around, barely able to see through the spikes of fear contentedly driving themselves into my skull.

"For whatever it's worth, if it counts for anything at all . . . I do still want to be with you. You don't have to say anything, but I want you to know that."

My vision doubled, blurred, righted itself into one singular look: Nick's face. Troubled, sad, handsome.

I gave him a tight nod—all I could manage to do—and somehow made it to my bed before I blacked out.

I was not asleep. I was not unconscious. I could see, though there was something like a darkened screen over my eyes. I trembled, soaking my sheets with a cold, clammy sweat, a lamb balancing on the edge of a cliff. One motherless move away from a freefall. Throughout the night, I lay in bed, cycling through the events of my life in Woodland.

My everything.

(Saving Mr. Francis.

The article, and Nick in the dugout,

Cam and Cam and Cam.

Ice cream and a sliced arm, the hospital, and Sim. Evan. Sim + Evan.

Driveway kisses and movies,

pirouettes with Sophie,

school and the sudden rush of Nick at the grocery store,

confessing to his dad. And through this,

through *all of this*,

me. My brain. My foreknowledge.

Getting in the way too much

and not enough at all.)

As the dawn light filtered in through Uncle Evan's immaculately washed windows, I tried to figure out what was amiss. Why it seemed as though my brain was trying to plug its imaginary electrical cord into a bowl of pudding. I could not make sense of this—could not make sense of any of it.

Flashes of memories lay before me, but they were . . . paler, almost?

I rubbed my temples. Gasped.

When I was a kid, I'd had this recurring dream where I ran up a wooden spiral staircase, and after I left the step behind me, it fell away. Gone. If I paused, the stairs paused. If I sped up, so did the stairs. They were never-ending, heading up to the sky, raining away like lost piano keys.

It was what was happening in my head now.

The knowledge of what had happened to my mom locked something inside me. Stole my gift, overturned the gumball jar, turning everything I used to be able to do into one giant, unending Blank Spot. As soon as Nick recounted the details, a switch flipped from on to off.

Everything I had that made me . . . me. Everything I'd struggled with my whole entire life. All the joy and pain and love and hurt and

(all my gumballs)

gone.

Leaving me, a motherless daughter. Someone who knew why her mother had gone, but not why she had left me.

—

The world was a nightmare.

How did people do this?

I drove Evan's car to school, refusing to let the speedometer get above twenty-five the entire trip. Hyperaware of the sound of the rubber tires against the dirt and gravel. My past perception of future events was like a wisp of smoke—I could smell that there had been a fire burning, but it had been snuffed out. I no longer had the insurance policy of knowing my own future, especially since I didn't know if the world had changed or shifted due to anything I'd said or done. I had no idea if I'd crash the car, hit a deer, run out of gas, nothing.

Was this how people actually lived?

I steered beyond the entrance to the school, parking in a far corner of the lot where the white lines were painted extra wide. The day was overcast. Leaves had spilled from their perches overnight. I pulled my jacket tighter, watching out of the corners of my eyes for people or cars or UFOs or something, because *what the hell was going on?*

I'd spent so much time caught up with wishing I didn't know everything that I didn't truly consider the side effect: *not* knowing everything.

People were a lot braver than I'd ever given them credit for.

"Hey, you okay?"

I whipped my head at the voice. "Oh. Yeah."

Jake Dirks, asking if I'm okay. Irony was alive.

His face was the picture of concern. "You sure?"

"I'm fine. Do you happen to know where Nick is?"

"Which one? Dostoomian? Farley? Irving?"

"Irving."

He dimpled. "Haven't seen him."

"Thanks anyway," I muttered, nearing the entryway to the school. I fumbled for my phone, since I had no clue as to the whereabouts of anyone. Which was, to say the least, as unsettling as walking through this world like a newborn baby stuck in the body of a teenager.

CHAPTER FORTY-SEVEN

Nick

December: Hey, where are you?
Me: Don't you know already?

I grinned through my yawn. I'd spent the entire morning recounting the events of last night, poring over the predictions she made that came true, wondering if I'd dreamed it all.

Me: Kidding. My locker

Moments later, she rounded the corner. She clutched the straps of her backpack, maneuvering through the halls. A locker door slammed, and she startled. When she drew closer, she leaned against the locker next to mine and sighed.

"It's C Block today. We've got Human Studies first," I said. She rubbed her eyes, her expression troubled. "Hey. I'm sorry we stayed out so late last night."

Her squint brought her dark lashes closer together. "I must look terrible."

"What's wrong?" I looked around and lowered my voice. "I mean, besides everything happening between us. And your mom. Never mind. I guess I know what's wrong."

"It's more than that." She tucked an escaped lock of hair into her ponytail. "Obviously, you remember what I told you last night."

"Uh, yeah. Kind of hard to forget when your girlfr—when the girl you *like* who coincidentally just dumped you confesses her aptitude for something pretty remarkable and tells you she altered your future by saving your teacher's life."

"Point taken. But all of that . . ." She leaned closer. "It's gone," she whispered. "Everything is gone."

"Gone?"

"Everything I knew ahead of time? It's all"—she waved her hands—"slipped away. Ever since you finished telling me about my mom. It's like . . . that information left a gate open in my head and let all the animals out to pasture."

I pulled away, staring at her face. The logic and order of my world had been under siege since last night, but as I'd come around to the possibility that *maybe* she was telling the truth—that there was something miraculous about her—she was saying it was gone? "I'm going to ask you this just one time," I said slowly. "I promise I'm not trying to doubt you or anything. But are you sure you didn't, I don't know, *exaggerate*, or—"

"Nick." She slid her backpack from her shoulders.

"I'm sorry, but it seems incredibly hard to believe. You tell me one day you know everything that's ever happened, and the next that you don't."

She dropped her bag. "You wrote Maisie a love letter in fourth grade that you then ripped up and threw away because it only said that she was pretty and you realized you didn't *like* her like her. When your grandmother died, your grandfather gave you her favorite ornament. But you didn't hang it for Christmas. You kept it out year-round." Color rose in her cheeks. "You studied all night before your history test—*you know the one.*" I watched in disbelief as she did my study-prep moves: three fingers for the Triple Entente, a small, in-place leap for aerial dogfights, holding up her finger and outlining a square in the air. Sophie, Duchess of Hohenberg.

"*Okay,*" I said, stunned. "Okay. I believe you."

"Instead of saying *fair and square,* you said *flair and swear* until you were, what, five? You slept with your first swimming medal until the summer after middle school. Your mom makes you home-made Popsicles when you're sick."

I stayed silent, waiting for her to finish.

"And now all that is gone."

"Okay," I whispered again. "But you just told me all these things about my past. How are they gone?"

She blushed. "I mean. I may remember things from when I acci-dentally dug into the past a bit. The things I took the time to think about personally, not the things that drifted by."

She looked like she wanted to spiral into the floor, but a gentle hum of joy filled my chest. "You checked me out?" I shut my locker and leaned over to bump against her. Trying to be playful. Trying to say, *Hey, remember us?*

She picked up her bag, and we set off toward Mr. Francis's class. "Maybe."

"How does my mug shot look? How'd I do? Tell me more."

"I called it climbing." She walked my fingers upward in the "Itsy Bitsy Spider" hand motion. "It was like mental gymnastics to get to a specific event. I'd never met someone who I knew I'd begin hanging out with like this, so. Yeah."

"So you're saying I was a research project?"

"Think what you want." She nudged my arm. "I remember that stuff because it was about you. But I don't know anything coming anymore. I only know what I'd climbed to figure out before." Her face darkened. "It's gone."

The smile slipped from my face. "No one else knows what's coming next."

"I know. But for the first time ever, I honestly have no idea what I'm doing," she said, her voice soft. "I'm on the same playing field as everyone else now. Even with my—with whatever ability I had, gone—*I* can choose." Her face opened with it, this sensation of unknowing, this possibility of what could be.

"It's a fair game, then. I've never had a real girlfriend before, and ditto that to a breakup. I have no clue how to navigate this. Or even if *this* is a thing. You know. Us."

She pressed her lips together. "We're an us. Let's see how it goes, huh? And even if there isn't, there will always have been an us."

"I think I can do that."

Maverick sidled beside us, shaking the last of a bag of pretzels into his mouth. He raised his eyebrows at the sight of the two of us together but made no comment. "Can you believe we're getting a blizzard tomorrow?"

December slid into her seat and groaned. "I forgot."

"What are you talking about?" I asked, walking backward to get to my seat. "It's October."

Stella Rose slid into the seat beside December. "You have to come to my house tonight. Ever since third grade, we've done a pre-blizzard party the night before a snowstorm. It's tradition. Friends, gossip, nails, food, old-fashioned crap like that. Then, since Carrie was too scared to sleep over in third grade, it ends by going home to the comfort of your own bed, where you can wake up in blizzard bliss."

"Sounds perfect," December said.

Maverick leaned back in his chair. "I was watching this TED Talk last night. Did you know there are four hundred and twenty-one words in the Scottish thesaurus for the word *snow*?"

Stella Rose raised her eyebrows at him. "You know I love your brain, Mav, but you're not crashing our non-slumber slumber party."

———

Me: Something's bothering me

After school. It had taken me at least fifteen minutes to work up the nerve to send the text. It made me feel funny—like I was emotionally naked, or something. Vulnerable. I scratched my nose, paced my room, checked my phone. Three dots.

December: A girlfriend with a broken alternate reality brain not enough for you?
Me: No, that's not it. It's something you said about all that tho
December: I'm going to Stella Rose's soon, but I can stop by?
Me: No. I want you to tell me one thing
December: ⏰
Me: I'm thinking about how to phrase it

"Nick?" My mother strode into the living room, where I was sprawled out on the couch, my feet crossed at the ankles. I hadn't even turned the television on.

"What's up?"

"I was putting some laundry away in your room, and I found this."
She brandished Mara Jones's wishing well. "Where's it from?"

I flipped my phone over. "Why were you going through my stuff?"

"You call this going through your stuff?" Mom gave a low laugh.
"Honey, I'm a principal. If you think I don't have the skills to track
you from here to Hawaii at this point, you're out of your mind. But I
usually trust you." She arched a brow. "See where that got me during
finals week in May?"

A rush of air left my lungs. "Mom, I—"

She held up a hand. "I'm more curious about this." She wiggled
the figurine. The fake stones were silvery, the mossy green paint sur-
rounding it scuffed in spots to reveal the clay or ceramic beneath.

"It's December's mother's."

"The woman who's been gone for a decade?"

I nodded.

She propped her free hand on her hip. "Does this have anything to
do with that whiteboard in your room?"

"Um." I paused. "I've been helping December track down her mom."

My mother's eyes narrowed. "Come again?"

"December didn't know anything about where her mother went,"
I explained. "Her uncle and grandmother—before she went into the
nursing home, that is—were tight-lipped about it. She left a few days
after Christmas when December was seven."

Mom frowned. "And December gave you all her mother's stuff
because . . ."

Sure. Tell Mom I was not only a cheater but also a crappy, lying
lifeguard, when I was already banging the top of the Delilah Irving
Disappointment Scale. I wanted to tell her so badly. I really did.

But I squashed the lie deep into my bones and pressed my tongue
against my teeth. Hard. "Because I owed her a favor." Because asking

her to save Mr. Francis's life and then having her try to fix my mess with that rotten reporter was too much for one person.

"Mm-hmm." She ran her finger along the bottom of the wishing well. "I asked about this because I had one when I was a kid."

"You had a wishing well figurine?"

"Yeah, they were sold as a place for people to hide their keys."

I sat up. "What?"

She dug her fingernail into one of the tiny bricks. A sharp click filled the room, and the bottom popped off.

My mouth fell open. "I knew something was funky about the bottom. Can I have that?"

She handed it over. A square of paper, like a corner cut off from an index card, was wedged inside.

"See?" Mom sat on the edge of the couch.

I pried it out. In familiar handwriting were lines from a poem we'd read in English last year.

"E. E. Cummings," Mom said. "Famous poet. And poem."

"I know." I picked up my phone. "Why would she leave this in here?" I asked, snapping a picture.

Mom traced the worn fabric of the seat. "I would guess," she said slowly, "that whether or not December was meant to find this isn't the point. It's that her mom wanted her to have it, even if December didn't know it was there." Mom stood up. "Maybe you can pass the message along." She brushed her palms over her pant legs, clearing away imaginary lint. "And, Nick? Don't be hard on yourself if you can't find her mom, okay?"

I met her eyes. "I already did."

She crossed her arms. "You already are hard on yourself? Or you already found December's mother?"

"Both. But mostly the latter. Kind of."

Mom hit me with her signature Principal Look and waited for me to continue. When I didn't, she exhaled. "If anyone could do it, it's you."

"Why do people keep *saying* that?"

"Probably because it's true." Mom pressed her lips together and closed her eyes for a moment. She'd lightened her hair a shade or two last weekend, and it somehow made her look both older and younger. She opened her eyes. "What happened to her?"

"We aren't sure, but we think—*I* think, at least—that she's working as some kind of secret agent?" It sounded so absurd. Like something from a movie. But I was already two feet in the lake, so I plunged ahead. "She traveled all over the states on a path that's one of the major drug routes."

Mom's eyebrows arched higher.

"And she kept track of fitness training in her journal. Exact exercises that match up to the FBI training at Quantico."

She relaxed a fraction of an inch and studied my face. "If that's true, then she's probably led a difficult life."

"Yeah, but it still doesn't explain why she cut everyone out of it. People in the government have families."

Her face was troubled. "I can't imagine it."

Me: My shirt. The one you're calling the sherbet orange shirt. Why can't I wear it?
December: It's offensive to the eyes
Me: That's not it. My neon yellow sweatpants are offensive to my eyes, and I still wear them. Can you be real here?
December: Ok. Remember all my gumballs? And how saving Mr. Francis basically shook up my jar?

Me: Yeah

December: Well, when everything readjusted, I saw something bad happening to you while you wore that. So I was thinking for a while that you not wearing the shirt would mean the bad thing didn't happen

My nerve endings tingled. I ran my thumb over the ajar wishing well, pressing hard to increase its pressure on my skin, struck by my choice in this moment.

The *something* that was bothering me.

A while back, my mom's sister went through a hard time that could have gone a lot worse. She'd found a lump in her breast, and after several sleepless nights and the early morning biopsy, distracted from the deviation in routine and distraught from the possibilities, she'd forgotten her regular day-care drop-off. She had run into the grocery store and left my toddler cousin sleeping in the car by mistake. Thankfully, by some kind of divine intervention, she'd realized before she left the first aisle that she left her wallet in the car. On the entire ride and jaunt through the store, she'd been preoccupied with her own mortality; she was skating in the waiting period of a biopsy, thinking about her son growing up without a mother, without realizing that in that moment she could have become a mother without a son.

When she jogged to her car for her wallet, she was startled to find her son awake and screaming, his cheeks dark tomatoes. My mom and aunt had devised a charity that night to spread awareness about the perils of leaving kids in cars. Now, every time she drove with my cousin, she took off her left shoe and put it in the back seat, banking on the shoeless sensation to flag her memory.

But for the next week, my mom agonized over the fallout of

biology, because if her sister had breast cancer, that meant she could lose her. It also meant my mom could have the same genes. Could mean Sophie had them. Or me. It became something she couldn't stop thinking about, sitting with her through every second of the day. Until the lump came back benign, my mother worried. She would have to choose. Get tested for it? Or not? What if she had a mortality clock that was sped up faster than she'd planned?

I hadn't understood it at the time, but right now, I was in my own kind of uneasy waiting game. Something unknown sat in me, something I'd never had to think about before. I didn't know what it was, and I didn't like being left in the dark.

Me: What do you mean? What bad thing?
December: Well. That's the thing. I did some thinking during Mr. Francis's class, about the worldview project? And I kinda think . . . what if the whole goal of me having precognition was for something—the universe, or whatever, to lead me to you? And now that you've found my mom, it's like the "spell" . . . it's been broken. And so has the bad thing.
Me: . . .
December: ?
Me: How confident are you in this analysis?
December: <u>100</u>
Me: What project?
December: The essay for Mr. Francis's class
Me: What essay
December: The one on our worldview? Weltanschauung?
Me: Groan
December: Was that a verbal groan?

Me: It was. But I also found something I think you might want. I'll give it to you later, if I can pick you up from Stella Rose's?
December: Okay. I'll see you later
December: And, for once, I actually have no idea what this is
December: It's weird. I can't believe people live like this. How brave is it that people go through life without knowing what happens next?

—

I put down my phone, completely and wholly unsettled.

CHAPTER FORTY-EIGHT
December

STELLA ROSE'S DAD opened the door. "Come on in, girls," he said, his hands stuffed into the pockets of what were very much dad jeans. "Must be a blizzard coming!"

Maisie smiled. "You know it, Mr. Goldman."

"You must be December." He shook my hand, his eyes crinkling at the corners. "I've heard only good things." He gestured toward the basement door. "If the snow starts early, come shake me awake. I'll drive you home."

"It's not supposed to start until midday," Carrie said. "They canceled school because of bus routes or something."

"Well!" he said. "Well." He walked away, nodding, leaving the conversation unfinished. We looked at one another.

"Well," Maisie joked.

At the bottom of the stairs, we stopped. Every flat surface in Stella Rose's basement was covered in food. Pizza from two different places—one from "the good place" in town everyone liked, one from the place that serves gluten-free pizza to accommodate Maisie. A plate of those peanut butter cookies with a Hershey's Kiss stuck in a thumbprint depression. Toothpicks lined with a ball of mozzarella, a baby cherry tomato, and a sprig of basil. A Pyrex of rolled empanadas, "baked straight from the freezer with super-explicit directions" from Stella Rose's mom.

"Oh, and there are chocolate-covered strawberries in the fridge from my dad. No doubt ordered by his secretary." Stella Rose flopped over on the couch. "You know, the one he's banging."

Carrie's eyebrows drew together. "Isn't it just the four of us?"

Stella Rose cast one hand across the basement. "Welcome to the land of the trial-separation only child. My parents rented a loft above the café downtown. They're trying this thing where they switch off every two or three nights to 'minimize the disruption' to my 'life experience.'" She punctuated half of her phrasing with air quotes.

"That's miserable," Maisie said.

"Tell me about it. I can hardly wait for Hanukkah. Both of them want me on all eight nights. I'll probably wind up making like Molly Ringwald in that old movie and lighting sixteen candles by the end of it." She rolled her eyes. "I made the mistake of texting my mom at school about our pre-blizzard party because I thought it was her night. She freaked out and overcompensated."

Carrie reached for a slice of pizza. "Pizza three nights in a row for you," she said to Maisie.

Maisie laughed. "Good thing I love it."

Stella Rose frowned. "You should've told me. We could've done Thai or Greek or wings or—"

"I'd have pizza seven nights a week if I could. It's not a big deal. Besides, there's enough food here to last us until New Year's." Maisie took a bite, as if to prove her point. "Carrie and I went to Papa Gino's last night, and my mom and I got it the night before. That's all."

My stomach sank when Stella Rose crossed her arms. "Anyone want a napkin?" I asked.

Stella Rose stared at Maisie. "When I texted you last night, you said you weren't doing anything."

Maisie glanced at Carrie, then back at Stella Rose. "Right. I wasn't when you texted me . . ." She trailed off. Her words hung in the air.

"It's fine." Stella Rose pasted a smile on her face. "How about the gossip portion of the evening?"

"I'll go!" Carrie said, her voice much louder than usual. "I heard Jake Dirks is going wild trying to figure out who dontbeaDirk was. The teachers all know about it, but no one's looking into it because Jake hasn't reported it."

"Neither has Ava Prey," I pointed out.

"Well, I mean, why *would* he?" Stella Rose speared an empanada with her fork. "What's he going to do? 'Oh, hey, administration and all my past and present educators. I'm actually a jerk-off who thinks less of everyone but men. By the way, can you help me identify the badass who took me down in an excruciatingly public way?'"

I hid a smile. The plan had worked.

Stella Rose popped a bite of her empanada in her mouth. "Oh my God. December," she said, enunciating the first syllable of my name. Dee-cember. "I totally forgot about it, but after homecoming, Nick said *you* were the one who saved Mr. Francis."

I stared at my plate. Right. I was the sort of person who forgot now. "Yeah. I did."

"I'm sorry, what?" Maisie handed a salad skewer to Carrie. "How did this come about?"

I told them the whole half story, shading the part about Nick hesitating. Implying instead that I was closer to Mr. Francis when it happened, so it only made sense for me to go in after him. I shrugged. "I'd been exposed to a bunch of CPR training, too."

(I left out the exposure by gumball. Way back in 1740, a group of

Parisian scientists recommended mouth-to-mouth for drowning victims. Since then, countless progress has been made in the technical practice, but I'd climbed to eavesdrop on trainings in time to breathe life back into Mr. Francis.)

"But that *article*," Carrie said. "My parents cut it out and saved it because they tangentially know him."

"I know. Nick didn't lie, though—the journalist didn't get the details right and then filled in the rest." I shrugged. "Happens all the time."

"But Mr. Francis never mentions you." Carrie wiped her chin with a napkin.

"He was unconscious. Nick tried telling him what happened there." I bit my lip. "I think Mr. Francis likes the idea that he knew the student who saved him, maybe? I don't know."

"Why didn't the paper print a correction?" Maisie asked. "You see those online all the time. 'Updated with a correction,' or something."

My face flamed. "Because I sort of told Nick I wouldn't come clean about it?"

Silence. So silent, you could practically hear the clouds outside, blanketing space with dusky gray, bringing that cold, *it's going to snow* smell with it.

Stella Rose pointed her finger at me. "Spill, girl."

"I . . . I'm not proud of it," I hedged. "I didn't know anyone in town. And Nick was freaking out that he didn't save Mr. Francis in the first place. Plus that article. He started getting all this attention he wasn't ready for—"

"Remember how tense he was at the pool that day?" Stella Rose interrupted.

"I thought he was being all modest or whatever," Carrie said. "But shhh, Stella Rose. Let her finish."

"I hadn't met you guys yet. And I knew I'd be coming to school in September. For senior year. With no friends." I ripped my pizza crust in half and threw it back on the plate. I also wanted to experience love and save his life, but I didn't say that. "I didn't want the attention."

"There are worse things than secretly saving someone's life," Maisie said.

"Yeah," I said. "I guess there are."

Last summer, I would have been sitting alone in my room while my uncle went on a date, or maybe eating one of Evan's well-intentioned attempts at fine dining. Again. It was fine then, but now? Now, somehow even with knowing less, I could feel there was *more*. More connection. More beauty. More joy in the world, no longer reserved for everyone else that I saw when I climbed, but for me, too.

It was a good night.

One of the last good nights.

—

Later, Nick picked me up. He left the car in park when I got in. Instead of taking off, he handed me a tiny square of stiff paper.

"What's this?"

"I found it." He cleared his throat. "In your mother's wishing well."

My lips went numb. "Oh," I said softly. A message. Something she left for me? My breathing hitched, then started a fast drumbeat in the center of my chest. If I was about to find out what happened to her . . .

"I didn't want to keep it from you."

"Is it—Does she say why she left?"

His eyes widened. "Oh. Oh, sorry. No. It's just—" He shrugged. "You'll know it."

I tipped the letter toward the streetlamp to get better light and mouthed the words while I read.

(anywhere
i go you go,my dear,and whatever is done
by only me is your doing,my darling)

Lines from E. E. Cummings's "[i carry your heart with me(i carry it in)." A concrete, tangible sign, the first I'd ever had that leaving me was complicated for her, too. I brushed my thumb against the loops of her letters. "I recognize her handwriting from the journal. The way she makes her *y*'s."

I tucked it in my pocket, comforted by the barest of pressure it placed against my hip. "Let's go."

Everything was falling into place. Maybe leaving me was hard for her. Maybe this was where I was supposed to end up, after all this time.

CHAPTER FORTY-NINE

Nick

WE DROVE THROUGH town, coasting by the baseball fields where I'd had my existential crisis two days after not-saving Mr. Francis. The ice-cream shop. The hospital. Our high school.

Before I picked up December, I had gone to my room for a sweatshirt. Mom had left my favorite orange shirt folded on the end of my bed. I'd shoved it in my bottom drawer, but no matter how much I tried, the warning not to wear it volleyed in my head.

"I can't believe how much this place has become a home," December said. She tucked a stray strand of hair behind her ear. Her smile spilled across her face, and my stomach sank, because I knew. I had to push the doubt down. Let go of the shirt, let go of the warning. Enjoy the now.

I returned my eyes to the road. Reached over to her thigh, traced my fingers along the smooth black fabric of her jeans. "I'm glad."

She took my hand. "Is there anywhere we can go for a little bit? Pull over?"

—

We wound up in the parking lot of the Little League fields at the rear of the Bright Acres Complex, sprawled on the laid-down seats of my dad's Explorer.

Something about this moment—secluded in the dirt lot, huddled together in the leftover heat of the car—felt greater than all our other moments. We were more together, more desperate, more in love, more everything. I wanted to soak myself in the Now of all of this. Wrap in my fist the feeling of December curling up against me, her lips to mine, clench it to the axis of whatever made me tick. The night was inky, lit only by the moonlight curling through a passenger window, illuminating the liquid brown of December's eyes when they met my own, the fringe of her eyelashes stark against her skin.

She took my hand and brought it to the hem of her shirt. "Okay?" she whispered.

"Okay," I said.

She slid it under her shirt. "Do you want to stay here awhile?"

Forever.

My voice stampeded into my throat; my ears screamed. "If you want to, then I want to," I said, my voice cracking. Grateful I could hide my flushed cheeks in the dark. "If it's okay with you, that is."

"Yes," she said simply.

We settled together, warmth in a cold evening.

"Oh." She inhaled sharply. "Nick, look."

I followed her gaze to the windshield. The first snowflakes flecked the glass, stars against the black night.

"Wow." I nudged her. "Hey."

"Hey," she echoed.

My heart pounded so loudly I felt it in my ears. "I love you."

"I love you," she whispered back.

CHAPTER FIFTY
December

"DECEMBER." POUNDING ON my bedroom door.

I cracked open tired eyes. Stretching, I cleared slumber from my throat. "Evan?"

"Can I come in?"

I hauled myself to a seated position. Gray T-shirt, black sweats, residual happiness from last night. The light in my room was dim, strange—snowlight. It was only then I realized how early it was, before six, probably. "Sure."

Evan entered, his hair sticking up in several directions. I didn't need precognition to know he'd be shoving it under a winter cap to plow.

"You heading out?" I asked.

He sat on the edge of my bed. Timid. Lowering himself like a ballet dancer instead of like the big, brawny landscaper he was.

Alarm bells clanged in my head. "Evan?"

He smoothed his palms along his thighs. Once, twice. Looked at me. "It's Cam," he said finally.

I leaned back against the headboard. "Is she . . . ?"

"Not yet." He inhaled through his nose. "Got a call from the nurse. You know the one who does her hair? Cam had some kind of episode this morning."

I hugged my knees to my chest. "Episode?"

He wouldn't meet my eyes. "Yeah. Don't you know that?"

I racked my brain, but I couldn't remember anything about this event. My stomach dipped. Had I—or someone else in the world—done something free willed enough to alter the future? "What kind of episode?"

"The nurse said she opened her eyes. Asked for a broccoli-and-cheddar omelet, which is what she used to get when we went out to breakfast on Sundays when I was a kid." He paused, plucking at my quilt with his index finger. "Said she 'had plans to do a crafting project with her granddaughter, so the kitchen better get going.'" He let out an enormous sigh. "She said to call Mara to see what time she'd be by, said to ask me to trim the hedge before August was over and it grew too big."

I remembered the duplex's gigantic hedge, which gave us much-loved privacy from the street. But in summers, if left untended, its branches obscured the view of whomever was trying to turn out onto the busy intersection.

But none of this made sense. None of it.

Cam couldn't do anything Evan described. She couldn't summon my name, couldn't string together a parade of words to form sentences. Didn't know who I was. Who her children were.

If it were before, I'd climb into the highest of spaces to figure this out. But I couldn't do it, so I did the next best thing and asked, "What are you saying?"

"The nurse thought it was maybe something called terminal lucidity. Happens to less than ten percent of Alzheimer's patients." Evan scrubbed his face with his hands. "It's where they have moments of being something like their old selves before they die, December." His eyes were a question.

A few short months ago, I happened upon the knowledge that I'd only see Cam three more times. I guessed this was it, unless knowing about my mom had changed things for us, the same way I'd felt so certain that being in the dark had broken the chain of events that led to Nick's death. I dropped my head in confirmation. Resignation slithered into my belly. I'd known it was coming, but nothing really prepares you for the end. "How much time does she have left?"

"She didn't say. I'm guessing not much." His voice was raw. Thickened by my unspoken endorsement.

I gestured to the window. "It's not exactly the best visiting weather, is it?"

For the first time, a smile. "Luckily, your uncle drives a plow."

—

In the car, I tucked my hands beneath my thighs, having forgotten my gloves. Apparently, when you lose your all-knowing identity, you gain forgetfulness.

We trucked at approximately fifteen miles per hour through a real-life snow globe. The center of Woodland was nearly unrecognizable. The wind gusted snow sideways, layering the street, sidewalks, fire hydrants, and center businesses with a clean blanket of at least a foot of white.

It had only been hours since Nick picked me up from Stella Rose's. Not long since those first snowflakes. I pressed my lips together, thinking of the delicious pressure of Nick's on my own. Trying to temper all that glowed inside me with all that was to come: The last time I'd see the woman who never abandoned me, the one who always believed in me, before she died.

I wedged my hands farther under my thighs, shivering.

"Cold?" Evan asked, swinging into the Wisteria Hills parking lot.

He'd turned up the heat as high as it could go. I could tell he wasn't asking out of concern, but out of making conversation, because how the hell do you act when you suddenly find out your mother was coherent when she hadn't been for so long? "I don't know what I am," I said finally.

"Me either," Evan said. The lot was empty. We parked in the first spot. I put my hand on the door handle. He toyed with the keys. "December?"

I stared at him, waiting.

"You know I don't ask you to do this." Evan kept his eyes straight out the windshield. Jingled his keys. "I don't want to now, either."

"Evan . . ."

"Can you tell me what I'm about to walk into?" He turned to me. His face twisted my heart into pieces. "With your—with whatever you have. This is my mom, you know? I know it's not fair of me to ask—"

"Evan, I can't," I interrupted, shaking my head.

His gaze fell. "I'm sorry. I shouldn't have asked."

"No, it's not that. I should have told you." I traced my fingertip along the door handle. "It's that I can't anymore. I lost it. Whatever *it* was."

An expression of disbelief crossed his face. "You did?"

"I did."

"When?"

"I knew for sure yesterday." After Nick broke my Blank Spot by solving where Mom was. I dug into my shredded cuticle. I didn't think Evan could ever forgive Mom for leaving, even if it was for a good reason.

"Why didn't you tell me?"

"I didn't know what to say."

We waited a moment, a gust of wind whipping a wall of snow across the glass. "I guess this means we have to face this like everyone else." Evan leaned over and nudged my shoulder. "Let's go, humble plant."

"I'm not sure you should call me that anymore." I wiped tears from my cheeks. "I lost it. I don't have that special ability to know things like the *Mimosa pudica* anymore."

"You're the single most resilient person I know," Evan said. He smoothed my hair from my forehead, his hand warm and reassuring on my head. "And one person can't carry all that weight with them for seventeen years and be unscathed from that experience." He straightened. "Now we're on the same playing field. Can you imagine how difficult it was to argue with a person who is literally correct *all the time*? We can be wrong together, as a family! It'll be fun!"

"I'm not sure I'll ever get used to being wrong." A laugh broke from my throat. "But I'll take ordinary any day."

—

It was before visiting hours—on a hellacious blizzard day, no less—which meant the nursing home must've thought Cam's event was serious enough that it warranted a rule break. "I'm glad you two could come in," the nurse said, depositing a pump of hand sanitizer on my frigid hands.

"Can you tell us more about what happened?" I rubbed my palms. "This terminal lucidity?"

"It was quick. And surprising." The nurse pressed the elevator UP arrow, then steered us inside. Automatically, I lifted my foot and toed the 4, thinking of Cam's admonition: *Never touch public elevator buttons. Those things are germ factories.*

The nurse nodded, impressed. "Yogi-level flexibility."

I swallowed back tears. Even though Cam had been gone for years,

I was going to miss her. We'd mourned the loss of the real Cam once before. Now, it seemed, we'd be grieving what was left of her, too. A double funeral.

The elevator crept to the fourth floor. In the painful silence, I turned to the nurse. "Was she aware of what her life's been like?"

"I don't think so. I went in to braid her hair before the end of my shift, and . . ." She shrugged. "I'm no expert. But it was basically as if she woke with an agenda."

"But how could her body do that? I mean, after how much the Alzheimer's has affected her—her brain, who she is, her body. Her everything. How could she suddenly wake up?"

"Honey," the nurse said. She clasped her hands. "I wish I knew what the answer was here, but the truth is, no one I know is certain how it happens." She paused. "We call it 'the rally.'"

The elevator opened. My uncle held his arm across the doorway, making sure the elevator door didn't close on me. When I brushed by him, Evan squeezed my shoulder, his reassurance traveling all the way to my toes. We followed the nurse down the hallway to the last door on the right.

It didn't make sense. None of it did. Fire doesn't start in an empty matchbook. How could she unexpectedly be her—be *Cam* again, with her brain the way it was?

"Evan?"

He looked at me.

"I'm scared," I whispered.

"Me too, plant," he mumbled.

Somehow, without admitting it to myself, I'd gone down the path of magically finding her well. Sitting in bed, with perhaps some knitted blanket over her legs, talking about going to yoga or reminiscing about when my uncle and mom were kids, or something. Recovering.

But in her room, Cam was propped on a half-dozen pillows, her expression unchanged. Her eyes didn't track my uncle when he moved around the edge of her bed.

Evan cleared his throat, but he couldn't keep the warble from his voice. "Mom?"

I closed my eyes. *Mom. You're missing this.*

"I don't know if she can understand you," the nurse said softly. "But I'll leave you here. Stay as long as you want."

Evan sat on the edge of Cam's bed, as he had on my own less than an hour before. I curled up in the pleather armchair, listening to him talk about Sim, the plow, the storm raging outside in pillowy snow-flakes.

"I'm glad we had this time together," Evan said to me.

I cleared my throat. "Me too."

"This feels so final. Like the end is coming." His eyes brimmed with tears.

"I know," I said, trying to pinpoint exactly what it was I felt.

Powerless.

I felt powerless.

The lucid moment might have led us here, but so long as everything hadn't changed, these would be our last moments together with Cam. The image of Evan's head bowed in funeral prayer haunted me.

Now I was only a girl, smoothing away the hair across her grandmother's forehead to kiss her one last time. A girl who wanted to change the world. Who maybe had. But was it enough? That girl had held the entire weight of what had come, what would come, and what was happening right now. But when it came down to it, *she* was just one person. Me. Watching Cam now, all I could think was that all I've ever been was a lie, an illusion, and maybe I've never had any power at all.

CHAPTER FIFTY-ONE
Nick

Maverick: DUDE, SAVE ME

Me: From?

Maverick: MY MOTHER DECLARED TODAY A NO-
PHONE SNOW DAY

Me: Ouuuuuuuuuch

Maverick: THIS IS AWFUL. HOW DID PEOPLE LIVE
BEFORE INTERNET OR PHONES? I'VE WANTED TO
GOOGLE LIKE 50 EFFING THINGS TODAY

Me: how are you talking to me now?

Maverick: I STOLE MY PHONE AND TOLD MY MOM
I WANTED TO TAKE A BATH WHILE SHE PUT IN THE
SECOND BATCH OF BANANA BREAD ON HER BREAK
FROM CROSS-STITCHING

Maverick: WHAT GROWN MAN TAKES A BATH? HOW
DID SHE EVEN BUY THIS?

Me: You know you aren't supposed to have your phone
in the bathtub, right? That's *actually* dangerous

Maverick: HOW THE HELL WOULD YOU KNOW THAT?

Maverick: SHIT. GOOGLE AGREES WITH YOU,

LIFEGUARD. HEY, NOW YOU REALLY DID SAVE SOMEONE!

Maverick: I'M NOT IN THE BATH, ANYWAY. I'M NEXT TO IT. AND NOW FEELING GUILTY FOR WASTING WATER, SO I'LL PROBABLY GET IN THE GODDAMN BATH.

Maverick: THIS WOMAN IS ONLY ON THE THIRD LETTER OF HER CROSS-STITCH. THIS IS GOING TO BE THE LONGEST DAY OF MY LIFE.

Me: Of how many?

Maverick: I DON'T KNOW. COUNT THE NUMBER OF LETTERS IN "BLESSED TO HAVE FRIENDS WHO ARE FAMILY AND FAMILY WHO ARE FRIENDS." CAN YOU BELIEVE THE SHIT THIS WOMAN BUYS FROM FACEBOOK?

Me: You don't need to make me a cross-stitch, Mav. I know you love me

Maverick: HA. HA.

An hour later:

Maverick: WELL, SHIT. GUESS WHO'S A NEW FAN OF BATHS?

—

My parents sat on the couch, head to toe like Charlie Bucket's grandparents, cradling cups of black coffee.

"I vote we do a huge round of cooking," Dad said.

Mom scoffed. "I dislike huge rounds of cooking."

"But think of all the prep work we could save for next week."

Mom's eyes gleamed at that. My parents were in a constant discussion over how to save time, especially after workdays. "Valid point," she murmured. "But what if the power goes out because of the storm?"

"Then we store everything outside in the snow until it comes back on."

"The weather's forecasted to turn around tomorrow. It's going to be unseasonably hot, in true freaky New England meteorological style." Mom sipped from her mug. "And then everything would spoil."

On the floor, Sophie lay sprawled on her stomach, painting with the instructions from a muted YouTube video. She swooped a large smear of blue paint on the canvas. "Don't even joke about the power going out," she said. "There's nothing to do here."

"Can't survive without a device?" Dad teased. "Your generation."

"You couldn't, either," I said.

"Even eight-year-olds can survive on their own," Sophie said, dipping her paintbrush in a glass jar of water.

We all waited a moment. Dad cleared his throat. "Care to explain that one, child?"

"If you're eight and abandoned, you can figure out how to survive. You steal food, find a place to sleep. Like in *Aladdin*. That's the first age they think you can do it. If you leave a pack of six-year-olds, though . . ." She adjusted her earbuds. "You don't want to know what happens."

Mom and Dad exchanged a glance. "Where are you *getting* this, Sophie?" Mom asked.

"NPR."

While Mom made a show of pretending to hide under the blanket, a knock sounded at the door.

Dad frowned. "Who's coming out in this mess?" He pointed to the window, where *this mess* raged away, piling snow against the sill.

I opened the door to find December, wearing a light blue coat and stomping her feet. Her cheeks were rosy from the cold, and snow stuck to her eyelashes. "Got bored home alone," she said.

I stepped aside to let her in. "You should've told me you were coming. I could've met you halfway."

Her teeth grazed her bottom lip when she smiled at me, and I took a moment to think about her and me and the car, and the world before this snow. She slipped off her coat and shook her hair from a knitted hat. Her hair cascaded down her back in rich brown waves. "Hey."

"Hey, yourself." I took her winter stuff from her, letting my fingers tap against her freezing ones while my family descended on her, begging her to paint (Sophie), asking how Cam was (Mom), inquiring with genuine interest what Evan's overtime schedule might look like (Dad).

My phone lit with a notification. I opened the lock screen to find a red bubble attached to my email app. I tapped it.

Inbox (1)
Swimming Trials Farm Team Update

"Holy shit," I said, tapping the keys to open my screenreader.

"Language," Mom said. Predictably.

"No. Mom. It's the farm team email."

Mom froze. "Oh. *Oh*. Open it!"

"You've got this," December said.

I brandished my shaking hand. "I didn't expect to be this nervous."

"Look at me," December said. I met her eyes, and a wave of calmness radiated through me. She leaned close. "You've got this. Be brave, Nick. Be brave."

"Brave," I repeated. "Right." I opened the email and jammed my thumb against the READ NOW button.

Dear Nicholas Irving,

Congratulations! You have been selected to be a part of the Massachusetts Elite Chapter of the Swimming Trials Farm Team. You are one of three new swimmers selected among fifty-two applicants to join our team, all coached by former Olympian Derrick-John Lewis.

Together with your team, you'll train until reaching a qualifying time for the events you selected on your form. You are welcome to attend trainings for other events as well. We will swim in four to six competitive meets in the winter, and each year, we come up with a service project to complete as a team. We hope you'll join us there, too.

Please e-sign the attached form at your earliest convenience.

Keep swimming!
The Swimming Trials Farm Team

Before I knew it, everyone had stood. Sophie danced around us, ad-libbing a song.

Mom wiped her eyes. "I knew it."

"You did it!" December squeezed my arm. "*You* did it."

I stared at my phone. This was it. Everything I'd worked for my whole life, right in front of me. I thought of the dozens of pictures Mom had printed and tucked in albums, of the swimmer's ear infections and missed birthday parties and all I could think was this was another thing I didn't deserve. "No way."

"You should be proud of yourself." Dad beamed.

"I am," I said. "But I've barely been in the pool lately. I'm not ready. And my backstroke start . . ." I flicked my eyes to December, thinking. "Oh. No."

"What?"

"Do you . . . ?" My brain stalled out while I tried to form the words I wanted to say. "Think this has anything to do with Mr. Francis?"

"No," December said, cutting my parents off before they could answer.

I gave her a hard look. "But do you know so?"

She trailed her fingertips down my forearm until she found my hand. I thought of the scar that trickled onto her own forearm. "Final answer. This was all you."

All me. Something flickered then swelled inside me, my lungs bursting with energy. And even though that doubt and guilt lingered, I realized these feelings could sit with all kinds of good things, too. I felt like I could conquer anything.

"I like you," Mom said, grinning at December. "Let's keep you around."

CHAPTER FIFTY-TWO

December

THE WEATHER TWENTY-FOUR hours post-snowstorm was unseasonably hot. Nick's mom was right: New England had an identity crisis. When Evan got home from plowing, he'd thrown the windows open before he crashed in his room, exhausted from being out all night. The springtime sound of melting snow running into the gutters filled the air with a satisfying, busy hum.

The same kind of hum filled me now because I was doing something I hadn't done in years.

Drawing.

I sprawled on my stomach, drawing on the back of everything I could find: computer paper, discarded mail coupons, old receipts.

Everything about today was off in a thrilling sort of way, like eating breakfast for dinner or ice cream for lunch, and I wanted to capture that. Instead of remaining comfortably in their assigned months, all four seasons competed for today's attention. I sketched the grass from yesterday, blanketed with wet leaves in raging hues: tangerines, honey maples, marigolds, some cherry red, poking through the record-breaking two feet of snow. Leaves clung to the tree branches despite the thick white icing that now frosted each limb.

I sat back to confirm. I still wasn't any good at this, but at least it felt great. Enjoying the ride instead of worrying about the destination, and all that.

In the galley kitchen, Evan had left me a perfect treat: pre-measured coffee, the hard-ground kind I like, nestled into the bottom of the French press. I checked the copper kettle, and sure enough, it was filled with precisely the right amount of water. Evan again. Warmth filled my chest, a smile curving my lips. He had plowed the entire night, and yet he took the time to prep me some coffee before drawing the shades and passing out. I flipped the burner on and yawned, jumping when I heard three quick raps on the tin screen door.

Before, this wouldn't have startled me. It was delightful to be surprised by Nick's silhouette, recognizable by his head of curls. He pulled earbuds from his ears.

"You scared me," I said, opening the screen door. *"Mystery Buff?"*

"Sorry." Nick wore a gray hoodie and light blue shorts. He came inside, stomping his feet on the mat. Pulling me in for a hug, he pressed his lips against my forehead, sending sparks of satisfaction into my bloodstream. "And nope. I need a break from death and destruction and mysteries for a little while."

"Cosign." I pulled away. "Want some coffee?"

"Sure, but actually—can we take it with us?"

"Where are we going?" I asked, leading him into the kitchen. Puffs of steam rose from the teakettle, and the beginnings of a whine grumbled within it. I pulled it from the burner and poured it over the French press, watching the ground beans soak up the hot water.

"Sledding."

"Sledding?"

"Yes. Actually, we're going *boogie* sledding."

"Sure we are." I pulled two of Evan's takeaway cups from the cabinet. "Going boogie sledding, I mean. Because I totally know what that is."

"This is the weirdest weather," Nick said, accepting his cup and squinting his eyes against the midday sunlight. "Which calls for boogie sledding. As in, boogie boards from the lifeguard shack, which we can use out on the hill behind the complex."

"Does that work?"

"Yeah, they're oversized. Three or four little kids hold on at the same time to practice kicking across the pool."

I grinned, picturing it. And everything after it. We were making plans to go sledding on boogie boards. I wasn't digesting the knowledge of the world, worried about car accidents or campaign funding or mortgages. "Can we get in the pool shack?"

A smile spilled across his face. He pulled a silver key from his sweatshirt pocket. "Can we ever," he said.

"Awesome. Let me write Evan a note." I snagged the pad of sticky notes from the junk drawer and scrawled:

> Uncle,
> I'm out boogie sledding with Nick. (I'll explain what
> that is later.) Hope you got some good sleep!
> xoxo, your humble plant <3

"Ready?" Nick asked.

By the door, I looked down at my black leggings and the charcoal-gray short-sleeved shirt with the pin tuck collar I'd thrown on this morning. "Is this appropriate attire?"

He nodded. "It's nice out. Borderline hot, but the ground is wet. Wear your boots." Nick lifted his coffee to his nose, inhaling deeply. He frowned. "Do you smell something funny?"

"All I smell is coffee."

"It smells like eggs. Or something."

"Eggs?" I said, but then gagged. The smell of sulfur cut through the earthy coffee smell that still hung in the air. "What *is* that?"

"I don't know . . . ," Nick began, but then his eyes changed. Without a word, he turned around and charged toward the stove.

My throat plummeted into my stomach. Had I . . . ?

Nick jerked the knob to the right. Abruptly, the sound of hissing—which I'd missed, beneath the running water in the gutters—cut off.

I covered my mouth with my hands.

"Forgot to turn off the burner," Nick said. "That was something old December never would've done."

"Wrong," I said. "No one got hurt. Old me would have remembered and let that whole thing play out as it did." I gave an exaggerated curtsy. "The new me knows nothing at all."

CHAPTER FIFTY-THREE

Nick

THIS HILL. THE winters of my childhood were punctuated by the times I'd gone sledding down it. When the snow was powdery, we'd fly down, almost as if we were catapulting through the air itself.

But this snow was the wet, clumpy kind. It gave way to a carved-ice path. At the top of the hill, December gave me a sideways glance. "You sure about this?"

"What was it you said?" I pretended to think. "'Be brave,' right?"

"Challenge accepted, Irving," she muttered, lowering herself onto the boogie board.

The combined weight of December and me sent us skittering down the icy surface. We sledded over and over again. Her alone. Me alone. December's warmth pressed in my lap, on my stomach, my arms hugging her closer. Warm air gusted against our cheeks, buffeting each trek. Between the adrenaline of the trip downhill, the closeness of this beautiful girl, and this news about swimming, I was on the precipice of a different space or place. Sledding down this hill, I felt on the brink, on the edge of something else.

New girlfriend. Senior year. New swim team. Maybe I wasn't always the person I wanted to be, but I was starting to like the person I'd become.

"Ta-da!" December sang at the end of another run. "This is so much fun."

We set back up the hill. "Isn't it?" I kicked an unearthed stick out of the way. "I probably won't have time for this in the winter, so I'm sort of glad I could catch this one."

At the top, December tossed the boogie board on the matted snow. "Do you have to quit the school swim team for your new one?"

"I'm not sure if the meets will conflict yet, but I don't think so. When I was a freshman, one of the seniors was on both. The elite team has adults on it, too, so they need to make time for people with jobs. They hold practices at some off-kilter hours—five in the morning, ten at night."

She sat on the boogie board and scooted forward so I could arrange myself around her. "Can I watch your swim meets?"

I kissed the back of her neck. "You better." Since hearing the news yesterday, I'd thought of little else. I found myself squeezing my glutes, engaging my shoulder blades at all times of the day.

We pushed off. Instead of looking around us—at our homes, below us, at the pond to the other side of us, or way off in the distance, toward the pool and the pool shed from which this boogie board had come from, dusty with its lack of use—I tucked my forehead against her neck and closed my eyes, breathing her in. She smelled of coffee and cookies, of sleep and blankets and warmth.

When we came to a stop, I twisted to the path. In the late-afternoon light, dark grass had begun to show through the worn, snowy track. Around us, tendrils winked from beneath the matted piles. Worn down until something revealed itself underneath.

And in that moment, I knew I couldn't let it sit.

Instead of getting up and doing it all over again, I held on to her, burying my face back against her neck. "Wait."

"What is it?" She tried to pivot to face me, but instead, I held her tight.

"I want to ask you something," I said. "Remember what you said when we were texting the other day?"

"We text a lot, no?"

"Yeah. But you know what I'm talking about."

"I remember," December said, her voice strained.

"You said the reason why you and I were together was a 'bad thing.'"

"Why won't you let me look at you?"

"Because *I* don't want to look at your face when I ask you this."

I'm afraid of what your answer will be, I wanted to say.

I'm not sure if I want to know the answer.

In case you need to lie to me.

In case you tell me the truth.

She stiffened in my arms. "Okay."

"I'm going to ask you this one time. One. And after that, I'll never ask it again."

Beneath my forehead, her vertebrae shifted with her nod.

"Was it that I was going to die?"

Heavy snow crashed through the trees near the pond. Below us was the careful whir of a car as it crested into its spot before the driver cut its engine.

Below me, her skin. Warm and tense. She drew a breath, her chest making the smallest of contractions before she spoke. "Yes."

I wasn't surprised to find my eyes well with tears. I blinked them into the cotton of her shirt. "Oh," I said. "Oh."

"I wish you didn't ask me that."

"I wish I didn't have to."

And then she twisted to face me, stumbling over herself on the foam of the boogie board and crashing into my arms, wrapping her legs around my waist. "I needed to save you," she said in my ear. "And I didn't know how. But I *did*, Nick. I know it."

What would I have said, if she'd come to me back in the summer? Telling me she'd foreseen my death? I took in my own ragged breath, trying to fit into my brain what she'd known about me dying. Because sure, it's coming for all of us at some point. But most of us don't write our own narratives—nor should we. I couldn't even begin to picture what would happen to my family if I died.

It was something I'd probably be unpacking at three in the morning for the rest of my life.

"How?" I asked.

She tipped my chin upward with her forefinger. "I'm sorry, but that's classified."

"If you're so sure you fixed it, then why is it classified?"

She made a sound of frustration. "I can't *see* anything anymore. I don't know how this conversation was supposed to go."

"You're stuck with navigating it like the rest of us, December. Congratulations."

"I don't want you to experience any more pain than you have to, okay?"

"Try again."

She wrinkled her nose. "Fine. What I do know is I don't know if I'm supposed to tell you or not, but it feels wrong to do so. So if I'm *not* supposed to tell you, and I *do* tell you, then we could possibly end up with a bigger free-will action than had been forecast, and it could change things, and I'd have *no idea*."

"Again. Also known as living life like a person."

Her fingers circled both of my arms. "Can it be enough that I've told you the truth?"

I had the dimmest realization then: If I pressed her, then she'd lie

310

to me. The girl in my arms was relaxed, with a clear expression. If I asked her to give more of herself to me—more of what she knew—her eyes might cloud over, her muscles might tense, her mouth might lie.

I leaned over and brushed her lips with mine. "It's enough," I said. "It ends here, December."

CHAPTER FIFTY-FOUR
December

THE SUN DIPPED toward the west, the temperature going with it. Leftover sweat from clomping uphill and flying down dried, leaving my skin damp but chilly. I shivered alongside Nick as we walked back to the pool shed.

I couldn't believe I'd told him the truth.

I almost hadn't—my lips parted, teeth and tongue poised to begin the word. *No.* But at the last moment, I'd replaced it to answer with the affirmative.

Yes.

I'd let my guard down.

The truth was a funny thing because it wasn't always a certain thing. Lying had been part of my life, like it or not. I understood why people were so comfortable with the truth—it was sort of an agreed-upon social rule to either tell it or massage it for the sake of being nice.

But I'd never met someone else like me. Not someone I knew of, at least. I didn't know if my father was like me—I sure as hell knew my mom and Evan weren't. And people like Past December couldn't live life by the same rules as other people.

But now my rules had changed, so along with that was a personal recalibration. Truth telling.

Alongside me, Nick balanced the boogie board above his head like a surfboard. He'd pulled his hood up, and his hair poked out of it wildly.

He caught my stare and grinned. "Rate boogie sledding on a scale of one to ten."

"Ten," I assured him. "Most definitely a ten."

"Best thing ever, right?" he said. "What could be better?"

I thought for a moment, as if the question were real. "You know," I said slowly, "I'm thinking about reaching out to the FBI. To see if they can give me any information on my mother." I squeezed my hand into a fist, then released it. "I think I owe it to my seven-year-old self to try and get some answers."

"I think you're allowed to decide what you want to know," Nick said. "You dealt with so much when you were little. When I was a little kid? I used to ask everyone I met what color their tail would be if they were a mermaid."

I smiled, picturing it. A small, curly-haired boy quizzing aunts, uncles, mail people. Reds and blues and purples. "Oh, yeah?"

"Yep."

"That's adorable." I crossed my arms and leaned back against a fence pole. I'd never come across that memory in my Nick-related climbs.

He nudged the pool fence open with his hip, holding the gate for me. "What's yours?"

"Silver," I said immediately.

"I can see that. You're all kinds of sparkly." He waggled his fingers in my direction. "But what I meant was, what's your thing? Are there any stories Evan tells from when you were a kid?"

My childhood memories were of plants that shrivel when they're touched, of taco trucks and misremembering who braided my hair.

313

I suppressed a smile, looking around at the place where we'd first met. The place where I'd changed everything. A woven cover spread over the pool, attached perfectly on all sides. Beneath, I pictured the drained basin, devoid of its aqua water. No more shifting and churning, the way everything I knew of the world used to. Adjusting and falling into rhythms and space. Now the pool water had been drained until next summer, the sleek ceramic surface beneath dry and porous. I thought harder. Back and back.

"Flip-books," I said. I hooked my index finger around one of the chain links and tugged. A large clump of melted snow fell from above, landing with a soft thud on the surface of the pool cover.

"Flip-books?"

"Yeah, do you remember those? On each page there was a similar image—like a guy riding a bike, for instance—if you turn the pages quickly, it appeared to ride across the page?"

"Sure, I do. My grandma used to call them thumb cinemas."

"Thumb cinemas! I love that." I shaded my eyes with my hand. Snow clung to one shadowy corner of the fence. Everywhere else, it had been burned away, like running hot water over a Popsicle. I leaned against the fence while Nick got to the pool house. He pulled the key from his pocket, resting the foam board at his feet.

"What should we do tonight?" he asked.

"Tonight?"

Nick turned the knob, then propped it open with his hip. He slid the boogie board along the floor, making loud scraping sounds. "I was thinking pizza, a movie, and ice cream. Hey!" He braced himself against the edge of the pool house wall and leaned in, grabbing a baseball hat. "I've been looking for this everywhere."

"Your sweatshirt's soaked," I said.

He glanced down and took in the muddied front of his sweatshirt.

"Oh, shoot." He flipped his hood and, on second thought, removed his sweatshirt.

I drank in the inches of smooth skin on his stomach before he pulled down his white T-shirt.

Nick jammed the baseball hat on his head and draped the wet sweatshirt on his arm like a waiter at a fancy restaurant. "Voilà," he said.

"Ready to head home?"

I opened my mouth to say *ready*, or maybe I'd say *sure*, or *no, let's stay a while*. But I never got a chance.

He stepped toward me, right in the path of the late-afternoon sun's rays. The sunset was gorgeous that night, all syruped pinks and golds and

(sherbet orange)

the same shade as his favorite shirt. The one he wore in my cloudy, hazy, impossible vision.

We heard the overhead crack at the same time. In unison, our heads tilted up, but Nick was hit in the face with falling snow. I froze against the fence for a beat, and then I ran toward him.

He ducked. The rest of the slushy mess hit the brim of his hat instead. My lifeguard—the same one who could not make himself move on the day we met—lifted his hand to block the onslaught and made a sound that was a cross between an *ahh* and *oh*.

I would never get there in time. "Nick," I called, my heart in the back of my throat. "*Move.*"

And somehow, somehow. He did. He pinwheeled backward, his body arcing in the most beautiful, most perfect backstroke start motion, his hat flying off and away, his shirt returning to a shadowed white in the shade of the pool house.

I stopped. Bent double. Relief rushed my ears, silencing my terror.

The air stilled, the snow settled, my heart climbing back where it belonged.

"Holy," he said, his voice breaking.

I sucked in a breath. "That was so scary. I—"

Another crack, and the branch fell.

—

Struck by thrown, projected, or falling object was a cause of death listed by the CDC. If you search far enough, it even has an insurance code.

Not listed: a mistaken girl screaming a warning to the wrong person.

A boy who wore a white T-shirt that appeared to be on fire with the sherbet orange of the sunset. The boy who she'd first met in July, the un-hero, the boy whose face she'd seen broken and bleeding against the ground.

It matched my vision after all. But instead of the boy dying, it was me.

I was wrong. How could I have been so wrong?

I'd spent all this time thinking I knew everything except for what happened with my mother that I didn't even stop to consider that, perhaps I was

(irrevocably)

wrong.

—

He crawled to where I lay on the ground. I think he shouted my name, but I couldn't hear anything beyond a faint buzz.

It hurt everywhere; it hurt nowhere.

My vision went multicolored with static. The edges of pain were a lightning bolt that fractured along my skull.

Of course

(of course)

I was never able to see anything about my mother. She'd done the same thing that I'd tried to do for Nick by breaking up with him.

She had left me, the way I left him. To protect someone we loved. To try to change what I said was the truth. To try to save a life.

And when I learned where she was, my mind took away my gift so I wouldn't remember this awful truth.

All at once, I remembered a slice of my own time with her:

Her arms, smelling of Jergens lotion, encircling me.

The sensation of being carried, my head lolling on the bone-hard cleft of her clavicle.

Her firm resolve. Unyielding. Protective. Her eyes, crinkled in the shadow of her black-and-white hat she removed and left on the nail by the open window.

The memory was mine, but it was also hers. The memory of leaving.

(Leave me to save me.)

In this tiniest of slices of time—a fraction of a fraction of a second since the crack from above—I saw her life as it was without me.

She left in the deepest, darkest part of the night, two nights after I told her what I had seen.

No matter what I did,

I

would

die

when I was seventeen.

She lived the story Nick had brought to life for me: catching the bad guys, removing herself from my future, because if she went against the grain of the world, then couldn't she change things?

(The way I had, with Mr. Francis. With Jake Dirks. With my lifeguard.)

(Nick)

Everything I hadn't known flashed before me in a rush of returned gumballs. My gift had presented me with a trinket of its own: protecting me from knowing about my imminent death. By creating the Blank Spot, it linked itself inexorably to my mother's life, her last desperate attempt to change my future. And when I learned of her real-life whereabouts—even sort of—it had done the only thing it could and removed itself to protect me. Preserve the reality of what I knew.

Nick had been right. She'd lived long days and nights in hotel rooms, trying to stop the spread of opiates as they leaked into this country, seeping into living rooms, Friday-night football games, gas station bathrooms, and morgues.

I saw her visiting Cam. During Cam's decline.

She'd been in this *area* during Cam's decline. Near me. Watching me. Tracking.

My vision had also been right: I'd only had three visits left with Cam, after all. But it wasn't because Cam was about to die.

It was because I was.

Nick's face had my blood on it. At that moment, he was in full-on no-hesitation rescue mode, pumping my chest and listening for my heartbeat, breathing for me. All futile.

What I'd thought was Nick's death wasn't his. It was never his.

All of this. My mother leaving. Mr. Francis's avoided death, falling in love, believing Nick was going to die. My gift morphing in ways it never had before, linking me to his emotions to keep stringing me

318

along. Keep me believing I could change things. *Everything* played out as it was meant to. This gift I had been given had led me here.

The death was my own.

He pressed his cheek against the ground, searching for my eyes with his. But mine were so heavy.

A lifetime of mourning for what I'd lost:

for my uncle and his future,

for my new friends,

for my tall and guilty, guilelessly unheroic lifeguard.

And I was gone with a leap into the gray.

CHAPTER FIFTY-FIVE
Inside the Blank Spot

WHAT'S THE END *of the story, Mama? What happened to the rock?*

—Do you really want to know?

I wouldn't ask if I didn't want to know, would I?

—You ask a lot of things I wouldn't want to know, sweets.

That's because—

—I know. I know. Anyway, the rock left the beach, slowly but surely. The opposite way it arrived.

How?

—Remember how the rock took up almost the whole beach?

I remember.

—Only the earliest arrivals, the people who pulled up before dawn to park, were able to comfortably hang out on the beach after the rock came. The town set up all these rules to try and get more people to fit. One small cooler per family, a chair only if you had an accommodations permit.

That's so strange.

—Sounds it, doesn't it? But soon . . . those people began to spread out a little more. Instead of a small family crowding onto the sand, more and more people could. There was more room.

The rock was moving.

—That's right. Plus, people still walked the beach every day, because it connected to a few other beaches. You could cross over a dune and be on a huge public beach. Before long, those people realized they had less room to walk on the strip of land between the rock and the water . . . you okay, sweets?

I'm okay. Just thinking about the rock rolling into the ocean.

—Bit by bit. Started out a few inches here, a few there, until it took grander leaps. A few feet a day, until . . .

Until it reached the water.

—That's right.

Then what?

—It kept rolling and rolling, until it was half submerged. Then it was gone.

Gone?

—Gone.

That's sad.

—Why?

Because when it was here, no one liked it. Then it was gone.

—I liked it.

You?

—Me.

But then when it was gone, did you miss it?

—The rock was where it was supposed to be. I'd guess it was probably still there. Right under the surface. It taught people a lesson while it was here, though.

Rocks don't teach lessons. And was this rock even really real?

—Yes.

Really?

—Really.

The rock was there, and then it was gone?

—The rock was there. It left an impression. It made people fight.

It made them get along. It told a story. And then, when its time was up, it was gone.

That's like me.

—Like you? How?

Exactly like me. I'll be here, and then I'll be gone.

— . . . What do you mean?

I mean when I'm seventeen. I'll be gone.

—What are you saying?

Door.

—No. No. Don't say door. Tell me what you mean.

I can't.

—Sweets, are you saying you'll be gone from the world when you're seventeen?

Uh-huh. Why are you crying?

—I don't want to hear this.

It's just what is, Mama. It's how it's always been.

—I need to do something to change that.

You can't.

—Why not?

Because that's what's supposed to be. Please, please stop crying. It's okay.

—How does it happen?

It changes all the time.

—Do you know how much I love you?

You always tell me more than the universe.

—I do tell you that. But why don't you know that?

Because I'm too much of you.

—What if your whole life changed in some big, huge way?

It isn't going to save me. Nothing will. Please stop crying, Mama. You're making me sad.

—Then how can I change what you're saying?

You can't.

—I'll do everything I can to try, my love.

CHAPTER FIFTY-SIX
TWO MONTHS LATER

Nick

Dear Mr. Francis,

If you'd asked me to define my worldview last year, you'd be getting a different essay.

I used to think the world was a safe enough place. I lived with a kind of benign invincibility. I don't live that way anymore. Someone once wrote to me: *How brave is it that people go through life without knowing what happens next?* And, well, I think that's how I conceive of the world now. How life is one unknown after the next.

I can't pinpoint when it was, exactly, that my worldview shifted. Was it when I spotted December's foot tapping a melody I couldn't hear—the clue that something wasn't right with you? Was it when she saved you—because Mr. Francis, let's start there. She's the one who saved you. Not me.

I *wish* I had been the one to save you. I thought it was important that people knew the truth, but I'm not so sure. I have always prided myself on truth. But once that article came out, I didn't know how to fix all my half-truths and lies.

This is the coward's way out, but here goes, Mr. Francis. One more confession, because I don't want to carry this with me for the rest of my life.

Last May, I cheated on my history final.

My parents have always prized honesty, and I'm ashamed that I cheated. My dyslexia isn't a bad thing. It makes me think outside the prescribed box. But I'd stayed up the entire night studying, and I can assure you I will never forget the name *Lusitania* now. I panicked, and I blanked, and the pressure of it all boiled over in my head and my eyes . . . they landed on Sara-Beth Seaborn's paper.

I've been living with guilt over both of those matters, but here's the thing. I'm angry, too. Because I believe different is good. Maybe it isn't my brain that's wrong. Maybe whoever decided to structure school and reading and learning and standardized testing is the one who had it all wrong. I've decided I will fight to prove that there should be more than one way to take a test. That education is not one-size-fits-all; that it is not a checklist we can blanket-apply to every student in the country.

Maybe we all think differently.

I know December did.

Was it last May? Was it the time I froze in place in July watching a girl I did not yet know saving a man I did, or was it the late-August falling in love with that same girl—the one whose name belongs at the end of a calendar, not on a gravestone?

Was it when she died?

I can't say with certainty when my worldview shifted, and maybe that's the whole point. What I can say is that I now believe we all affect one another more than I realized. All our gestures, all our actions, all our tweets and posts and facial expressions and the most impercep- tible reactions—they change the course of history. And even though doing one or two wrong things doesn't get canceled out by doing a million right ones, it's still a better bet to try and do the good.

That's a pretty powerful thought.

That maybe holding the door for the kid behind me will redirect our lives. That befriending a boy named Maverick Tate in third grade was one of the smartest decisions I ever made, though I couldn't have forecasted it then.

I believe we all sail through this life of ours thinking we're right—and I also believe we have the power to learn otherwise. For example, I used to think the word *bravery* meant courage, or valiance, the kind of plucky fearlessness reserved for superheroes. Now I'm pretty sure December was right. Bravery is simply facing a world of unknowns.

Things I wish I didn't know: The sight of December's mother's face when she cries. The angle December's uncle holds his head when it is bowed in sadness. That time passes when someone dies, marked for me when her uncle leaves us cut flowers, a Thanksgiving basket, and we drop off meals for him and his boyfriend. What it feels like to suggest Woodland dedicates the key to the city to December instead, or to tell my parents that I wasn't the hero everyone thought I was. The feeling of anticipation about submitting this essay to you, someone who's going to read it and never think of me the same way again.

Right now, I'm hoping I feel the worst I'll ever feel. My hands are cold. The name that used to light up my phone and kick-start my heart in my chest? It'll never do that again. I'm afraid I'll never feel that irresistible spark I felt with her again, that the greatest love I'll ever have is gone.

But I don't know that. I can't know that. No one can, even if they think they do.

I'm sorry I couldn't save you, but I'm so glad she did.

I'm sorry I couldn't save her.

I'm sorry she couldn't save herself.

Sometimes, I go to the pond out beyond Bright Acres and sit way high up in a tree, straining as far as my eyes will take me to the line where the sky meets the earth. I look for her there, because if she was the kind of miracle on earth I believe she was, then maybe I can hope for a different kind of miracle to happen.

One thing I know for sure is I will carry her with me. I don't have this thing called a worldview without her. For the rest of my life, when I drive at night with the windows open, when branches break, when I dance in a crowd, when I'm alone underwater, when I feel joy and when I feel loss, when I think of every event I cannot control, I will think of the girl with the liquid eyes and the gift of perception who tapped her foot to music and fit into the part of me that was missing.

I will think of December.

ACKNOWLEDGMENTS

The concept for this book came to me when I had a newborn, a time when many amazing and terrible ideas are also born. I'm glad this one made it out into the world.

To my agent Kerry D'Agostino, for your warmth and passion and keen eye, and always especially your thoroughness. I treasure your insight and I am so lucky to have it. And to the rest of the team at Curtis Brown, Ltd., especially Sarah Perillo, thank you for all the support.

To Kat Brzozowski. Two of my favorite email subject lines from you include your first—"New England," and the one that came after the offer for this one—"YAY!" Thank you for your vision, your appreciation for Little League snacks, and, most importantly, your passion and drive for your work. I appreciate you every day. Thank you to Jean Feiwel and the whole team at Feiwel & Friends, including Hana Tzou, Liz Szabla, and everyone who touched this book along the way.

To the Macmillan Children's Publishing Group: Thank you for the behind-the-scenes work in bringing this book to life, especially my patient production editor, Lelia Mander, brilliant copyeditor, Jacqueline Hornberger, and stellar proofreader Ronnie Ambrose; to art director Beth Clark and designer Samira Iravani; and to my marketing and publicity team, especially Sara Elroubi. To Beatriz Ramo, who brought December and Nick to life on this cover: You are brilliantly talented. Special thanks to Crystal Patriarche and team.

To my writing partners, Laura Taylor Namey and Allison Bitz: You are friends, gutchecks, genius wordsmiths, and two of my very favorite people. I love you both. Thank you.

To everyone who read versions of this book (under a different title!) and gave their input on it, including Jesse Q. Sutanto and Erin King, I am so grateful to you. And you, Julie Ritchie. A huge thank-you to all of the sensitivity readers for this project.

To all the writers who I've met along the way: I love every ounce of engagement we have. Thank you for being you, and gifting me with your words. And to my readers, thank you for the kindness and truth in your notes. I hear it with all I've got. Thank you to the Milton Public Library for my time as the Writer-in-Residence; I am so grateful for the space to write and engage with the community. Librarians are heroes.

To the neighbors I was standing with when I heard about this book deal: Thank you for being part of my village. Shoutout to the Jones family: Your last name matching December's is a giant and fun coincidence.

And to my dance family: I adore you always.

To childcare! Especially to you, Juliann O'Connor, without whom this book—nor any of my subsequent ones—would exist in their current forms. To Barbie and Steve, and your willingness to cross the bridge to come off-Cape.

To my friends, especially the ones who are my family (10143), and to all of my real family from Massachusetts to California: I love you. Kevin: to always. Lucy and Teddy: You are my whole infinity.

And lastly, the idea for this book would not have come without the profound loss of someone else. To Nick Farley, and the Farley family: Though the Nick in this book is an entirely different person (whose name I never changed), not a day goes by where I don't think of your Nick and his influence on my universe.